FALLING FOR YOU

STACY TRAVIS

FAST TURTLE
PRESS

FALLING FOR YOU

~

STACY TRAVIS

Cover Design: Shanoff Designs

Copyediting: Evident Ink

Publicity: Social Butterfly PR

CHAPTER 1

sla

WEDNESDAY FELT like a great day for a breakup.

To the kind of person who thinks things through—like knowing in the morning which dessert I planned to eat after dinner that night—Wednesday made the most sense.

For the record, it was apple pie, preferably à la mode.

Wednesday was far enough away from the previous weekend to blur the memory of the beautiful brunch Tom and I had eaten at Sam's in Tiburon and far enough from the upcoming weekend that I wasn't worried about sitting on my couch alone with no plans.

If I waited until Friday, there was a chance I'd get lazy, decide that kissing the wrong guy was better than kissing no guy, and decide to wait another week.

Like I'd done for the past two months.

So Wednesday it was—the day I'd tell my unfairly handsome, highly accomplished, noncommittal boyfriend to pack his things

1

and find someone else to shower with lukewarm affection and expensive jewelry bought by his assistant.

But first, I needed to bake two hundred and fifty loaves of bread.

My day started at three in the morning, as it always does, when my babies needed my full attention, and I arose before the sleeping roosters to feed them. I threw on a pair of comfortable cotton pants and a long-sleeved shirt and tied my long, blondish brown hair up in a knot to keep it out of my face.

My morning wasn't flexible, and I had the routine down pat, including a little wiggle room for the unexpectedly long red light, the coffee spill in my car, or whatever other trouble could befall me at three in the morning.

The first snafu came in the form of bad parking karma.

My usual parking spot was occupied, odd considering it was a non-space wedged between a blue dumpster and a telephone pole in an alley. I managed to find a semi-legal space that only covered a quarter of someone's driveway.

In San Francisco, which had zero parking ever, that was practically valet.

The sourdough starters were sleeping when I opened the back door to Victorine, my bakery and café, and felt the cool outdoor air mingle with the warmer humidity of the industrial kitchen.

And there they were, lined up in jars under a length of burlap cloth. So pretty. So much potential.

"Hello, loves," I said, uncovering them and smiling at the way they'd bubbled overnight.

Yes, I knew it was a little crazy and they weren't actually human children, but honestly, they were as well-tended as some of the kids whose parents I knew. And they behaved a lot better.

If I took care of them and kept their lives consistent, they did exactly what I wanted. I paid close attention to their development, I fed them, I made sure they had what they needed to grow and thrive . . . and the result was an award-winning sourdough that sold out every day since I opened my first bread bakery seven years earlier.

In the time since then, I'd ended up authoring a couple cookbooks and selling my bread to restaurants—some of which had the most sought-after reservations in San Francisco. That led to write-ups in epicurean magazines, invitations to bake for events at the mayor's residence, and a devoted following of sourdough die-hards who treated me like a celebrity—a bread celebrity.

Normally, when I turned the key in the back door, I felt excited—new day, new loaves. Each time I baked, it was a chance to discover something, even though I was starting with the same ingredients every time.

Flour. Salt. Water.

It might seem like there were only so many ways baking a sourdough round could go. But depending on how a farmer changed the soil or how the grains were ground, or which strains of wheat were blended with other ones, the bread would taste different. If there was a heavy fog in the city that day or a light rain, the bread would be different. Normally, I loved it all.

Not today.

Today, I was so fixated on the impending breakup that it was ruining everything else.

"*Bonjour, copine.*" Camille, my pastry chef, was the only other one who got to work as early as me. She had her own morning ritual that consisted of laminating dough for croissants, which meant layering cold butter between sheets of dough and folding, chilling, and folding umpteen times before they were ready to bake. Then she'd start on the other baked goods that we sold in the pastry case in front.

Classically trained in Paris, Camille wanted to open her own shop, but she needed her green card and some financial backing before she could do it.

We'd struck a deal early on—she only baked for me, which

allowed my café to offer some of the best pastries I'd ever eaten, and I showed her the ropes of running a business.

Today, a blue beanie covered her blond hair because it was forty degrees outside and she was crazy enough to ride to work on a moped. Even with the beanie under a helmet, thick gloves, and a leather jacket, the fierce chill had her shivering.

"Hey, Cam. You get wet out there? The fog was practically rain."

"Yeah, it was a treat. No big, though." She unwound a scarf from her neck and started hanging her layers up on a hook in the back. I'd already put my jacket and scarf there.

Camille had moved to the Bay Area from Paris four years earlier and I'd hired her immediately. Her English was flawless, thanks to a few years she'd spent at a high school in England, and she still didn't know many people in San Francisco, so she spent a lot of time at work. Like me.

"You're a beast. Someday, I aspire to be you," I told her.

"You want to ride around in the cold because you can't afford a car or a parking space?"

"No, I just want to be cool and ride a Vespa and pretend I'm French. But first I'll have to learn how to ride one," I said.

"It's easy. I'll teach you. The key is balance." As if proving her exceptional skill in that area, she climbed on a stool and stood on one foot as she leaned to grab a fresh box of parchment paper off a high shelf.

"Hey, can you grab me a stack of baskets while you're up there?" I asked. I had a special order for a dozen extra loaves.

She handed down the baskets and I added them to the stacks that were waiting on the lower shelves for the day's bread. Then, I fed the starters and waited while they consumed the new flour and water and started to bubble.

"*Alors, quoi de neuf?*" she asked. I'd gotten used to her habit of interspersing conversations with French. I understood she was asking me what's new, but despite a few years of high school French, I always answered in English.

"Same old. I think I dreamed of bread starters."

"Waste of a good dream. You should listen to poems read by French men before bed, dream about that."

I went to the front where we had an industrial coffee brewing setup and turned on the machines. The crew of bakers who'd be coming in over the next hour would want coffee and I always made sure there was an urn filled in the back for us.

When I came back with the urn, Camille was in the walk-in fridge foraging around for her butter. She was almost as crazy about the origin and provenance of her butter as I was about my flour. She imported five-pound slabs of it through a cheesemaker with a connection to a dairy farm in Normandy. "It's practically black market. Probably illegal," she told me. "But it's worth it for the perfect butter."

"I won't tell a soul. Can't afford to have you hauled to jail for trafficking in illegal dairy."

Camille slammed the door to the walk-in. "So . . . how'd it go with Tom?"

"I didn't do it," I said, quickly moving to the other stacks of baskets and counting them. It was pure avoidance because I knew exactly how many baskets were in each stack.

I hated telling her I'd chickened out of the breakup. Again. But Tom had brought me flowers from a place I liked, and I'd wilted like last week's blooms.

"Tonight. I'll do it tonight."

"You're a broken record, you know."

She cast a judgmental stare my way. I didn't even mind. I deserved judgment. "I know. I was just exhausted by the time I got home and didn't feel like dealing with a confrontation."

She shrugged. "So what, you left him sleeping in your eight-hundred thread count sheets under your warm down comforter so you could come to work and he could live to dream of having lukewarm sex with you another day?"

Admittedly, it wasn't a pretty picture.

Part of the problem was that from the outside Tom and I looked perfect.

I was tall, he was taller. Both of us were driven and independent. Most people figured that no one in her right mind would dump a billionaire venture capitalist with a hard jawline and searing green eyes.

Hugely successful and gorgeous, Tom knew how to live well.

He was exactly the kind of guy I'd dated over and over again, the captain of industry types. They liked that I baked—they thought it was cute and homey—and they thought I'd accomplished enough, but not too much. I could be arm candy at whatever business thing they dragged me to, but not too pretty, smart, or accomplished to overshadow their physical splendor, brilliance, and success.

And once again, the relationship left me wanting.

Wanting what, I wasn't exactly sure, but I had a feeling it had something to do with the wild melding of minds and the hot, sexy melding of everything else.

Tom and I didn't have that.

For a year, it didn't matter.

Then I'd rounded the backstretch of thirty-four and was heading into my last months before thirty-five. As the oldest of five sisters, I felt responsible for setting some kind of example for women as we aimed for work-life balance. Our brother, the oldest, was already engaged, and by the logic of our birth order, I was supposed to be next. Or at least taking meaningful steps in that direction.

Somehow a bell started ringing in an empty belfry in my brain I hadn't visited before. *Clang, clang, clang. Commitment, adulting, babies.* It was loud and annoying, and it got my attention.

I knew I should stop wasting my time if Tom wasn't the guy. He wasn't. I just hadn't done anything about it.

My phone buzzed with a text.

Tom: Call me.

I felt a pang of nerves rush through my body. Breakup time.

I had to do it. I would.

But my fingers wouldn't dial.

A few minutes later, another text.

Tom: Please.

I felt my resolve weakening just at that one word. *Please* tugged at my heartstrings. Maybe I could wait another week. Maybe something would change, and Tom would want something more than arm candy.

Maybe I was deluding myself. Again.

sla

By seven in the morning, my three baking assistants and I had gotten a hundred and fifty sourdough loaves out of the oven and cooling onto racks in plain view of the small café in front.

People liked to see the process of bread making and they'd pay a little extra for something made by hand from locally farmed ingredients. Sure, they could go down the block and buy baguettes from the high-end grocery for four bucks, but the dough was brought in frozen and heated in their ovens.

The trick was used all the time—shops heated baked goods onsite so it smelled like fresh bread and no one gave it a second thought, assuming it was made fresh for half the price I charged.

"These frozen baguettes don't hold a candle to your sourdough goodness," a voice intoned in the doorway. I didn't need to look up from the pastry display to know it belonged to Owen Miller, my most *regular* regular.

He held up the loaf he'd just bought from the grocery and

ceremonially dropped it in the trashcan, as he did about once a week.

We'd had lengthy conversations about it. I hated waste. But Owen claimed he was "saving one more unknowing soul from bad bread," and couldn't be dissuaded. I'd fish it out later and feed it to the birds in the back alley.

My bread was too good for the birds. On that we agreed.

"Morning, friend," I said. "And thanks for the undying loyalty to my bread cult." When the grocery had first opened, Owen had checked it out and dismissed the place as an Eataly wannabe with hipster lettuce.

"How're the kids?" I noted amusement in his eyes when he asked about the starters. He probably thought I was a loon for treating them like the living organisms they were.

Or maybe he was one of the few souls who appreciated the molecular magic that was fermentation.

"They were blooming with bacteria. Sour smelling. A little sweet and yeasty."

Owen nodded. "What I like to hear." There weren't many people who'd find that description appealing, but sourdough nerds united with a common purpose—fresh, amazing bread.

Owen was an enigma who came by himself several mornings a week and never brought a newspaper or a laptop or even a sudoku puzzle. He'd sit at the table closest to the kitchen and crane his neck to watch the bakers finishing up the loaves with rapt interest, as though he hadn't just done the exact same thing the day before.

He also showed up early—too early—a good hour before we opened to the public. He said it was because he wanted to smell the bread baking and he was an early riser. That, or he was a bread mole feeding dough secrets to MI6.

Ordinarily, I wouldn't let customers in the door before we opened, but Owen was nice to everyone and seemed harmless, a bread diehard who had nothing better to do. Anyone who paid attention to what we did and felt so passionately that he'd dump someone else's baguette in the trash was okay in my book.

When I had a free moment, I liked chatting with him—always about the flour I sourced from farmers in the fields northeast of San Francisco and the care and maintenance of starters. At this point, he knew enough to start his own bakery.

"Can you sit? Do you have time?" he asked. He always asked, I always said no. Normally, it was a knee-jerk response. But today was different.

"Actually, sure. I made good time on the baking today because I have three assistants back there." It was the first time I'd ever baked with three and although we crowded each other initially, we'd quickly figured a system and had been super-efficient.

We'd made all the loaves for the morning and finished the dough for the afternoon, so it could do a bench rise instead of going in the warmers later. I was excited to see how that would change the flavor. But more importantly, it saved me time.

"You normally have two. Plus, Camille, but she doesn't help with bread." He said it matter-of-factly because he'd watched us enough mornings to know the order of things.

"It was a scheduling mistake, but it made my morning so much easier. And now I'm kind of fantasizing about having three assistants every morning . . ."

"You should," he said, stirring milk into his coffee. He drank the coffee I made for the employees and poured the milk from a carton I plopped on the counter when he walked in. He ←never complained that I wasn't making him a fancy latte from the machine. Good thing, because in seven years, I'd never bothered to learn how to use it.

"Too expensive," I said. But I let my mind wander to how luxurious it would feel to have an extra assistant every day. I might have moaned.

"You're tired," Owen said, again as a statement, not a question.

And again, he was right. I was on my second cup of coffee and

I was starting to feel my energy drop, which was unusual for me. I didn't normally hit a lull until after noon.

"Yeah, didn't sleep well." I opted against telling him why. He didn't need to know that I'd spent half the night awake chastising myself for not woman-ing up and pulling the plug on Tom.

Owen nodded, and I looked him over—about my age, maybe slightly older, always with a couple days of scruff on his face, which I might have noticed if I wasn't in the throes of a breakup that had so far only happened in my head.

Okay, fine, I absolutely noticed, and it was damn sexy, especially when he scrubbed his thumb under his chin while his eyes moved lazily over my face.

A bloom of heat took me by surprise as it rose in my cheeks and on the back of my neck. Was it my imagination or was he staring at my lips like he wanted to bite them?

Look away. Save your dignity. And . . . no, impossible.

If he saw my blush, he gave no indication. His eyes stayed fixed on me, while mine roamed and took in the healthy tan of his skin and the generous, pillowy lips which he pressed together when he was thinking.

And as long as I was noticing . . . holy hell, those eyes. They flashed a tranquil, deep blue that made me stare unabashedly. His hair was brown, mixed with subtle streaks of gold, like he'd spent a lot of time on horseback, at the top of a mountain, riding shirtless in the sun.

Ahem.

Or maybe that was just his normal hair color.

All in all, with his easy smile, Owen painted a nice picture. It felt life-affirming to know that my lackluster year with Tom hadn't dulled my senses completely.

"Tell me about the flour blend you're using," Owen said. Again, not phrased as a question. I couldn't recall if he made a habit of speaking in declarations. He was hardly bossy, but his authoritative manner was kind of appealing, like he knew what he wanted and asked for it.

It made me wonder if he did that in bed. And…my mind was off and wandering again.

"The flour?" I forced myself to focus on his question. "Did I tell you about the farmers in Vallejo? I was out visiting their crops a couple months ago and they've been harvesting like crazy after the rains we had."

It wasn't easy to find farmers who'd reliably grind and deliver grain that they harvested within two days, so more of the protein remained intact. That was the key to good flavor.

"Amazing. I love that you found those guys," he said.

I could feel the subtle difference in the air that came when the bakers opened the ovens to take out the fresh loaves. I tipped my head up like a dog who'd just heard a high-pitched sound.

Owen's eyebrow popped up. "Ready?" He checked the time on his phone. He knew the timing of the place almost as well as I did.

"Soon," I said.

Owen nodded and smiled. I always let him take a loaf of bread before they were done cooling. And I always said the same thing to him when I sent him off with bread fresh from the oven. "You'll wait a half hour before you eat it, right?"

"Yes. I promise," he'd say, with a wink and a flash of a smile that told me he probably wasn't going to do what I asked.

Owen sat back in his chair and looked around the room. "You replaced the wall sconces. I like these," he said, pointing to the tulip-shaped glass that held candle bulbs. I'd swapped out the heavier brass sconces a couple weeks earlier because they didn't emit enough light and I never liked the brass.

I nodded. Of course he'd notice anything that was different. He practically lived here. "Owen, what do you do? For a job." I didn't mean it to sound accusatory, but I realized my mistake when he visibly deflated.

"You mean, other than make observations about your lighting? That's not a robust enough job in your book?"

"Ha ha. I'm serious. I never have time to talk and today I do. So tell me something. What do you do all day after you leave here?"

I kind of expected him to say he didn't do anything. Or he was retired or independently wealthy. There were a lot of those types around the Bay Area who'd made their money on stock options and had to find ways to spend it.

Lurking in a bakery four mornings a week smacked of wealth and boredom.

Owen raked a hand over his face as though answering the question pained him.

Nailed it. He's a wealthy boring guy.

"I work in hotels. Generally small ones in cool locations. I'm kind of a jack of all trades."

Oh. That was kind of interesting and different.

I wanted to know more. Was he a hotel manager? Handyman? Groundskeeper?

"Hey, Isla, do you have a sec?" Camille asked, peeking out from the kitchen. The grimace on her face made it seem like she felt guilty to be interrupting. I gestured her over to let her know it was fine.

"Camille, you know Owen, our lurker?"

"Wait, I'm a lurker?" he said.

"Of course you are. You hang here and lurk," I said.

"I'd rather be referred to as a hanger than a lurker." He smiled and leaned back in his chair.

"*Salut* Owen," Camille said. "Isla, will you come look at something?" she asked without even glancing at Owen. It was odd.

She beckoned me to the other side of the café, almost out of earshot of Owen, and leaned against a table for two, where I noticed a pot of lavender that needed watering. And the salt and pepper grinders were half-empty.

"What's up?" I asked.

She crossed her arms and looked down, so I braced for bad news—her telling me she needed time off, or worse, that she'd found another job. I didn't have time to look for a new pastry chef. "I hate to be the one to tell you this."

"Just spill it. You're freaking me out. Are you quitting?"

"What? No. Of course not," she said.

I heaved a sigh of relief. Short of that, any news was tolerable.

"Okay, good. You scared the crap out of me."

She still had that pained look on her face. Finally, she blinked heavily and showed me her phone, where there were several photos and a headline about Tom Stone, head of Fletcher-Stone, having a night out with his "new flame."

Only problem was that despite my breakup plans, I was still Tom's old flame.

Lo and behold, the gossip sites felt the need to bring that up two lines later. "Celebrity baker Isla Finley spurned by billionaire financier." It was supposed to be one saving grace of being a baker—photographers didn't follow me around and gossip rags didn't care to know my name.

But once my photo had started popping up in San Francisco food blogs and travel magazines, people sometimes recognized my face and snapped a photo. I ignored it unless they got pushy.

"Wait, what?!" With shaking hands, I took the phone from Camille and scrolled through the photos. Tom coming out of a restaurant with his arm around the blond woman. Tom getting into a car with the blond woman. Tom . . . kissing the blond woman outside a Starbucks.

"Damn him, he went to a chain coffee place?" I said, pushing the phone back into Camille's hands.

"That's what you're upset about? That he didn't shop local?" she asked, incredulous.

"No. Of course that's not what I'm upset about. But geez, he knows how I feel about that. It's like an extra hot turd on top of a flaming fuck you." I didn't know what I was saying or who was listening, and I didn't care. I'd moved to the center of the shop and was gesturing wildly with my arms.

The bakers had all stopped what they were doing and were staring at me. "This isn't a circus side show. Keep baking!" I shouted.

Crap. Now I'd have to apologize to them. It was a good thing we hadn't opened for business yet or there would probably already be a viral video of the insane bread lady.

"I'm sorry. This is so not cool of him," Camille said. I nodded. It wasn't her fault, but I appreciated the sympathy.

"I can't believe that a guy that smart would be dumb enough to get photographed. And who the hell is that woman?!" Out of the corner of my eye, I saw Owen taking all this in but I didn't have the wherewithal to run interference between my mouth and my best customer.

Camille guided me farther from the prying ears of my baking staff and tried to calm me down. "Do you want to get out of here for a little bit? Take a walk? Clear your head? I can run things."

"No. I don't need to clear my head. It's been clear for weeks. I was supposed to break up with him. Before there was cheating and humiliation."

"Maybe he knew it was coming. Maybe this is why he moved on before you could do it," she said.

I couldn't believe she really thought that made sense. "He moved on to spare himself being dumped? If you want to spare yourself, you do the dumping first. You don't go out and get photographed with some blonde you're banging."

"No, you're right. Of course you're right." She looked anguished and I realized I was taking everything out on her. I pulled her in for a hug, which she may have found strange, but she said nothing.

"Thanks, Camille. I'm fine. Really. I just can't believe he took her to dinner, then came to my house and slept in my bed. He's such an asshole, a blonde-screwing, egomaniacal asshole."

"You sure you don't want to get some air or something?" She looked wary, the way you look at a crazy person.

I nodded. "No. I want to bake. It's fine, I'm fine. I'm just really, really pissed off." I turned back toward the kitchen, where everyone was making a point to make extra noise so I'd know they weren't paying attention to me. And because I was insane, I contradicted myself in the next second. "You know what, maybe I should get some air. We're ahead of schedule."

My brain spun off making a wish list of pain for Tom.

Gah, forget him. He just proved he's not worth it.

And goddamn him for making me lose it in front of my staff and a customer. I'd apologize to the bakers in a sec, but first I needed to say something to Owen who'd clearly overheard.

After barely having a conversation in over a year, I'd gone from bread starters to airing my whole sordid personal life. I rolled my eyes before even turning around to see the evidence of pity in his eyes.

But when I looked over at Owen's table, he was gone.

CHAPTER 3

wen

IF ANYTHING CAN BE SAID about me, it's that I pay attention. I'd been hanging out at that bakery almost daily for over a year and I'd gleaned a hell of a lot of information about how bread was baked.

I'd learned the difference between cracked wheat and milled wheat. I knew how gluten and water interacted and why fermentation was the holy grail of bread making. Sufficient moisture in the bread oven was a no-brainer.

But I didn't know Isla Finley was dating the head of Fletcher-Stone.

Was it willful avoidance because I preferred to think of her as gorgeous, sexy, and unavailable only because of her baking schedule?

Perhaps.

Tom Stone was legendary in the startup scene—legendary for

17

being both a rainmaker and an asshole. I'd mainly experienced the asshole side.

About ten years ago, my company had been one of the region's many startups. Now we were solid, but in the early days, I'd prayed for someone like Tom Stone to cast a glance my way and sprinkle some of his venture capital fairy dust on my fledgling operation. He didn't.

Back then, I was small potatoes for a company like Fletcher-Stone, so I did what most other small companies did—I worked twenty-four-seven to find tons of tiny investors—literally everyone from my next door neighbors who pitched in a hundred bucks to my college roommate's parents, who made a bigger bet because I'd saved their son from choking on a goldfish during a fraternity pledge dare.

Eventually, I scraped together enough money to open a boutique hotel in Sausalito. Then I sweated for the next two years to make sure I could pay all of those kind folks back, with interest. I couldn't bear the thought of my elderly neighbor Beatrice losing a quarter of the nest egg she insisted I sink into the hotel.

She was one of the first ones I repaid once we had money coming in. It felt good to tell my investors they were getting their money plus an eight percent return inside of two years.

It was a bloody, sweaty, and tearful two years.

But the investors were happy, so they were ready and willing when I was ready to open a second hotel.

And so on, and so forth.

Now I was looking at opening a seventh hotel and most of my early investors had happily cashed out and been replaced by larger backers who could write checks for tens of millions instead of thousands.

But I digress...

What really surprised me was that Isla was dating that VC guy at all. I'd finally had an opportunity to get to know him better a couple years ago. My impression of him . . . well, I hated his damn guts.

He'd taken notice of what we were doing and asked to have lunch. Still cowed by his influence in Silicon Valley and curious what he had to say, I took the meeting.

It was a Tom Stone dog and pony show where he brought in three-dimensional renderings of sprawling hotel complexes and sick video presentations with maps dotted with all the places he'd envisioned for domination by my hotel brand.

He proposed some big changes that would have doubled down on the quaint uniqueness of each property by making cookie cutter versions in far-flung locations, amping up the corporate money-making machine, and selling the company to the highest bidder.

The local charm of the architecture would remain, but behind the scenes, everything would be replaced by a corporate structure that would snuff out all the local artisans I normally hired and raise prices in the process.

All so rich investors could get richer.

I hated the plan and told him so. He told me I was being naïve and proceeded to launch a petty spite campaign aimed at some of my celebrity clients—names we kept under a cone of silence, so it took some underhanded dealings for him to discover them—and said nasty things intended to make them stop staying at my hotels.

It's a point of personal pride that not one listened to him, especially given the money he spent trying to lure them elsewhere.

Tom Stone hated to lose, that much was clear.

So he went after me personally. That meant hitting me where it hurt more than a business transaction—my girlfriend. At first, it was a chance meeting at the coffee place near her office. He unleashed his charm offensive. He dangled his Amex Black Card and lavished her with attention.

She flew to him like a paperclip to an industrial magnet.

Maybe it says more about the frail state of my relationship than anything glorious about Tom, but the son of a bitch won that big dick contest and made sure I knew it.

I couldn't imagine what Isla saw in him other than the obvious—his brain, his irritating Dudley Do-Right chiseled jaw, or the money he made hand over fist through the ownership interest he took in every company he helped drive to billion-dollar success.

Okay, fine, maybe she saw those things.

Regardless, I had an impression of her as being oblivious to those trappings. She handled real dough every day for a living, not the venture capital kind. The bread baking made me think of her as a grounded, logical woman who was more concerned about the effects of annual rainfall on wheat berries than the strike price of stock options. Maybe I'd watched too much *Little House on the Prairie* with my sister as kids.

It's not like Isla and I talked—ever—about anything other than bread, but you'd think I'd have picked up on the Tom Stone thing at some point.

And now, with news of his new girlfriend splashed all over the internet for anyone to see, it seemed like her personal life had become instantly complicated. That made me sad for her because it was clear she had no idea. I figured the best thing I could do to save her from embarrassment in her own shop was to get out of there.

I thought about all of this as the train zipped me to the Palo Alto station, which was only a couple blocks from work. I'd clocked it, and it took me a half hour longer to get to work on foot and by train than if I drove door to door. But in traffic, the train was actually fifteen minutes faster. That's how bad Bay Area traffic sucked, especially for people who worked south of the city, in Silicon Valley.

When I walked into my office building with the image of Isla still stuck in my mind, I was so out to lunch that I didn't notice Rafael sitting at the front desk until he waved his hands in front of my face.

"Hey, man. In the clouds much?"

I snapped out of my reverie and stared at Raf, my business partner. He handled all the financials and management issues, and I took care of the creative and development side of the business, but we both wore all the hats all the time.

Still, despite all the hats, he wasn't usually our receptionist.

"You're at the desk. Where's Julia?" A trained architect, Julia was also our newest hire, and as such, she got some of the scut work, like answering phones.

"Working on the sketches for the new Sonoma location," Raf said like it was obvious.

Right. I was the one who assigned her that project. I needed to get my wits about me and stop thinking about Isla and her problems which most definitely weren't my own.

"Yeah. What's on your plate today?" I asked.

He quirked an eyebrow at me like I was the idiot I'd already proven I was. "Finding a GM for the Healdsburg property."

"Great. Right. Perfect," I said, looking down at the files spread all over the temporary desk where he sat.

Our company had grown to the point where we'd run short on offices and even desks. That meant that a lot of people moved from desk to desk when they didn't need quiet space in an office in order to accommodate the people who were onsite.

It had worked out well for five years and I saw no reason to change it up. We had a big open-plan office with a communal kitchen, lots of meeting spaces, and the requisite foosball table and pop-a-shot basketball. We had air hockey too at one point, but the slamming noise became a problem, so now it took up residence in my apartment.

"Hey, did you see the dirt on Tom Stone? Finally got some bad ink for being a cheating asshole. Figured you'd enjoy that come-uppance," Raf said.

I didn't enjoy it, not when it led to the look I saw on Isla's face earlier.

"Dude, all good?" Rafael asked. I realized I was still standing over his temporary desk and staring at his piles of paper which he probably found unnerving.

I nodded and backed away from his desk. "Yup, all good. Saw the Tom Stone thing—guy's a Grade A douche."

A douche who doesn't deserve a woman like Isla Finley.

Raf was staring at me. Had he asked me something else? "Sorry, didn't sleep enough. Need coffee."

"Don't have that flavored shit that's in the first drawer. It tastes like moldy blueberries," he said, going back to his files.

"Noted. Thanks," I said, making my way to the kitchen. I'd bought the flavored coffee and happened to like it, but I didn't want to get into it with him. We had a new hotel to build and I needed to find a new company that would give us a decent deal on mattresses that normally cost ten grand apiece.

I looked at the clock and made a mental bet with myself that I could get it done by lunch.

TWO HOURS LATER, I'd gotten a decent deal on organic handmade mattresses, talked a developer into selling a piece of land at a discounted price, and put out fires at three different hotel locations where the in-house restaurants were spending too much money on ingredients and not making it up in wine sales.

There was an ebb and flow to these things. We lost money on Wagyu beef and hangar steak but we made it up on locally sourced salads and wines.

It was all in the story. We were running curated vacation destinations that made people feel like they'd left their lives behind and entered a haven of sustainable farming, lavender spa therapies, and food as medicine.

The customers needed to buy into the farm-to-table philosophy or they wouldn't spend the money on heirloom greens.

We were falling short there, and it wasn't something one phone call was going to solve. I needed to visit the properties and rewrite our entire marketing strategy to speak to the right customers. Preferably by yesterday.

No wonder I preferred to escape it all to hang out and eat bread. I rubbed my eyes and tried to decide if it would make me look like a charming, dedicated customer if I started showing up twice a day or if I'd look desperate and pathetic. Probably the latter.

My mind was drifting back to Isla when Julia knocked on the doorframe of my office and waited until I invited her in with a wave. Even then, she looked hesitant.

"I apologize, I know I'm not on your calendar," she said. Having worked for a stodgy architecture firm for a year, Julia had a hard time breaking out of a corporate mold.

"No one here is on my calendar. What's up?"

She stammered and stood stiffly in the doorway and I marveled, as I always did, at how uncomfortable and formal she was, despite the fact that our workplace was anything but. Her dark brown hair fell in a shoulder-length bob and she wore a navy blue dress with a scarf tied around her neck. She could've moonlighted as a flight attendant at Delta Airlines, except that at barely five feet tall, she'd be too short to reach the overhead bins.

Julia was a contradiction if I ever saw one—probably the most artistic person I'd met with a degree in architecture and a self-proclaimed heavy metal music fan, who wore conservative clothes and was scared to death of people. She was one of my favorite hires at the company, mainly because I'd yet to figure her out.

I pointed to one of the chairs on wheels that were out in the hall. "Come. Have a seat. Did you bring sketches?"

She brought the chair over and presented the tube of drawings as if it were a gift. "Yes. I have a couple alternates for the new location."

She was still sitting about nine feet away from me. I waved her over and stood up so we could unroll the sketches and look at them on my desk.

"This one has a bigger footprint, but because of the way it's facing and the option of putting up solar panels, it's more cost-effective to build but it would have fewer rooms."

"Why fewer rooms if it's a bigger building?"

"Just the way it lays out. There's wasted space, but the aesthetics are better." She'd also brought three dimensional renderings that showed what the building would look like from the ground, which was crucial for someone like me who only knew what I liked once I could see it.

"And this version costs more to build but it looks worse?" I asked pointing to the other sketch.

She looked guilty at my conclusion. "Yes. In my opinion, it's less pleasing, but I'm only one person."

"You're the one with vision and a degree in this stuff. That's why I need your opinion. "

She blushed and started to back away, leaving me with the drawings. "I'm going to work on a few more ideas. I just wanted you to see what I had so far," she said, backing up some more until she was in the doorway.

She was so strange and oddly intriguing, maybe because I had no fucking idea what was up with her.

"Great. Thanks." I waved but she'd already turned around and scurried away. I squeezed my eyes shut, as if I could open them to some sort of clarity on her weirdness.

"She's got the hots for you," Raf said, striding into my office without knocking.

I looked at him like he was nuts, which he clearly was if he thought Julia's behavior was some sort of mating call. "I'm gonna say *no* to that. But man, is she . . ."

"Awkward in a completely sexy and awesome way? So crazy town that she might be a serial killer, might not? Buttoned up at work but hot in bed?" he asked.

"I was going to say strange. But now I see where the hopped up pheromones are hiding out," I said.

He shrugged. "Yeah, sure. I'd tap that if it was an option, but it's probably not. So be it. I might be getting beers later with a couple of the guys if you're interested. Did you finish looking over the numbers?"

Raf's brain was a meat grinder of thoughts that came out in no particular order but somehow all made sense and didn't waste valuable words.

"No to the beer, almost done with the numbers, but I might want to add in a few new costs, so prepare for that. I'll tell you more when I know what I'm doing."

"Cool, man. But trust me on the Julia thing. She's weird with everyone, but she's especially strange with you. Just something to think about . . ." He left my office as abruptly as he'd appeared. Maybe everyone I worked with was weird. The last thing I needed was to consider dating an employee, especially someone who acted the strangest around me.

Besides, I was pretty sure she didn't bake bread.

CHAPTER 4

$\mathcal{I}$sla

THE SAVING grace of my job was that I was so busy all day baking and talking to people that I didn't have time to think about much else. It was my Zen place, my version of meditation.

Being all-consumed was key on days when boyfriends were caught cheating and my cell phone was buzzing nonstop with social media updates, calls from a couple gossip-hungry reporters, worried check-ins from friends, and even a few photographers outside the café taking pictures.

It still struck me as nutty that relationship drama between a financial guy and a baker would qualify as social media fodder. But when the financial guy was a billionaire and a player, people followed the money.

Now I had messages from gossip blogs asking for comment. Anything pithy and sassy I might have wanted to say about Tom would only fan the flames and lead to more attention, so I said nothing.

But when things slowed down toward the end of the day, my resistance caved.

My baked-on armor melted away and I was left with the visual of him with his lips all over some tall blonde.

I went back to my phone and by now there were more salacious details about the Swedish model that Tom Stone was linked with, in addition to some older photos of me with Tom at a charity event. According to social media gossip, Tom and the model had met in New York a month ago and had been seeing each other on the down low ever since.

The painful realization that he'd been seeing her behind my back made me feel sick.

"You okay, *cherie?*" Camille asked, looking past me to where Tom was now standing outside the bakery. She was wrapping her scarf around her neck and getting ready to leave.

He didn't hesitate before pulling the heavy door open and flashing a broad smile like he owned the place.

She put a hand on my shoulder. "You want me to stay? When he's gone, we can drink absinthe in the back and bake something really weird."

I laughed. "I do want to do that with you someday, but nah, I'm good. Your twelve-hour day ends now."

She kissed me on both cheeks and glared at Tom before heading out. He had the good sense to look contrite, but just barely.

"No. Not who I want to see right now," I said with my arms folded as Tom stood there the way he had so many times before when he'd met me after work and whisked me off to some fancy dinner at a new restaurant. He always knew where the hottest tables were in San Francisco and he always got reservations.

"Isla, please. I need to explain," he said extending his hands to me.

I shook my head. "I'm not sure what explanation you could possibly have that would make cheating okay."

He reached a hand out and touched my shoulder, but I backed up a step. "I had a plan . . ."

WTF, he had a plan?

"Oh, tell me, Tom. Tell me about your plan. I'm fascinated." I couldn't keep the sarcasm from my voice.

"Can we just . . . let's sit and talk somewhere." He looked around the room like some five-star options were going to magically materialize. I gestured to the rustic tables for two against the walls.

He walked over to a table and pulled out a chair for me, ever chivalrous. I took the one on the other side and he glared at me. "That's mature."

"Says the man with high school bleacher moves. So explain your plan or whatever the hell you have to say and go, please," I said.

He ran his hands through his hair, which I knew he did when he was aggravated. Since I'd known him, I'd seen him do it a hundred times while he was on the phone with investors or recalcitrant startup founders. But never with me.

Now I'd become frustrating just like the people he dealt with every day.

"I've only been seeing Giselle for a month," he said. As though I wanted to know her name and bra size. She and I were not going to become shopping buddies, getting mani-pedis on the weekends.

I blew out a breath and shook my head. "Only? A month is a long time when you're still having sex with your girlfriend and sleeping in her bed."

The scumbag.

"I had standards. I never spent the night with her. I wouldn't do that. We only met in hotels. It was tawdry, I admit." He kept his voice calm and even, like he was telling me a relaxing bedtime story.

"It astounds me that you somehow think that makes it better."

28

"That's not what I meant. I meant that I had what I assumed was a fleeting interest in her and I thought if I acted on it, I could put it in its place as a mere distraction and move on to a more substantial future with you. It was like a safety check to make sure I could only be tempted physically, not emotionally. My heart belongs to you. Being with Giselle made me certain. I want a future with you." He folded his hands when he was done talking.

Tom presented his explanation so matter-of-factly it felt like he was trying to sell me on an investment. It was why he was so successful as a venture capitalist—he made his reasoning sound logical and even flattering.

Also insane.

"That's how every cheater rationalizes it. If you wanted a substantial future, cheating was not the way to get there," I said. As I heard my own voice, I realized that in his backward way, he was proposing the long-term relationship I thought I should have by thirty-five.

But I didn't want it with him. I didn't want anything to do with him.

I just wanted to make sure he knew his logic was flawed.

Then he could go fuck himself.

He tipped back in his chair and nodded, conceding. "I know. I'm sorry. Like I said, this wasn't how I wanted it all to go down."

"Meaning, you wanted to dump me yourself instead of having me see photo proof that you're an asshole? Or you wanted to have me see the photos, say everything's still cool, and work out how to be a throuple? Sorry Tom, not doing that."

He ran a hand through his hair again. It made me smile. I liked that I was aggravating him. It was more emotion than I'd seen from him in weeks. Maybe ever.

"So now what? Is there any way to repair this?" he asked. His voice was strained and irritated, which I found funny since he had no right to be annoyed with me, and yet, he was always self-righteous about business.

I'd become a piece of business to him, a problem to be solved, a possession to be secured so he could check it off his list.

"Giselle . . . she was just entertainment. You're the kind of woman I belong with."

I shook my head. "See, that's the problem, Tom. I'm not a real person to you. I'm just the kind of person you think you should be with. That's not the same as love."

He huffed a laugh as though I'd just said something completely ridiculous. Then he shook his head and wagged a finger at me like he was lecturing a stupid person.

"No. You and I agreed. We wanted the fun. The good times. And we have that. We look good as a couple. We're both professionals and it works well for both of us."

I closed my eyes and took a deep breath. "That was the conversation we had in the first three weeks of dating, the time when no one thinks about anything other than fun. It's been a year, Tom. Fun doesn't work for me. Not anymore."

Tom looked annoyed. He wasn't used to people disagreeing with him.

He was a smooth talker and he was accustomed to breezing into a room, making a convincing argument, and having everyone—male and female alike—swoon at his feet and tell him he was the greatest thing they'd ever encountered.

Well, that's not me.

Tom rolled his eyes like he'd drawn a bad poker hand. "Do you need a bigger apology? Do you need a fucking diamond on your hand, is that what this is about? Tell me what we do from here."

"Um, we do nothing," I said because he didn't seem to see how obvious it was that we were done. "I should have called time of death on us months ago, but I got lazy. I'm sorry for that because it wasn't fair to either one of us. And if I'd done what I should have back then, I'd have saved myself some embarrassment. But the end result is the same."

He looked confused. He actually seemed to think he was going to apologize for getting caught on camera and "acting on a fleeting interest" and we'd be back on track. He wasn't used to unplanned outcomes, and I wasn't giving him what he wanted. "So . . . you don't want the ring?" he asked.

"No, Tom. No ring. I want you to go," I said, getting up from the table. We really hadn't needed to sit and now I wanted to be back on my feet. I needed to move around.

I wanted to punch some dough. Or Tom's pretty face.

"It's just . . ." He shook his head. He had too much pride to engage in a losing battle. "Okay then. I regret that it didn't work out for us," he said.

I choked out a laugh. "Really? Was that regret I saw on your face in the photos? Didn't really look like it."

He was staring at me like I was an out-of-control toddler. "Are you quite finished now?"

"Quite. Or possibly not. I'm not sure." I saw no reason to make it any easier for him.

You were going to break up with him anyway. Just let it go.

And yet...I couldn't let it go. I was too angry. And that anger needed to have its due.

"You know what, Tom? I am finished. Completely finished. So even though this wasn't the way I would have liked things to end, I'm glad to be free finally."

He looked dumbfounded and it wasn't a good look on him. "Okay, well, maybe we can talk down the line..."

"Sure, sounds good," I said even though I had no interest in keeping in touch. He leaned over and kissed me on the cheek. I didn't move to hug him or show him any of the affection I'd planned to bestow when I'd imagined our breakup last night. I didn't have warm feelings for him anymore.

"Okay, well, I guess this is goodbye." He focused his eyes on mine almost like he was daring me to disagree. Instead, I nodded. Left with no other options, he turned and went for the door.

I watched it close behind him with a mixture of relief and the grief that always came with endings, even when they were expected. I had to shake that off, and the best way I knew to do that was either running or baking.

Sex was also a good option, but probably not a viable one, given the situation.

I preferred the long weekend runs I usually went on with my running club, and they met over in Oakland, which wasn't quite as hilly as my neighborhood route, but I liked the camaraderie. Plus, it had gotten dark between the time Tom had shown up and the time he left.

I wasn't a huge fan of running in darkness, even though my sister Becca had bought me a headlamp for the purpose. I found that somehow I tripped on cracks in the sidewalk more often when I wore the headlamp than when I didn't.

All of that is to say that I rationalized myself out of running. So baking it would be. I headed to the kitchen to see what trouble I could get myself into now that everything had been put away for the night.

Before long, a noise came from the front of the shop. It sounded like a knock on the glass. I wasn't worried about intruders because the front door self-locked at six as a matter of safety. Ideally, I'd have left by six, but lately it hadn't happened very often.

I assumed it was Tom coming back to hit me with one more argument for why our relationship could still work. And because I was a glutton for punishment, I went back to open the door.

But the man I saw smiling under the streetlights wasn't Tom.

It was Owen.

sla

Maybe it was the mentally draining day, but my brain couldn't compute.

He looked like the same guy I was used to seeing at his corner table in the morning, but he was out of context now. It was almost like running into someone I only knew from the gym somewhere else in the city—hard to place in regular clothes without sweat—and I stared at him dumbfounded for a moment before opening the door.

"Hey," I said. "Am I confused and it's really six in the morning, not six at night?"

"Naw, it's night, as evidenced by the darkness. Then again, I suppose it's dark in the morning when you get here. Am I disturbing you?" he asked. Phrased it as a question—maybe he did that when he didn't know the answer.

Seeing him was nice, but odd.

Owen and I didn't have the kind of friendly relationship that encouraged stopping by in the evening. The conversation we'd had that morning had been the longest we'd talked in a year's time.

He looked at me expectantly and I realized I hadn't answered his question. His deep blue eyes searched mine for acknowledgement that it was okay that he'd come. "No. You're not disturbing me. What's up? Are you looking for an evening bread fix to go with your morning one? Is this about to become a habit?"

His mouth tipped up into a smile and I noticed how the corners of his eyes creased with laugh lines. I couldn't stop staring at the color, which reminded me of a late summer sky and bordered on too blue to be real. I wanted to ask him if he wore contact lenses, but it didn't seem like the most crucial order of business.

"Nah. I'm good on bread. I just . . . I kind of overheard your conversation this morning and I felt awkward about it. I'm intruding on your personal space by being at the bakery outside your normal opening hours. I wanted to apologize."

Is he for real?

My actual boyfriend could barely bring himself to say he was sorry for openly cheating on me and getting caught doing it, and this man had made a special trip to the bakery to apologize for crowding my personal space.

"Wow," I said, shaking my head.

He tipped his head to the side and considered my one-word response. Maybe he was waiting to see if I had more to say.

When the awkward silence became even more awkward by nature of us standing in the doorway, I backed up a few paces in case he wanted to come in. "I'm afraid we shipped everything that was left to a homeless shelter, or I'd offer you something to eat," I said.

We didn't sell day-old anything. It was a rule. I looked at the bakery cases as though some perfect ham and gruyere croissant would magically appear, but they remained bare.

Owen stepped into the shop. "I didn't come for free snacks. I came to see if you were okay. And again, I apologize if I'm over-stepping my bounds."

I held up a hand. "Stop. Apologizing."

"Okay. Is there . . . can I do anything to help you?"

"Help me?" I still wasn't sure why he was here. Did he want to help close up the bakery for the night?

He blinked hard. "I'm not saying this right. I meant that from what I could see, it seemed like maybe you were set up to have a shitty day. And I came back because I thought maybe I could buy you dinner or something and maybe end it on a better note."

I heard what he was saying, but I immediately felt suspicious. "Is that code for thinking you can get laid because I'm too distraught to say no?"

"Get laid? Seriously?" He folded his arms like he was waiting to see what other idiocy might spew forth.

"Yes. Is this a pity proposition?" I asked. I still couldn't under-stand why he was here. We didn't know each other outside of daily banter and I wasn't used to people swooping in on my worst days and asking if they could help.

No. Worse than that, I was completely ill-equipped to handle such acts of kindness because I'd never experienced that from a man who didn't want something.

He huffed a laugh and moved fully into the room, shaking his head. "What kind of an asshole do you think I am? You really think I'm here out of pity? No. Hardly. I just thought you might be hungry. Do you get hungry? Or do you just get by eating bread all day long?"

"I don't eat bread all day long."

"You should. Your bread is fucking awesome."

I felt an unwilling smile creep across my face. "Thanks."

I still didn't know what to make of him.

He'd practically become a fixture at the bakery like the twin chandeliers. He'd spent so much time sitting at his table in the corner that I'd written him off as some odd bread nut who had an outsized appreciation for dough.

He ran a hand over his forehead as though he was trying not to get exasperated with me. "So . . . I'm going to hope the third ask is the charm here. Can I buy you some dinner? Or even a snack? There's a CVS down the block. How about a Twix bar? Lays chips?"

It was like he was speaking a foreign language. After getting used to Tom's big fancy dinner invitations to private tastings at Michelin-starred restaurants, I'd forgotten what it felt like when someone suggested grabbing food because it was dinnertime and I might be hungry.

"Yes," I said, nodding at him, still a bit dazed. "Yes, okay. Except for Lays. I don't like them. I need a thicker chip, like kettle baked or Ruffles."

He nodded slowly. "Noted."

"And I like sour gummy worms, not that you asked."

I knew I sounded like a loon, but it felt important that he knew I wasn't going to be satisfied with any old snack.

There were standards.

Plus, he'd thrown me off and I was having trouble recovering.

The one thing I knew for sure was I wanted to get out of the bakery and have dinner with him. It didn't matter if he wanted to get KFC or make me a peanut butter sandwich on the hood of his car. I was hungry.

We were standing in the middle of the bakery floor and the only light came from the Edison bulbs hanging from two industrial chandeliers overhead. The night beyond him outside the shop was dusky and I could hear the occasional voices of people walking by on the sidewalk.

Watching me with his placid blue eyes, he waited for me to work out the questions that were still coursing through my brain. He seemed unhurried and I wasn't used to people like that in my life. My sisters were all crazy and my best hires tended to sprint around like caffeinated bunnies.

I had so many questions, namely why he, of all people, had chosen to show up here.

"I'm just..." I didn't know what.

He waited patiently to find out.

My bakers had watched my meltdown after seeing the pictures of Tom and none of them had asked me to dinner. They'd taken off as soon as their shifts were over, mostly without saying goodbye as though they didn't want to disturb the crazy person who might bite their heads off or cry. For the record, I was planning to do neither.

I'd called my middle sister, Becca, and the next-youngest sister, Cherry, and vented at them for twenty minutes apiece, but they hadn't shown up to make sure I remained well-fed.

So what's with this guy?

Maybe it was gratitude mixed with curiosity or maybe it was that I'd just noticed his lips looked particularly pink and plush, but I reached for his face and ran my fingertips over his cheek and over to his lips, which were just as soft as they looked.

His eyes clouded a little when I touched him and he stood frozen, as if waiting to see what else the crazy baker lady planned to do.

What I planned to do was kiss him.

It surprised me as much as it clearly surprised him.

And before I could think too much about the reason why or talk myself out of it, I erased the distance between us, looked up at him, and ran my tongue across my lips. I saw his eyes open a little wider in confusion, but he recovered when my lips touched his.

Or maybe I was too close to see his face anymore.

It felt good. My lips brushed across his, feeling them the way I'd done with my fingers.

I moved my hand around the back of his neck and pulled him

toward me a little harder, still unsure of what I was doing or what he'd do in response. He'd seemed genial and willing to help me, and my body decided this was what I wanted from him.

I didn't want a new boyfriend. I also didn't feel particularly broken up over Tom—that relationship had been over for months. Kissing Owen wasn't about anyone else.

I just wanted to kiss him.

After an initial hesitation where it seemed like Owen was waiting to follow my lead, he responded, his lips grazing mine with more intensity, his fingertips coming lightly to my jaw and guiding my face to the angle that allowed him to claim my mouth more fully.

He pressed his lips harder against mine and tangled his hand in my hair. I didn't feel rushed or wild with abandon, but I also didn't want to stop.

He swept his lips across my mouth and sucked gently on my bottom lip, which made me a little more bold and crazy. I ran my tongue across the seam of his lips, and he opened to find my tongue with his own.

As our lips melded like they were made for this, our tongues tangled and I took full leave of my senses. I didn't need senses for this. It was all feeling and zero thinking, which was perfect.

I felt the rise of heat in my chest and the swirl of desire let loose in my belly. Kissing him was sweet, almost tender, which set off alarm bells in my head.

Warning, feelings in the house.

I wasn't looking for that. That was too much, too soon. Or just too much entirely. I just wanted to know what his lips tasted like. I wanted to forget the pain of being humiliated by Tom.

I wasn't ready for tender.

Or am I? I don't know.

I jerked back and looked up to meet his gaze, which was calm and unreadable. He said nothing and he didn't take his hand away from my face. His fingertips felt hot against my skin and after a moment, I took a step back, needing relief from his touch and an end to the folly I'd started.

"Okay," I said, keeping my eyes locked on his.

He looked confused and maybe a little bit wary. "Okay?"

I nodded. I'd been reduced to the basic necessities—human contact, desire, food. "Yes. You mentioned dinner. Let's do that."

He smiled at me. "Okay. Dinner it is."

I grabbed my jacket and he held the door open for me. We walked through and I didn't look back.

CHAPTER 6

wen

IT WAS a good thing we had nearly a mile-long walk to dinner because I needed the time to figure out what the hell had just happened.

When I'd returned to the bakery to check on Isla, I'd done so as a friendly human. Isla and I were friendly, I told myself, even though we'd barely had a chance to chat more than a few minutes a day in passing and most of those conversations were about bread.

I was a customer, and as such, she paid attention to me when I came around because that's what a good business owner does for her customers. And despite what seemed like a sudden impulse to kiss me, I didn't harbor any delusions that we were suddenly more than friends.

Hell, I wasn't even sure we *were* friends. But I didn't mind waiting around to find out.

It was a perfect San Francisco night, the light fog kissing

our skin and adding a chilly coda to the unexpected heat of the spring day. Everywhere I looked, people were walking or biking or snaking through the streets in cars. The workday was done and the hour of errands and dinner had everyone in its grip.

As we walked down Market Street in the direction of the Castro, I snuck a look at Isla, whose honey brown hair was still pulled up into a high ponytail, although I'd messed it up a little by running my hands through it. Her cheeks were pink from the cool air and she'd reapplied a deep plum lipstick that only made me want to kiss her again.

Slow down.

I didn't have a dinner destination in mind, but there were lots of places in the direction we were walking, so I figured we'd pick someplace on the fly.

Watching her walking next to me, I realized that even though I'd had my eye on her for over a year and exchanged pleasantries on a daily basis, I barely knew anything about her. What little I'd occasionally glimpsed in a splashy article in San Francisco Magazine was mostly about how many celebrated local restaurants exclusively carried her bread.

Never anything personal.

I knew she was a baseball fan because she'd mentioned that it was a point of contention in her family that she was a Giants fan when the rest of them followed the A's. So she had a family of some sort, but we'd never gotten much beyond that.

"You mentioned you're the only holdout in a family of Oakland A's fans," I said, hoping to remind her of the conversation.

"Yes," she said, striding quickly as though on a compass point to some destination in The Mission.

"Your family lives locally, then, in the East Bay." It was the logical conclusion.

She stopped walking and stared at me. "You seem like you're

asking me questions, but you're really just stating facts. Do you know you do this?"

She sounded accusatory but she was smiling, her bright eyes searching mine for an answer. They were a pale hazel that seemed to change color with her mood rather than what she wore. I'd noticed it before and had always tried to avoid staring at them, but tonight I drank in every feature of her face.

"Humph," I said. "I never thought too much about it."

I did know this about myself but I didn't really want to have a conversation about it.

"No one's ever pointed it out before now?" She seemed incredulous, but it was true. Most people didn't pay attention.

She did. I liked it.

I shrugged. "Okay," she said and continued walking.

When I'd gone to the bakery, I hadn't planned on asking her to dinner. I really did just want to make sure she was okay after how shocked and humiliated she seemed seeing the pictures of her asshole boyfriend kissing someone who was not her.

Then the words slipped from my mouth without permission, and before I could censor them, I got the pleasure of watching her stammer like it was a trick question. It was adorable, if not slightly alarming for the panic it seemed to provoke.

Had no one ever asked her to dinner before?

The idea seemed impossible, given that she was gorgeous, talented, and quietly brainy.

"We might as well get this out of the way so you're not curious and I'm not forced to spend dinner talking about my ex," she said, walking quickly. Again, not knowing her well, I wondered if she always walked so fast or if she set the pace to match the topic of conversation.

"Okay, but don't feel obligated to talk about it."

Are we going to talk about the kiss?

It almost seemed like she'd forgotten all about that. Her hands waved and gestured as we moved along, doing most of the explaining.

"I don't. I just want you to know the nuts and bolts. Tom and I dated for a year or so, it wasn't great, but it wasn't awful. Don't worry, I'm still busy judging myself for that choice. I know I deserve better than "not awful." I'd been planning to end it, but I got lazy and kept chickening out. One more date, one more day. Eventually, I'd do it. Then . . . as you witnessed, he beat me to it through cheating and public humiliation. So there you have it. It's over, it's fine, and I don't want to think about him anymore."

"Okay, that's a pretty short story."

"Yes."

I waited to see if there was more.

"O-kay...I'm not going to badger you, but if something occurs to you later that you think you'd like to share, have at it," I said.

She looked at me quizzically and I wondered if my response was as odd as her expression led me to believe. I thought I was being open and not too intrusive.

"Oh, and one more thing. He just swung by the bakery just now and wondered if we could patch things up and keep going like nothing had happened and I said no."

"Oh. Okay, well it's good that you know what you want," I said.

I had no idea how to talk about this with her. Should I be asking for more details? Offering advice?

My sisters had always told me women didn't want me to solve their problems. They just wanted me to listen. I'd done my best to adhere to that and it had served me well over the years. Most women I'd dated said they appreciated that I wasn't telling them what to do.

"I know what I *don't* want. And that's Tom Stone. Like I said, it was fine, but I'm not interested in being with a guy just because it looks good on paper. Or because I seem fun at first."

I had no idea what that meant. Did she not think she was fun anymore? I knew enough about her ex to imagine that he prob-ably took her for granted. He definitely did if he was sleeping with someone on the side.

It also meant he was out of his fucking mind.

Isla seemed fun to me. Kissing her was definitely fun.

"Sure. That seems like the wrong reason," I said.

Isla's head swiveled to look at me, her eyes unreadable but her sarcasm obvious. "You think?"

She amused me. I liked the spitfire side of her that I hadn't known existed before. She was always calm and focused in the morning when I hung out at the bakery.

I nodded and kept walking, trying to think of some trivia or clever getting to know you questions because I was starting to worry about how to keep her mind out of anger-provoking breakup territory over an entire dinner.

I was also still trying to read between the lines about her and Tom. "You're way too accomplished to be someone's arm candy. If that's how he treated you, I'm sorry," I said.

She looked at me. "You're a good guy, Owen. You don't need to be sorry. He should be sorry and he's not. He somehow turned cheating into some sort of romantic test of his devotion to me. But he's an idiot. So thank you."

She picked up her pace, if that was even possible.

A moment later, she was gesturing and explaining some more. "The thing that kills me is that it's really my own fault. I'm the one who dated him for a year. After dating two other guys just like him—alpha males who think they want to be with me because they've seen my picture in some fancy magazine, but then they don't want anything serious, they don't want a real relationship even when they say they do. It's just a line. And I keep falling for it, thinking I'd matter enough for there to be some kind of future."

"You belong in someone's future. That's a given," I said.

She halted and turned to me. Her eyes suddenly misted with

such touched gratitude that I feared I'd gone too far. Then she threw her arms around me and hugged me so tightly I may have briefly lost consciousness.

"Thank you. See, not all guys are assholes. I just have to keep reminding myself of that," she said.

I was feeling pretty good that I'd distinguished myself from her former bad boyfriends by merely stating fact. Then she threw me for a loop.

"I remember you saying you worked at a hotel. I love that. It's so normal. Like, just get up in the morning and stand at the desk and welcome guests or cart around luggage—a normal job. It says a lot about you that you're happy being a cog in someone else's wheel. Not everyone has to be a titan. I think there's something about those captain of industry guys that's like empty carbs for me."

I'm still back on 'carting around luggage.'

Somewhere along the way, I'd given her the wrong impression of my job. I thought back to our conversation that morning when she'd asked about work. I'd been intentionally vague because I didn't feel like going into a whole discussion about it.

Call it morning apathy or laziness or whatever, but I only recall being vague.

I didn't recall telling her I was a bellhop.

She'd drawn that conclusion on her own.

Isla didn't wait for the light to change before walking boldly into the intersection. I darted a look around and fortunately there was no oncoming traffic. Shielding her from cars and trucks was clearly a part of my responsibilities that evening.

But first, I wanted her to clarify that bit about not liking business owners.

"You don't like people who own businesses? You own a business. Isn't that hypocritical?"

"I don't mean it like that. It's the millionaire corporate types that I seem to fall for, and they end up breaking my heart. Those are the ones I'm done with."

"Got it." I decided it was not a good time to tell her I was a millionaire corporate type who'd grown my boutique hotel business into something somewhat big.

I was pretty sure I wasn't an asshole like Tom Stone, so it seemed like a fair decision to let the issue lie.

For now.

Then she stopped walking and put her hands on her hips, legs shoulder width apart, and I expected her to don some sort of cape and cold cock a criminal. "Okay. I'm done. You heard me say it first. I'm done with the asshole alphas with their big companies and their giant egos. Done. From now on, it's true love or bust."

She exhaled a deep breath and her shoulders dropped for the first time. Tilting her head from side to side and rolling out her neck, she seemed to be willing herself to relax. I still wasn't sure if she had more to say, so I waited.

"Okay, I feel better. Thank you," she said, picking up her pace again. "Where should we eat?"

I hoofed it to keep up. "Do you like Indian food? Pub food? Dumplings? There are lots of choices in this direction," I said, trying to remember if it was worth walking all the way to Castro Street. Although at the rate we were going, we'd be there in a span of minutes.

She kept up the crazy fast pace even though she was no longer talking. Maybe she just liked getting places as quickly as possible. Isla was tall, but my legs were longer, and I was still having trouble keeping up.

"Do you always walk this fast?" I asked, hoping it didn't sound critical.

She slowed her pace a tiny bit and gave me the side eye. "Yeah, mostly. Why, is it not working for you?"

"Oh, it's fine. I just didn't bring my stopwatch, so I have no way of knowing if we're actually breaking a land speed record. In case you're in competition for that."

That earned me a partial smile, and she slowed a bit more. Thank God.

"Are you one of those people who likes to *stroll*?" She may as well have tasted a bitter apple for the disdain she showed for the word. It made me laugh.

"Okay, I see what we have here. You're a force of nature who can't be slowed by mere mortals who need to take it easy for the sake of our knees," I said, marveling at her intensity.

She looked down at my legs. "Sorry. Do you have bad knees?"

"My knees are fine. I just didn't bring the right shoes for track and field."

She slowed way down. Now we were almost walking at a normal pace for two people enjoying an evening in the city. Almost.

"Is that better?" she asked, her tone impatient. She was taking smaller halting steps. I noticed it was almost a struggle for her to slow her pace and it amused me.

"Does anyone ever describe you as being . . . passionate?" I asked.

She barked out a laugh. "Is that a euphemism for Type A or intense or annoying? Because I've been called all of those." She turned her head all the way to the side to look at me. I returned her gaze so she'd know that I was absolutely not making fun of her or accusing her of something negative.

"Nope. It's a compliment. I just wondered if you'd heard that before."

"Never." She tried to glare at me but there was a hint of a smile there. Then it morphed into a full smile and I felt like I'd won the Mega Millions Jackpot. "But I like passionate. So thank you for being the first."

Down the block, the marquee sign of a microbrewery flickered behind the leaves of tall trees that lined the street. I'd been there all of two times, but at least I could vouch for the beer and quality of the food.

I also feared that if we didn't choose a place quickly, I'd wear out the soles of my shoes. And I happened to like these shoes.

I pointed at the place as we approached. "This good? Beer and a burger, something like that?"

She nodded. "Perfect. My feet were starting to hurt." I looked down and noticed she was wearing boots with a two-inch heel. They didn't look comfortable.

Yet she'd kept going without complaint and with no idea of our destination.

It told me more about her than a year's worth of conversations.

CHAPTER 7

 sla

THE BREW PUB was a great pick. I'd been walking down Market
like a freight train bound for nowhere because Owen asking me
to dinner and me agreeing to dinner was freaking me out.

After the very public end to my relationship with Tom, the
last thing I needed was anything that could be mistaken for a
date.

And apparently, I was the type of person who used kissing as
a way to spell that out. If Owen had any clue what to make of my
absolute muddled clarity, I'd be shocked.

Fortunately, after a few sips from a pint of lager, I felt much
better about my life and the world around me, so I decided not to
dwell on the kiss.

I could always chalk it up to post-breakup insanity.

We were sitting at a high-top wooden table with coasters
from pubs around the world secured under a piece of glass on the
tabletop. We'd spent the first couple minutes looking at all of

them to figure out where the most far-flung coaster acquisition had occurred. It looked like an Amsterdam pub was the winner.

"Have you always been a bakery lurker?" I asked, figuring we could start with common interests and go from there.

"Do you really find me to be lurking? That sounds creepy. I think I may have to take my bakery appreciation somewhere else," he said.

"Don't you dare. I was kidding. You aren't creepy, but you are devoted. I kind of love that." His eyes brightened when I said that, and I realized I needed to be careful about doling out effusive sentiments. I didn't want him to get the wrong idea.

He was a customer and sort of a friend. I wasn't even sure I saw him as a potential hookup. It would be too weird to see him every day after that.

"Anyway, my question was more about what made you stumble into my bread place and start hanging out?" I asked.

"That's easy. And obvious. The smell. Anyone within a four-block radius would be insane to wake up to that bread smell and not wander over. I live slightly farther away, but I walk all over the city and one day I got a good whiff, and the rest is history. So I'm sorry. Unless I move away or you kick me out, you're stuck with me in the mornings."

"I'm not going to kick you out."

We talked and ordered our food and both dug into a basket of fries when they came before our burgers. It was easy and for a while I forgot I didn't know him that well. I didn't need to know him in order to have a good time with him.

I wondered if he was going to bring up the kiss. If I were a guy, I probably would, if for no other reason than to know if I was going to be getting some more.

Owen said nothing.

Instead he asked me about two hundred questions about other things, mostly in the form of a statement instead of an actual question.

The pub was semi-busy, which made it noisy enough to feel comfortable but not so loud that we couldn't hear each other. Owen ordered a bacon cheeseburger but substituted a veggie patty for the meat. I planned to quiz him about that, but for the moment, I was taking note of the design of the place.

"I like the chalkboards on the walls," I said, pointing to the large boards mounted in between the exposed wood beams. "Someone's an artist. Are you required to have at least one person on staff who knows how to draw if you put up chalkboards at your business?"

He nodded. "I always wondered that. It seems like at every Trader Joe's someone knows how to do artistic lettering on their chalkboards. Maybe they ask about it on the job application."

"I should start doing that. Baking skills can be taught, but artistic ability is genetic. And sadly for me, my sister got all those genes. I've been taking a watercolor painting class to try and encourage my inner artist, but it's kind of a losing battle. Fun to make a mess with the paint though."

I watched Owen pick up his burger and arrange the bacon strips and the tomato slice so he'd get a bit of each in the bite he was about to take. I approved of his technique.

He chewed and washed the bite down with a swig of the dark beer he'd ordered before putting the burger back on his plate. "You don't consider baking to be creative," he said.

"It's not. It's science. And it can go very wrong if you try to be creative. Trust me, been there."

"Yes, but you try new things out all the time. They may not all work, but you're doing that seed loaf no one else bakes. There's artistry there."

The way he talked about it caused a swell of pride and affection for him. "Thanks." I couldn't articulate a better response.

"So who's the real 'artist' in the family?" He made air quotes and rolled his eyes like I was being overly modest.

He was so nice, so easy to talk to, and so . . . freaking attractive.

How had I breezed past him day after day without taking time to notice the waves in his dark brown hair and the way he casually raked a hand through it when he was trying to think of what to say?

The blue eyes had already done me in several times over since we'd sat down for dinner and when he spoke, I caught myself watching the curve of his lips and wanting to kiss them again.

I grabbed a fry from the basket we were sharing and tried to satisfy my mouth with that instead. They had seasoned salt on them and I had no doubt I could polish them off by myself, but I had my eye on an apple pie that sat under a glass dome at the corner of the bar, so I was saving room.

"There are three. My sister, Cherry, is really creative with fashion, and my other sister Becca sews and makes stuff for her house. Then, there's my youngest sister, Tatum. She's crazy smart, like rocket scientist smart, and she doodles stuff on napkins that could be professional book illustrations. And she has no interest in ever doing anything with it."

"Sounds like you're all creative, but hang on . . . You have three sisters?" He looked at me agog.

"Four. Sarah's like me, not super artistic, so I left her out. And I have a brother. How about you?"

He shook his head. "I'm still trying to get my brain around a family of six kids. I have one sister. And most of the time, she's a lot, and she doesn't even live nearby."

It made me laugh. "Yeah, I could probably say that about any one of my sisters at a given time, but I love them. I guess if you don't grow up around a big family, it seems overwhelming, but it's all I know so it seems normal. And crazy to say, but we all pretty much get along. My dad died of brain cancer when we were young, but my mom still lives locally and we see her a ton too."

"Oh. I'm sorry about your dad. That's tough." He looked sympathetic. And curious.

"It was awful. We were close, but I was in college for the last few months of his life and I think I'll always regret not being there. But he insisted I stay in school, wanted me to live my life... I named the bakery after him—Victor was his name—I figured if I could make it work, I'd be a sort of victor. It felt like a good omen when the place started thriving."

He smiled. "That's a great story. You should share that with your customers on the back of the menu or something. People love it when there's a personal reason for things. But I get that you might want to keep it personal."

"Yeah, I feel protective of him, I guess. I'm that way with my siblings too."

A tiny flicker of something passed over his face, but he quickly blinked it away. "Good that you all stayed close." He looked like he wanted to say more, but instead he took another bite of his burger.

"Are you and your family close?" I wanted to know more but I could see that as soon as he mentioned his sister, his smile was a little forced and he seemed slightly uncomfortable. Would it derail the easy banter if I pushed him on the family stuff?

"My sister and I are, yeah. She doesn't visit often but technology helps." He held up his phone. I waited and watched him, assuming he'd finish up his thought or comment some more on the conversation with information about the rest of his family. But he changed the subject.

"What got you interested in baking?" he asked, grabbing two fries and dipping them in barbecue sauce.

I studied him for a moment, still trying to figure out what was going through his head. Baking was the one thing we had talked about a lot over a year's worth of morning visits to the bakery. He knew the answer to his question, so he'd asked it in a quick attempt to ditch the conversation we were having. I didn't want to pry, but I kind of did.

He picked up another fry but didn't eat it. He gazed at it like it was fascinating.

"Hey," I said, reaching for the hand holding the fry and wrapping my hand around it. He met my eyes, and I noticed their deep blue color again. They looked like a sea that could carry me away if I let it. I wasn't planning to.

He put the fry down and brought his hand to the table, turning it so he was holding my hand instead.

I couldn't have said what made me reach for him. It was instinctive. My rational side would have told me to keep my hands to myself. But something in the way he'd shut down made me want to bring him back out.

"Can you tell me more about your sister? Or the rest of your family? Do you mind?" I wanted to tread lightly in case they didn't get along or on the chance that there was some sort of trauma that he wanted to avoid discussing.

But he shook his head. "Well . . . my sister lives in Vermont. She met her husband in college and they moved there to be closer to his family, so I lost the draw on that one. And I don't have any other family."

With nothing else to go on, I wasn't sure how to interpret that information. "You don't . . . or didn't—?"

He took a deep breath and blinked a few times. I could tell it wasn't a conversation he wanted to have and I felt bad about pressing him on it just for the sake of my curiosity. "Actually, you know, we don't have to talk about that," I said.

I picked up my beer and waved my other hand dismissively. "This is supposed to be a fun night of not thinking about stressful things. We should probably order another round of beer and just not—"

He quieted my apologetic stream by leaning across the table and claiming my mouth in a kiss that was not apologetic at all.

It was heaven.

As he deepened the kiss, all my words evaporated.

I was confused, because nothing about our conversation was romantic, but then, nothing had been earlier when I'd done it.

He scooted his chair around to the side of the table so we were closer and his lips found mine again. We kissed. For a long time.

I forgot we were in a restaurant.

I forgot about the well-seasoned fries that before now had been the best thing I'd ever tasted.

Now I had him to compare them with and the fries fell flat like useless cardboard.

This was the kind of kiss I'd write about in my diary if I kept a diary.

Since I didn't, I closed my eyes and tried to commit it to memory because I was certain this was something I'd want to remember. Owen's lips were sweet and tasted faintly of barbecue sauce and beer, but the way they moved over mine felt like delicious sin.

There's no way the sweet bliss he made me feel with a brush of his tongue could possibly be legal.

I felt the blossom of heat over my skin and an urgent need to be closer to him—more contact, more skin, his lips in more places.

We were at a corner table in a dark pub. No one cared what we were doing.

He kissed me until the only available next step would have been tearing at each other's clothes. He nipped at my bottom lip and I was grateful for the noise in the place so he wouldn't hear me moan.

When we broke the kiss, I met Owen's eyes for a hint at what he was thinking. Did he see me as an easy hookup? I'd probably given him the wrong impression earlier by practically jumping him at the bakery so I couldn't blame him for thinking that's where we were headed.

But he didn't look at me with a smirk or an impish gleam that said we should take this show into a back room somewhere and have at each other.

He squeezed my hand, which was still clenched in his on the table, and looped a strand of my hair around a finger on his other hand and brushed it back.

The gesture was more intimate than half the nights I'd spent with Tom, not that I was comparing.

Okay, I was comparing.

This guy was not what I expected. Owen looked peaceful and content like a man who did exactly what he wanted to do when he wanted to do it. He wasn't apologetic and he wasn't leering at me like I was dessert.

He seemed confident that he'd read me correctly and done exactly what I wanted and needed. The crazy thing was that I'd been the one caught off guard, wholly unaware I wanted and needed it. But he was correct.

I'd sort that out later.

My eyes hadn't left his. There was something grounding about looking at him and it didn't feel strange that we hadn't looked away from each other for probably a full minute. Then I shook myself free and tried to regain composure.

"Well. You must've really not wanted to answer my question," I said.

He smirked. "I want to answer your question. And I will. I just wanted to do that more."

"Oh." It wasn't often that someone left me speechless, but Owen continued to surprise me. He also sent alarm bells sounding because, excuse me, what the hell was I doing kissing him . . . in a restaurant . . . on the heels of a breakup?

It was a rebound kiss, plain and simple.

I just hoped he had the good sense to know that.

I did my best not to think about it for the time being because I was having a good time, and that didn't happen every day. There would be plenty of hours for self-analysis and annihilation later.

Sometime late at night when I should be sleeping, I'd be lying awake thinking about that kiss.

Owen grabbed a French fry and popped it into his mouth. When he was done chewing, he leaned his elbows on the table and folded his hands in front of him. "I was born in Pleasanton, about an hour from here, and I have one sister. She and I grew up pretty much alone. Our parents were missionaries and spent their time traveling to remote locations to indoctrinate people into Christianity. From what little I know, they were zealots on a crusade to spread the faith. Honestly, I kind of think they were part of a cult."

I didn't know what I was expecting, but Christian zealots wasn't it. The way he said it almost robotically made it seem like he was hurrying to get the words out without having to think about them. I didn't want to judge what I didn't understand.

"Oh. So did you grow up pretty religious?" I didn't know much about present-day missionaries, but I assumed that if people wanted to spread a religion they started with their own family.

I'd learned about the early California missions in school because it was part of the fourth-grade curriculum, but it always seemed like something in the remote past when new ways of life were forced on unwilling settlements in the name of religion. I mentally flogged myself for not being better informed.

He looked at me like I was crazy. "No. Not at all. I'm about as close to an atheist as a person can get. Maybe they taught me that, indirectly. They were so devoted to the church and their mission that they spent six months a year traveling. Sometimes more. It got to where I resented Christianity as a concept because it cost me my family. My sister and I were pretty much on our own from the time I was sixteen and she was twelve. Since I was older, I helped her with schoolwork until it became clear she was smarter than me. She liked to cook so she handled that stuff, and I had a solid after-school job at a sub sandwich place, so I had spending money for both of us."

I couldn't be hearing this right. "Wait, they left you two alone for weeks at a time when you were sixteen?"

"Yeah. They created an imaginary aunt who supposedly stayed with us when they went out of town, so the school never bothered us and they were free to come and go whenever they found a new place to spread religion."

I couldn't imagine it. Unlike my childhood full of siblings and fights and laughter, even when my dad was sick, Owen's childhood sounded quiet and sad. "I can't believe you only had parents for part of the year. Who paid for groceries and rent and . . . everything? You couldn't have supported two people working part time making sandwiches."

His face was unemotional. "To their credit, they set up accounts for both of us and they were well-funded enough that we managed. That's how it was for a while, then when I was seventeen, they left for somewhere in Mexico—they never told us exactly where they were going, maybe because their itineraries could change on the fly or maybe they were just really irresponsible—but on this particular trip, there was an ambush of their bus by some mercenaries who were part of a drug cartel and I'm pretty sure they were killed."

I stared at him in shock. "Pretty sure? You don't know for sure?"

He shook his head. "It was a dicey situation. I tried to get some information from the missionary group they usually went with but I was just a kid. They weren't going to tell me they sent my parents to Mexico and put them in the path of Mexican drug lords. But over the years, I've collected more information and that's the likeliest explanation for why they never came back."

"Wow. So who raised you after that?"

He made air quotes. "My aunt."

"Who didn't exist."

"Exactly, but no one knew that because they did a great job of making her seem like a real relative. There were photos of us with some random lady in my file at school. I never knew who she was and I have no recollection of taking the photos. For all I know, they were photoshopped. So when it became clear they weren't coming back, I let our school know our aunt was staying with us on a more permanent basis and they never questioned it. I only had one more year until I was a legal adult, but I was desperate not to let anything happen to my sister. I couldn't let her end up in foster care, so when I turned eighteen, I applied to be her legal guardian and stayed in the house until she was ready for college."

At some point while he was talking, I noticed my hand had migrated to where his was resting on the table and I'd reached out protectively. I couldn't hear that story without offering some physical connection.

I shook my head, unsure what to say. "That's . . . unbelievable. I'm so sorry to hear that. Really. I can't imagine what that must've been like."

He smiled sheepishly. "Bet now you wish you didn't push me to talk about my family."

I threw a wadded-up napkin at him. "Stinker. I'm glad you told me. It makes me appreciate that you seem to have it so together after what sounds like a hellish childhood."

When he spoke, his voice was calm. "It wasn't hellish. I mean, imagine growing up without parents around. Ice cream for breakfast whenever you want! No bedtime!" He smiled, but I could tell he was trying to put a positive spin on his story.

For the first time since we'd left the bakery, I didn't know what to say. I was at a loss for how to comfort a person who didn't seem to need comforting, but who I was sure deserved a hug and more. My anguish must have shown on my face because he reached for my face and ran one finger across my forehead and between my eyes.

"I didn't tell you to stress you out. I'm fine. It all ended up fine," he said.

"I . . . okay. I just wish I'd known you back then. I'd have invited you over for dinner at least."

His face softened and I could tell the idea touched him. "That's maybe the nicest thing anyone's ever said to me," he said.

The hint of a smile played against his closed lips, but in his eyes I could see the residual pain of not feeling the parental love he should have had. It was heartbreaking.

I didn't have much interest in the rest of my food, so I pushed the plate aside. We needed a change of tack from the heavy conversation so I gave his hand a friendly nudge and delved into Owen's burger anomaly. "So explain the logic behind a veggie burger with bacon and cheese on it. Are you a part-time vegan?"

He laughed. "Hardly. I'm a full-time guilt eater. I'd rather go a little healthier by not getting a meat burger if it means I can have the bacon and cheese."

"Ah, very logical. But burgers aren't completely unhealthy unless you eat them all the time."

"Are you just rationalizing your meat burger?" he asked. "I'm not judging if you are. As long as you can sleep at night."

I really wished my mind wasn't so easily swayed that his casual reference to sleeping made me immediately think about sleeping with him, which was not something I did on the first date.

Not that this was a date.

What had happened to me? I was seriously losing it.

Our waiter came and cleared our plates and asked if we wanted anything else. Owen didn't even look at me before ordering two slices of apple pie.

"À la mode?" the waiter asked.

"Are you kidding?" Owen said, nodding like the answer was

obvious and the question crazy. The waiter left with the dishes and said he'd be back in a minute with the hot pie and ice cream. "Do we want it à la mode? What kind of a question is that?" He shook his head.

"It's a question from an inexperienced pie eater," I said. "But how'd you know I wanted pie?"

Now he looked at me like *I* was crazy. "You've been staring at it the whole time we've been eating."

"I have not." I'd mostly been staring at him, but I had been wanting pie since breakfast. If he'd read my mind about the pie, who knew what he was capable of? It scared me a little.

"You eyed that pie case the second we walked in, you took this seat instead of mine so you could ogle it, and you agreed to share a plate of fries instead of getting your own because you wanted to have pie later."

I stared at him. How did he know that when he barely knew me? And because he was apparently a mind reader, Owen leaned in and whispered, "I do know you."

If that wasn't reason enough to be intrigued by him, the feel of his breath near my ear had my insides twisting into a knot of lust and begging him to linger there forever.

But first, there was pie.

wen

THE WALK back to the bakery felt very different than our walk a couple hours earlier. Instead of worrying about whether it had been an impulsive mistake to ask Isla to dinner, I was worrying about whether I'd ever get over her. In the course of one night, she'd leveled me.

I wished that I could just look at her forever without having to blink. I resented even the tiniest lost moment, and that should have been a big flashing warning sign that I should back away slowly and take a breath.

For fuck's sake, she'd asked about my family and I'd told her the truth. She was the first person in years I'd bothered to tell about my sordid family saga and I didn't do it because I wanted to soften her shitty day by telling her about my shitty years. I wanted her to know me better and for once I didn't care if that meant knowing the messy parts.

Normally, no one asked and I didn't volunteer the information, especially with women I dated. I'd made that mistake once years ago and couldn't handle the awkward sympathy I wasn't looking for.

It was easier to be vague about my family details and most of the time I never dated anyone long enough for it to matter.

I had the same tendency to be vague about my job. It wasn't that I didn't like talking about my work if someone was interested for the right reasons, like a shared passion for design or sustainable landscaping. But some of what Isla had alluded to was true at our age—sometimes I got the feeling that women I was dating were looking at me as a dating resume, a set of criteria that were part of their ideal man portrait.

Was I relationship material or was I a one-night stand? It all came down to that. All the questions and surreptitious clocking of information was part of figuring that out and deciding whether I was "the kind of guy" they wanted to date.

I hated the whole dance. If I wanted to spend time with someone, I did it. There didn't need to be a marriage proposal in the offing or a promise of a date sixteen when we were only on date two.

But Isla was different. She was one of the few women I'd ever met who made me want to talk about date sixteen and get it locked down and recorded in pen.

It surprised me how much I felt like it was a foregone conclusion that I was going to fall in love with her after one date that wasn't even a date.

And yet . . . she'd made a point of talking about the "alpha males" with their big corporate jobs and empire building in such a negative light. She'd seemed relieved to think I had some sort of hotel peon job. Hell, maybe she really wanted to date a bellhop.

If it would get her to spend more time with me—and kiss me again—I was prepared to spend ample time at each of my hotel properties shuttling bags back and forth between rooms.

Of course, if we spent any significant amount of time together, I'd tell her eventually.

I would.

We'd chalk it up to a miscommunication.

When we got back to the bakery, there was really no reason for me to linger unless it was to linger for a lot longer. I'd been thinking about my lips on her skin since…well, since I'd met her a year ago.

So much of me wanted to bite her earlobe and lick my way down her neck. I pretty much hadn't thought about anything else for the past half hour.

Give me a break—I'm a guy and she's breathtaking.

"Are you going back to work?" I asked when she unlocked the front door to the bakery.

"Oh, not even. I've been here since four this morning and I have to be back in . . ." She looked at her watch and frowned. "Seven hours. No wonder I'm always exhausted."

"How often do you work fourteen-hour days?"

"Too often. Especially now. We didn't even get a chance to talk about it, but I'm trying to grow this little bread box and it's going to require training more bakers and expanding into a couple new locations."

"That's exciting. I'd love to hear about that sometime." To be clear, that was me asking her out in a completely surreptitious and probably unsuccessful way.

She looked at me and nodded. It was obvious she was exhausted. Her eyes were slits and her smile looked a little loopy. It was a good look on her, but I wasn't such a jerk that I would cut into her sleep any more than I already had. Mostly.

"So . . . can I make sure you get safely to your car?" I asked. I wasn't about to leave her alone to close up shop and walk in the dark to her car.

Even if I didn't have my parents around to raise me, I'd picked up some good life lessons from after-school specials.

"Not yet." Isla grabbed my hand and drew me inside as the lock on the door gave way. It was mostly dark inside the bakery, save for the dimmed wall sconces and twinkle lights that gave the place ambiance to anyone who looked in from the sidewalk at night. In other words, the room had the perfect romantic lighting.

I was never one to waste romantic lighting.

"Is this you inviting me into your house?" I asked, following her into the room.

She smiled at me and shook her head. "The House of Bread. I don't actually live here. You know that, right? Or do you believe I'm actually some kind of bread fairy who sleeps among the bread baskets and bakes through the night?"

"You're painting quite a picture. I won't pretend that doesn't sound hot, especially if you do it in satin lingerie."

"Stop," she said.

"Done." I kissed her again because kissing her was everything.

I was tempted to make use of one of the tables, which was barely big enough for me to lay her down on it, so I quickly aborted that plan and looked around the room for anyplace that looked remotely comfortable.

"This whole place is wood and angles and painful surfaces," I said. She nodded in agreement, then she held up a finger.

"I have an idea. Come." I followed her into the back, wondering if she was going to whip up a giant batch of fluffy dough to use as a pillow. Instead, she pointed at a stack of flour sacks. "They could be molded a little bit more to fit, kind of like a beanbag chair maybe."

"I don't know if I feel right messing with your flour. What if we get carried away and ruin the whole bread operation? The weeping of carb junkies will be heard across the city and I couldn't bear the responsibility."

She laughed. "How thoughtful."

I pointed to my chest. "I am a self-serving bread eater, nothing more."

And to hell with comfortable surfaces. I'd make do on the floor without a complaint, but Isla had other ideas, yanking my hand so I'd follow her up a flight of stairs. At the top, she opened a door to a small office. With a small couch.

"I was thinking about getting rid of this couch 'cause I never sit on it and I never have anyone else in the office with me," she said as though I was consulting on her interior decorating choices.

"I'm happy you're too busy to get rid of couches," I said, walking her gently backward and lying her down. I knelt with a knee on either side of her hips and my hands cupping her face. It was exactly where I wanted to be. "This is quite nice."

I leaned in and kissed her softly. I had no presumptions about how far this would go. It was completely up to her. She responded, pulling me against her and tracing my lips with her tongue.

We kissed for a long time, her arms wrapped around me and a leg hitched over mine. We took it slowly, the way we hadn't in the restaurant, and it felt just right.

That is, until she pushed me away. I sat up and saw the regret on her face.

"Ugh, I just . . ." She put her hands over her eyes. I waited but she sat frozen. So I gently removed her hands and leaned a little closer so she was looking at me directly.

"Hey. Talk to me." My voice was calm. I didn't want to push her, but I needed her to tell me what she wanted.

"Here's the thing. I want to kiss you . . . I mean, I really, really do, but . . . you should understand that I don't know what I'm doing," she said, raising up to her elbows so our faces were closer.

"You seemed pretty skilled earlier."

"I don't mean that. I mean my brain doesn't know what I'm doing."

66

I laughed. "Oh. Okay. That's perfectly clear."

She ran her hand over my chest, top to bottom, then she lifted the hem of my shirt and ran her nails appreciatively over my abs. I'd never been so grateful for the gym workouts I'd been forcing on myself since college as when I heard a quiet sigh escape her lips.

"I feel bad making you my rebound guy. You don't deserve that, but I'm just getting out of a relationship. I mean, it hasn't even been a day since my romantic crash and burn was plastered on social media and I've been single for like three hours, though that relationship was definitively over months ago," she said.

I liked the sound of 'definitively,' but I needed to focus on the rest of what she was saying. She was right. She hadn't even had a chance to sleep alone in her own bed yet, so I could hardly assume she was ready to sleep in mine. Or even on this well-placed couch.

"I'm sorry." She scooted farther away.

"Don't be," I said. "Really. I don't feel bad, so neither should you. I'm good with being the rebound guy. I'm not trying to swoop in and start something up with you right on the heels of your breakup—"

She held her fingers to my lips, which made me want to suck on them even though I doubted that was her intention. "Thank you. I can't start something up with you or anyone. I need to figure out my life for a minute. Or a month."

"Right. Of course. We're friends. And as your friend, I'm here for you, whether that means we sit and talk about bread or we make out all night. Whatever it takes to help you get over your ex." I quirked an eyebrow.

Her eyes twinkled. "You are magnanimous."

"As a rebound guy should be." As I said it, though, I distinctly disliked the idea and that should have been an immediate sign to get the hell out of there.

I had no business thinking of myself as anything more than her rebound guy.

So I nodded and hoisted myself off the couch. "It's late. You've had a long day, and you should get some rest. I'm gonna walk you to your car, okay?"

"It's probably a good idea." She looked like she wanted me to argue her out of it, but I wasn't going there. It wasn't a good idea for me to feel half of the things I was feeling and I needed to run —not walk—away from her, even if I wanted to kiss the hell out of her.

She grabbed her shoulder bag and a red and blue scarf that was hanging over her chair, and I put an arm around her waist and walked her down the stairs and out to the horrible parking spot she'd wedged into on the street. I was surprised she didn't have a ticket.

"Thank you for dinner," she said, her smile lighting up her face like the crescent moon overhead. "I'll see you in the morning?"

I was about to agree. I'd have agreed to anything she wanted to earn more of that smile, but I couldn't. "Oh, actually, no. We have a staff meeting in Palo Alto. One of the depressing days that won't start with the aroma of fresh bread."

"That kind of day's bound to be a disappointment," she said.

She had no idea.

"My thought as well. But there's no way around it. Maybe I'll stop in later when I get back. Will you be here?"

She shook her head. "Family dinner night. I'll be fighting traffic to Berkeley by then, but you should still come by if you want your bread. I'll make sure one of the guys saves a couple loaves for you."

That would solve all my problems if I was only coming for the bread.

"Thanks."

"You're welcome." We were awfully formal all of a sudden and it felt strange.

"See you on Friday, regular time, as in the ass crack of dawn before normal humans wake up." Then I realized that wasn't happening either. I needed to head to Healdsburg for the day to meet with the new general manager. "Actually, not Friday. I have to be at one of our hotels out of town."

She shrugged. "Okay, maybe I'll see you over the weekend. I'm working on Sunday though I'm sure you don't get up at five in the morning on weekends. But if you're around . . ."

I nodded. "I may be around," I said.

I would be around.

I already felt the void from not seeing her in the morning and the bite of disappointment surprised me. Damn straight, she'd see me on Sunday. And just for insurance, I asked for her cell number.

Then I kissed the hell out of her and reluctantly let her go.

sla

THE WEATHER HAD SETTLED into its traditional fog, but somewhere over my head there must have been a black cloud. By mid-Thursday, the embarrassment and hassle of Tom's affair was almost the least of my worries.

I didn't believe in fate or destiny. None of my siblings did. That meant that my four sisters and one brother went through life believing that anything could happen at any time without any particular provocation or reason.

Maybe it was having our dad die at an unfairly young age that led to our lack of faith, but it was rooted deeply for all of us. For that reason, I never said things like, "this week that's already proven itself to be a shit storm is destined to get even worse."

But maybe it was time to reconsider my lack of faith.

We got our bakes done and our breakfast and lunch orders filled at the Bay Area restaurants who we served every day, and the breakfast and coffee crowd had been replaced by a more boisterous, larger lunch crowd. Our sidewalk and inside tables were all filled, and a line snaked out the door for to-go orders.

Sometimes I hid in the kitchen when it got crazy busy in the front because I knew my staff was highly competent and completely capable of handling the ebb and flow of customers, like when the kitchen got slammed and messes were made by unapologetic toddlers or the best flakey croissants.

"Hey, the back line rang and I took a message from Frank Woods at The Tavern," Camille told me, handing me a slip of paper where she'd scribbled his phone number.

"Thanks. Tavern's a new contract as of last week."

"*Felicitations*," she said, following me to the front where I counted up the loaves still on the shelves. Coming into the café sometimes overwhelmed me when I was in my own groove and couldn't get into the flow of a crowded space. The chaos stressed me the hell out.

On other days, I loved the energy, the noise, the smells, the diversity of people coming through the door. That was why I loved having the choice of where to spend my time.

"Come to the office if you have time and we can go over the orders from the new restaurants." She nodded but didn't follow me back into the kitchen. I knew she was checking the pastry cases to see what was selling out.

When we'd started serving actual meals in addition to breads and pastries, I'd hired a new team of prep cooks and a lunch chef. They'd increased our profit margins by twenty percent, so even though it made the place complete chaos between the hours of eleven and two, it was worth it.

We were busting at the seams, but the thrumming pace of the place created its own energy and instead of feeling exhausted by it, I always felt invigorated.

The rush began to taper after two like it always did and the to-go customers had taken their lunches back to their offices. Enough order had been restored that I crept upstairs to the tiny office so I could prep for the following day and the upcoming weeks.

My phone pinged with a text from Owen and my heart started fluttering. I liked my rebound guy.

Owen: I missed my daily bread fix this morning.

Of course his text was going to be about bread, not some romantic declaration about how much he missed seeing me.

Why was I even thinking about that?

Me: Spoken like a true addict. My favorite kind.

Owen: I also missed seeing you. I should have led with that.

My heart did a little flip which made me admit that my spirits had sunk every time I looked at his usual table and didn't find him there.

But I couldn't tell him that. It was too soon and you don't say things like that to the rebound guy.

Me: We can remedy that on Sunday.

It felt wrong to not return his sentiment, especially since it was true. I did miss him. But I was also emotionally raw from Tom's antics and it wasn't fair to lead him on if I didn't know what I was doing.

Owen: Done. It's a date.

Me: You don't want to date me, Bread Boy. I'm still a mess.

Owen: Sunday the 7th is a date on my calendar. It's a date. That's all I was saying. But if you're asking me on a hot date, I say yes.

Me: Thanks for the clarity. See you Sunday.

He responded with a happy face emoji and I tried to refocus on the work I had ahead of me, but not until I'd reread our text string a few more times. He made me smile.

I reached for my phone and debated sending him another text. Bantering with him was much more fun than the work I had to do.

But no. I didn't want to give him the wrong idea since I was very committed to the solo time, the self-analysis, the reflection, and the wine drinking that it was going to take before I was in good emotional shape to start a new relationship.

Sitting in my office now, I couldn't help staring at my couch and realizing I'd never done much to give the office any character or style. It was basically an industrial metal desk and an ergonomic chair with file cabinets and a window. My desk had one framed photo of my siblings from a day we'd gone sailing a couple summers ago, but otherwise, there was nothing personal in sight.

Yes, there were aprons and towels stacked on an extra chair in the corner and files that had yet to be put away sitting on the floor, but that hardly counted as decor. Becca, my middle sister and the only one with a sewing machine, had offered to make me some throw pillows or curtains when she saw the spare space, but I told her I didn't spend enough time in the office for it to matter. I had her make me pillows and a tablecloth for my house instead.

Now I found myself thinking that maybe my office could be a little cuter just in case I ended up entertaining guests . . . on my couch . . . in the future. Better to be prepared. Maybe a candle here or there. Or at least some better lighting.

After firing off a quick text to ask Becca for some pillows, I opened my laptop.

"I love that sound," Camille said, standing in the doorway.

I listened to the chatter of voices and the banging of dishes downstairs in the dishwashing area. I'd always gravitated toward the sounds and smells of food service kitchens, so I'd spent my teen years working in restaurants.

"It is a soothing symphony for crazy people," I agreed.

She smiled. "You created everything down there. Amazing." She was right, but I never dwelled on that.

Thinking about the future had always led to a dead end after college, so I'd never pictured myself running my own place. But once I decided that bread was always going to be a part of my life, my business took off and I'd been in growth mode ever since.

I'd doubled the number of restaurants I was baking for just in the last year and I'd taken on three new contracts that I needed to finalize so I could figure out how much more flour to order. Maybe I'd be able to keep the third baker permanently.

"I just wanted to go over numbers with you. Berkshire and Chester's are asking for pastries and I don't know how much we can do."

So far, it had served us better to keep quality high and prices a little higher and serve fewer restaurants. The perceived scarcity of our product made it more valuable to the restaurants we did business with.

But we'd pretty much hit capacity in-house. There weren't many more loaves I could squeeze out of our ovens in a given day, no matter how many people I hired. And there was interest from restaurants in Oakland and Los Altos.

"Not much more. Time for new kitchen space and more locations," she said, excitement in her voice. She knew she'd be my number one pick to run a new bakery.

Expanding and training bread makers at a few more bakery cafés around the Bay Area made sense. I'd thought about it once before, but the amount of work involved to do a volume business and keep quality high felt daunting.

Now I felt ready.

I scanned the emails, looking for the ones from the new restaurants so we could start running the numbers. My quick back of the envelope calculation had estimated at least a hundred fifty additional sourdough loaves and some specialty olive and rosemary rounds, plus six dozen pastries.

But when I started reading the ones from the new clients, I noticed a problem.

One after another, I scanned the emails from the three restaurants I'd negotiated with, noticing they'd all been sent this morning. Oddly, they all said a version of the same thing—they were canceling their agreements for ongoing orders and wouldn't be signing a contract with me after all.

It was strange.

Of course, people changed their minds and a handshake deal doesn't mean anything until it's been signed and executed. I'd had clients back out before.

But never three in the same day.

"Hey, Cam, can we do this later? Sorry. I have to straighten some stuff out first."

"Of course. Lemme know," she said, popping back downstairs.

I texted my younger sister, Becca, whose fiancé Blake owned several restaurants and knew a lot of the owners in the city. They'd just gotten engaged and he was crazy about her. I needed to work any angle I could.

Me: Hey, any idea if Blake knows people at Zen Table, Berkshire Creamery or Chester's Bakery?

Becca: No idea. Ping him directly. He won't mind.

Me: You sure?

Becca: Stop being ridiculous. And quit fangirling my boyfriend.

Me: Not fangirling. Just being polite.

*Becca: Whatever, chef groupie. *smiley face**

I'd admit to fangirling Blake, a respected, high-end chef who'd opened a San Francisco restaurant that had already won a bunch of awards and accolades in its first few months.

I'd been supplying his restaurant with bread since it opened but I always felt like he indulged me as a favor to Becca. The guy intimidated me and I only got intimidated by a handful of food people.

But Becca said to text him, so I did.

In under fifteen minutes, he was calling my cell, after having done recon around town on my behalf.

"Hey, Blake. Thanks for this. I'm sure it's nothing and it's just me being paranoid, but it's so weird—"

He cut me off. "Isla, you're not paranoid. Something's definitely up. First of all, you should know that it's nothing about you or the quality of your product or anything about that. All three chefs were practically in tears when the owners told them they weren't going to be getting your stuff."

"Well, that's nice to hear, but not if they're gonna cry their way to another bread supplier. So what's going on?" Compliments did me no good if I was losing business.

"Someone's undercutting your contracts, offering what they claim is the same artisanal bread baked with flour from the same terroir. They're going by the name of Flour Artisan, but I haven't seen any shops with that name so it's either brand new or a renamed version of something that's been around. I'll keep hunting for more info. It's all a bit mysterious for now. But they're killing you on price."

I was shocked. "I can't think of any bakers in the area who are working with my vendors, whether they're changing their name or not. Seriously, none. My people are loyal. They'd tell me if a competitor was trying to buy from them."

"It might not be your vendors, but whoever this is found some farmer who will flood his field and grow similar wheat. It's someone who knows an awful lot about your business. Down to dollar amounts that you spend on flour and employee pensions. Usually that takes corporate muscle. You might be up against someone who's willing to take a loss in order to beat you."

My heart started pounding and not in a good way. I'd never had this problem before. I knew my farmers and I knew every Bay Area restaurant owner who cared about ingredients the way I did and I was selling to all of them.

Until now, apparently.

"I can't think of anyone in the area doing the same thing I am, at least not on a scale that would allow for a bunch of restaurant contracts."

"It might not be in the area. It could be an outfit out of state.

Who knows? I didn't have time to dig into an internet search. Flour Artisan could be a DBA for some other company, and they could be incorporated outside the US. If they don't want you to find out who they are, you probably won't."

"Shit. Well, that ain't good," I said.

"No, it's not. But I let those restaurant owners have it and I think they'll be calling you. They know better than to forgo local for some corporate outfit that's probably sending them frozen bread, even if they're selling it for a penny."

That got my attention. "You think it's coming to them frozen from someplace else?" I thought about the grocery down the block and wondered where they were getting their bread. I never cared to ask, but maybe it was time to strike up a friendship.

"Who the hell knows? All I can say is I think I shamed these guys into honoring their contracts with you, but you'd better watch your back. If someone wants to undercut you and is aggressively going after your business, this probably isn't the last you'll hear from them."

Intuitively, I knew he was right, but I didn't like hearing him confirm that fact out loud. "Thanks, Blake."

"Sure thing. Let me know if there's anything else I can do to help."

I felt depressed and in over my head, which was a new feeling. Maybe I'd just been lucky not to have been challenged by a serious competitor up until now, but it left me sorely unprepared as to what to do.

After I hung up with Blake, I immediately called my sister, Sarah. She'd be able to set me straight.

Sarah had been my unofficial partner in the business for the past few years when I'd expanded from just being a bread shop to having contracts with dozens of restaurants and a few small grocery stores.

She was a professor at Berkeley in physics with a subspecialty in something obscure that involved welding, but the woman was a genius with accounting and numbers and had whipped my bookkeeping into shape in mere hours when I thought I was going to lose my mind.

I knew I could afford to lose a few contracts and keep everything I had going. But there was no way to know how aggressive my mysterious competitor planned on being. What if all my restaurant clients bailed? Was someone actually trying to run me out of business?

Sarah would know whether the trend I was seeing was a blip or a big problem.

"Hey," she answered my FaceTime call on the first ring and I could see she was in her office on campus. It was a wood-paneled space with a brown desk. When she first got hired at Berkeley, she joked that the office made her panel crazy, but eventually she stopped noticing.

It always made me do a double take when I first saw Sarah's face on my phone because she and I looked so much alike. We were two years apart but there were several years when we were kids that we paraded around together in matching outfits telling people we were twins. Everyone believed it.

"You busy?" I asked. I could see students walking past her open door. I wasn't sure if she had office hours.

"No, just grading papers and using a new computer program to check for plagiarism. Have to stay one step ahead of my students and they're practically CIA when it comes to stealth. It's a joy."

"Don't you miss the good old days when the only way to get away with plagiarizing was to steal from a really good book? At least that meant they were reading."

"Seriously. So what's up?"

"Apparently, I've got a ruthless competitor who's going after my restaurant contracts. So far it just looks like I've got real competition over the new ones, but there's one big Oakland restaurant that hasn't ordered from me in a couple weeks and it's a little odd. I'm worried it might be the next one to jump ship."

"That sucks. Okay, I'll run all your numbers and let you know where you've got wiggle room and where you're going into the red."

I hated hearing those words, "in the red," and Sarah knew it. "Please don't give me a heart attack here. Blake feels pretty confident the restaurants that were thinking about bolting will come back now that he's talked sense into them, but I'm looking ahead because if I do end up losing restaurant clients, there goes my nest egg that I need for expansion," I said.

"Got it. I'll come up with a few scenarios of how this could look and show you where you need to be more efficient to compensate for any loss of business down the road. Good?"

"Thank you. You know, if you ever decide physics isn't your cup of tea, I'll hire you to be my financial partner."

She laughed. She knew I barely understood her job and was kind enough not to make me feel dumb for not being able to keep up with her brain. "I'm good doing both. Don't worry about any of the financial stuff for now. I'm on it. I'll see you tonight at dinner and we can have a little sidebar on this if you want."

"Nah, numbers don't mix with wine. We can deal with it later. But hey, would you do me a favor and send out a little preemptive text to the sibs, tell them I don't want to talk about the whole Tom cheating thing? I don't feel like group therapy from the fam."

"Yes, on it. I gotta run though. I teach in fifteen."

"Sure. Run. Go. Thanks, Sar."

I couldn't fathom how she taught particle physics classes at Berkeley, wrote articles for academic journals, and kept my bookkeeping straight, all in a normal week when most people had only one job.

Actually, I did know. She barely allowed herself time to do anything else.

I vowed to get her a really nice gift, something that would encourage her to enjoy some free time.

When I came back downstairs, Camille was cleaning up her station and getting ready to leave. The lucky thing about her job was that all the pastry prep and baking could be done in the early morning and by the time the lunch rush ended, her day was done.

Unlike bread, there wasn't a huge need for croissants on the dinner menus at most restaurants. She worked an eight-hour day that ended at noon. Something I was completely unfamiliar with since my twelve-hour day ended at four and I often stayed past then.

"Bye, *mon amie*, see you in the morning," she said, wrapping her scarf around her neck and tucking her motorcycle helmet under her arm.

"Actually, Camille, can you think of a good gift for someone who works too hard and doesn't take enough time for herself?" I asked.

She raised an eyebrow. "Is that your way of hinting that I should get you a present?"

"No, it's not for me. I want to get something for my sister. Something she wouldn't get herself."

She thought about it for a moment, her mouth rounding into a pout. Then she snapped her fingers. "Ah, yes, it's perfect," she said, her accent making her sound like Inspector Clouseau. "Get her a male escort."

Unfortunately, I'd just picked up a bottle of Perrier and taken a swig when she said it because the spray ended up all over her scarf. But I couldn't stop laughing.

"Oh my gosh, I was thinking about a nice candle or a necklace or something," I said, wiping the tears from my eyes.

Camille shrugged. "Or you could do that. Your call. *Au revoir*," she said, breezing through the kitchen like she hadn't just suggested I gift my sister with a hooker.

Sarah was bookish and brilliant but she'd never given me the impression she had much of a wild side. When we were younger, we were all rambunctious teenagers and I remember her having fun back then, but since she'd earned her PhD and started working as a professor, she'd become way too serious and responsible. I couldn't remember the last time I'd seen her cut loose.

Maybe a male escort *would* be a better gift than a candle.

sla

I TRIED NOT to feel like a stalker while I Googled Owen Miller.

I'd figured out his last name by going through old credit card receipts at the shop—okay . . . I was officially a stalker. Nonetheless, it made good sense to learn the names of our regular customers, first and last.

You plan on Googling all the customers or just the ones you kiss?

Obviously, we weren't dating, but even if he was just my rebound guy, I still wanted a little basic info that an internet search could provide in minutes.

Unsure what exactly I was looking for, I typed in his name, expecting to find some social media links or maybe evidence of a donation here or there. Or a nice photo. Instead, the first thing I found was a profile from a business magazine on Owen Miller, boutique hotel owner.

At first, I acknowledged the possibility that there was a different Owen Miller in the hotel business.

But . . . really?

It only took a few more clicks to read the entire text of the article and see a photo of Owen Miller—the one I'd kissed the night before—standing in the courtyard of a traditional Spanish hacienda which had been turned into a five-star hotel in Santa Barbara.

So he wasn't the night manager at a Holiday Inn, which was for some reason what I pictured after he said he worked at a hotel.

Wasn't that what he'd said?

Regardless of the actual words, I was pretty sure that he never told me he owned what turned out to be a collection of seven hotel properties in romantic California travel destinations. And even though we'd talked all about how I'd started Victorine, he'd given me no indication that he'd started his own business and had actual knowledge of how to do it.

No, that had not been the takeaway.

Unable to wait until Sunday, I sent him a text, couching it in more bread talk because that seemed like neutral territory.

Me: Hey, how's the bread withdrawal going? Asking as a concerned friend.

He responded almost instantly. I wondered if he kept his phone in his hand at all times.

Owen: I'm . . . weak. Can't move. Send carbs . . .

I laughed.

Me: Sadly, we don't deliver.

Owen: I think I've just found the first and only flaw in you. Please come over with bread.

Me: Can't right now. I'm stuck at my desk.

Owen: How's that going?

Me: Going alright. So . . . did I miss it when you told me you owned seven hotels?

I watched the three dots indicate he was typing. Then they

disappeared. Then reappeared. It was nerve-wracking. Finally, he responded.

Owen: No. I didn't mention that.

Cute. He was correct, but still . . .

Me: Why? Were you trying to mislead me?

I waited. Nothing.

Why did I text him? The waiting was excruciating. Finally, more dots.

Owen: Nope.

That's it? That's all I get?

Me: Didn't you tell me you worked at a hotel?

Owen: I believe I said I worked in hotels. I didn't mean I actually worked behind the desk at a hotel. But you're right, I didn't clarify. I'm sorry. Truly.

Me: Why didn't you correct me?

Owen: I didn't really want to talk about my work. I wanted to talk about yours.

Me: That's sweet. But in the future, please tell me all relevant details.

I got nothing after that for a full minute. No dots.

Maybe I'd annoyed him by being confrontational. Oh well, if he couldn't handle being called on it . . .

The dots were back.

Owen: You said you hate corporate guys. I didn't want you to hate me before I could prove my worth as a human.

He had a point. I might have been wary of him if he'd said he owned a hotel company right after the most recent corporate magnate blew my ego to bits.

Me: I hate some of them. I don't hate you. But I will if you make me Google you like a stalker.

I watched the dots appear and disappear again.

Damn him.

Owen: I like having you as a stalker.

Me: Not the point.

Owen: Gotta hit a meeting for my super impressive not-corporate hotel chain of which I am the owner. I'm in withdrawal from your bread and from you. See you on Sunday for my fix of both.

My smile made my cheeks ache.

I liked this guy. But if I wasn't careful, I'd ruin a friendship with a seemingly great man by abusing him as my rebound. Even though I hadn't been happy with Tom for a while, I needed to grieve the end of our relationship at least a little bit before I started up with someone new.

The next time I saw Owen, I'd make sure I was clear on my boundaries.

So . . . no more kissing. Sadly.

I sent a smiley emoji to Owen and went back to reading through the Google results, just to make sure there wasn't anything else he hadn't told me. I saw more articles about his boutique hotels—lots of them over the years, too many to read without seriously digging into my work productivity—and lots of information about the hotels themselves.

But nothing personal. No photos of him with a girlfriend, wife, ex-wife. It was almost like the human side of Owen Miller had been scrubbed from public view. I tried to decide whether that was a good or a bad thing.

Or maybe he was one of those rare individuals who managed to keep his personal life private. That possibility proved to be the most intriguing of all.

I LOVED LIVING in San Francisco, but if I ever moved to the East Bay, I'd fight my brother Finn for his house. It looked like it had emerged organically from the hill on which it sat, all wood and tall glass windows with gorgeous native plants and flowers blooming in planter boxes and vertical gardens.

Its wraparound porches afforded stunning views of the bay

and a secret staircase alongside the house tangled through the hills, leading to other hidden staircases and eventually a trail that led up to Grizzly Peak. I'd brought my running shoes on more than one occasion and navigated all the stairways I could find for the quickest route to the top.

Finn and his fiancée Annie bought the house eight months earlier after moving to the Bay Area from Los Angeles. Finn, an economist with a big brain and a bigger heart, had gotten a tenured position at Berkeley and Annie worked as a white-collar lawyer at a firm in San Francisco.

They'd been renovating a bit at a time, which meant they never had a huge crew working at any given time, but it also meant there was always something under construction.

"I'm so mad at you." My younger sister Cherry started in on me as soon as I walked into the kitchen where Finn was chopping things on a wooden cutting board.

He spun around to greet me and toppled a jar of olives. Juice went everywhere, but in typical Finn fashion, he cared more about hugging me than getting olive juice on his counters.

I ignored Cherry for the moment and went over to hug Finn. "How's it going? Can I help? Or at least clean up your spill?"

"Nah, I'm good. Annie's out in the garden and she's the other half of my team." He waved a kitchen towel, which said "Team Tamale."

"Ooh, are you making tamales?" I asked.

"No, but I didn't have a towel that said Team Vegetables."

"Got it. Now, why are you mad at me?" I asked Cherry. I glanced around the countertops to see if there were any partially prepared snacks I could help shuttle onto a tray and then eat.

With nothing in sight, I went to the fridge and grabbed some vegetables and started assembling a little crudité platter. Finn observed and nodded. "Good idea."

"I'm mad because you didn't kick that douche canoe out on his ass while you had the chance." Cherry was the second-youngest sister and at almost age thirty, she had the energy and appetite of a teenage boy. She was sitting cross-legged on a bench pulled up to Finn's kitchen table. She'd kicked off her stylish black faux-crocodile booties and was studying the swirling paisley design on her dark red blousy boho top.

"Yeah, not going to talk about it," I said, cutting the carrots into sticks with a vengeance. Then I went to the fridge to search out some hummus or other dip so I wouldn't have to look at my sister.

But Cherry was not one to be dissuaded. "So tell me about how it all went down. What did Tom say to you?"

I looked around hoping other siblings would appear and tell her to shut up, but Finn was the only other one in the room. He put his hands up and shrugged.

"Didn't Sarah text you all and tell you I didn't want to talk about it?"

"Sure, but I didn't think you meant me. You told me a while ago you didn't think you and Tom would make it through the year. You can't deprive me now of the end of the story. That's like taking someone to a movie and buying them popcorn and not letting them eat it."

"It's nothing like that. Finn, defend me please?"

Finn wiped his hands on an apron he'd taken to wearing while he cooked. It had a large pig on the front and said, "Every butt deserves a good rub." He went to the refrigerator and took out a fresh bottle of white wine.

"I'm not getting involved. Here. This oughtta help." He handed me the wine and pointed to the glass-front cabinets where wine glasses hung from the top shelf.

"Like I need you to point out where you keep the wine glasses." I smirked at his avoidance. "What are you cooking? Can I help?" I asked.

I could avoid conversation too. I just wouldn't answer Cherry.

Finn took the lid off a pot and gave it a stir. "It's a vegetarian chili recipe they gave us in our cooking class."

"They gave you the recipe or they taught you to make it?" Cherry asked. I was pleased she seemed distracted enough to leave me alone for now.

"They gave us the recipe. There's not really much to making chili. You kind of sauté and mix and stir and cook. But it goes with a bunch of things they did teach us to cook and I'm making all those."

"Ooh, like what?" I asked.

"Charred broccolini, cornbread pudding, and crispy fried garlic. Which I'm pretty certain I've royally screwed up. Annie?" He looked helplessly in the direction of the garden.

It amused me to see how lost he was without her cooking beside him.

"Yeah," came a voice from somewhere in the house.

"Can you come look at the garlic? I'm not sure I did it right."

"Be right there," she called.

Finn's eyes roamed around the kitchen and he seemed a little overwhelmed by his menu. I loved it. He was such an accomplished economist—he'd been short-listed for the Nobel Prize this year—that it was nice to see him unsure about how thinly to slice a clove of garlic.

I poked around looking in the oven at the bread pudding and at the piles of garlic he'd sliced. It all looked okay to me.

Annie breezed into the kitchen with a fistful of fresh herbs. "Sorry, I wanted to pick these before it was pitch black out there," she said, gesturing to the greens.

"Those smell amazing. Is that tarragon?" I asked.

"Yep. And flat leaf parsley and sage to go with the garlic. I'm gonna fry it together." She put the herbs down and came over to hug Cherry and me. I wasn't surprised Becca wasn't there yet because she was always late, but Sarah and Tatum were usually punctual if not early.

"Finn, where is everyone?" I asked. A part of me was worried everyone would ignore Sarah's instructions like Cherry had and I worried they were lurking around the house someplace.

Cherry, who'd gone to the cupboard for glasses when I was actively evading her questions, started pouring wine for the four of us and handing it out. Finn led Annie over to look at the garlic.

"Tater Tot and Sarah were here but I sent them on an errand so I could talk to you without Sarah yelling at me for ignoring her text." Tater Tot was our nickname for our youngest sister, Tatum, who worked in tech in Palo Alto.

"You're unbelievable. What fool's errand did you send them on?" I asked, rolling my eyes. I took a sip of my wine. I had a feeling I'd need a lot more of it to get through the evening.

She waved a hand at me. "Relax. I just had them go out for some wine. I told them there wasn't any here in the house."

"And they believed you?" Annie asked, incredulous. "We have a wine cellar downstairs. Have you seen how much wine is in there? Blake's friend hooked us up with something like a dozen cases and shipped them down from Napa. We need to start drinking that stuff yesterday."

"I haven't seen it, but I want to now," I said, walking away from Cherry.

I had seen it, but I'd do anything to avoid talking about Tom and the ignominious social media gotcha pics.

I started walking in the direction Annie was pointing, but Cherry hooked her finger in the belt loop of my pants and pulled me back. "Not so fast, cowgirl."

"You're really starting to annoy me," I said.

She grinned the way she always had as a kid when she knew she was getting my goat—which was often. "Fine. Let's check out the wine cellar. And in the privacy of dead grapes, you can tell me what happened with Tom." She raised an eyebrow at Finn, victorious, and he rolled his eyes and mouthed 'sorry' to me.

Annie gestured to a door in the middle of the hallway that the average visitor would mistake for a coat closet. I pulled the handle and a light went on automatically in the cool space below.

"Wow…" Cherry said.

"I know. It's a little bit glamorous in a hidden-panic-room sort of way and a little freakish, like there might be bodies down here."

"You have an active imagination. I was just thinking it was cool that the light went on by itself." Cherry followed me down a narrow set of stairs.

When we got to the bottom, I stood in the middle of what was really the basement of the house with a water heater in one corner and a furnace in another. A bunch of ductwork and WiFi routers and cables snaked overhead. But along one wall was a built-in refrigerated storage area with no less than two hundred bottles on display. The wall was divided into quarters, each one temperature controlled separately so they could house different kinds of wine. Reds didn't need to be chilled quite as cold, whites liked things a little more frosty.

"So this is really more of a wine wall than some custom-built wine cellar," Cherry said when we stood in the center surveying the ten by ten foot space. "It kind of makes me feel better about our brother not being a bougie hipster with a wine cave."

"Do bougie hipsters have wine caves?" I asked. I had no idea, given that no one had ever accused me of being a bougie hipster and I never imagined myself having a wine cave.

She shrugged. At the exact same time we both seemed to notice a folding chair sitting in the middle of the floor. We looked at it, looked at each other and immediately burst into hysterics. Then she ran up the stairs and yelled for Finn so loudly, he probably thought the water heater had rolled off its hinges and crushed me.

I heard his footsteps overhead come running. He leaned in the doorway and looked down.

"Yeah? What happened?"

"Finn, do you sit in this chair and gaze at your wine collection? Please tell me you really do that so I can tease you about it until the end of days."

I couldn't see Finn but he sounded annoyed. "Seriously, that's why you're screaming like a banshee? Because of a chair?"

"Just answer the question. Do you gaze at your wine?" she asked.

"No, I do not. I do, however, store stuff in my basement. Including chairs."

"I only see one chair, Finn. I think you're a wine gazer," Cherry said. I didn't dare interrupt. I was still hoping to distract her until my other sisters came back—the ones who knew the rules about asking me about Tom.

He stomped off, yelling behind him. "The rest of the chairs are up here, you lunatic. They're sitting around the kitchen table for dinner."

Cherry went to the chair and sat down in it before casting a glance around the small space. "It does make for a nice cool spot to contemplate a bunch of wine and a water heater," she said.

I'd moved on and was looking at some of the wine in the various refrigerators. "You think he'd mind if we grabbed a couple of these? I like Frog's Leap and he has a bunch from there."

Cherry shook her head. "I sent the sisters on a wine errand, remember? We can't bring up perfectly chilled bottles and have them come back and see them."

I shivered as a strand from an overhead cobweb came loose and brushed against my neck. "I don't care if there's wine down here. It's still a basement and it kind of gives me the creeps. I keep waiting for a mouse to scurry by," I said.

I was antsy to get out of there, so I figured I should make quick work of answering Cherry's questions. "So what do you want to know?"

"Who's the Swedish model? How stupid is he that he thought

he could be out in public with her without getting photographed? Why didn't you break up with him first? And are you okay?"

I was impressed. My sister was organized.

"She's some skank he met in New York and according to him, it was just sex, and I'm the one he wants to be with, which is not going to happen. How stupid is he? Um, very. Clearly. I meant to break up with him and got lazy. My bad. I'll regret that for a long time. And yes, I'm actually fine."

It was the truth. I really felt okay. In part that was due to the recent distraction provided by Owen, but that wasn't a Pandora's box of new gossip I was willing to open in front of Cherry. I loved her, but she had the biggest mouth of any of my sisters and less than average sensitivity about divulging secrets.

"Wow, good for you. I should have led with asking how you're doing. Sorry about that. And sorry for pinning you into a corner, or a wine cellar, and making you talk about this. It's just that I care and I didn't want to blow it off and not see how you are, you know?"

"Thanks, Cher. The truth is I've been over him for a while and even though seeing the pictures stung, it didn't tell me anything I didn't already know. He doesn't make me happy and he never felt like forever. He's not the guy."

"You've been saying that for a while. I just hated seeing those pictures and I wanted to check on you."

I nodded. "I wasn't trying to shut you out. I just didn't want this whole dinner to revolve around Tom and his idiotic behavior. Or mine, for that matter."

It felt good to talk to Cherry, and as much as I hated to admit it, I was glad she'd forced me to spell out my feelings about Tom and the reasons it was never going to work out. The more times I said it, the better I felt about my relationship ending.

"The problem is he keeps leaving me messages, saying he wants us to be together. I keep deleting them, but he's making me feel tied to him when I don't want to be," I said.

"You could change your number."

"I shouldn't have to. Ugh, I'm sure eventually he'll give up, but man, the guy is stubborn."

"Guess you don't get to be a billionaire by taking no for an answer."

"Well, he's not getting any other answer from me." I was getting worked up just thinking about how much I wanted Tom gone from my life. Maybe I would change my number. "On a positive note, my day ended well."

Then I caved and filled Cherry in on the past twenty-four hours with Owen because I wanted to say his name and have an excuse to think about him. And his lips. Cherry would set me straight if she thought I was crazy to hook up with someone so soon after Tom.

"I like him and he's fun and he likes to talk about bread, so what's the harm in having a good time with him while I get myself back on track?"

The loud stomp of footsteps on the ceiling indicated that Sarah and Tatum were back from their wild grape chase but I felt confident they wouldn't be able to find us in the basement.

"Sounds good to me. Go for it. Have fun, blow off some steam and get your mojo back. You need to feel like your best self before you're ready for a more serious relationship. But if he turns into another distracting guy who sidetracks you from getting what you really want out of a relationship, promise me you'll cut him loose," she said.

"I promise. Right now, he's the kind of distraction that I need. There's too much going on with my expansion plans and the battle it looks like I'm going to need to fight to get that lined up right to think about starting a relationship with anyone."

The stomping got louder. "Where are their voices coming from?" Sarah's voice intoned from the floor above.

I heard a muffled reply from Annie, then a shout from Tatum.

"Wine cellar? What wine cellar?" Tatum was only loud when

she started drinking, so I had to assume she and Sarah had either done some tasting at the wine store on Euclid, which was walking distance from Finn's house, or she'd been back for a while and just now realized we were missing—also thanks to the wine consumption.

Before I could come up with an excuse for what we were doing, Sarah and Tatum were descending the stairs, joined by our middle sister Becca, who I hadn't realized had arrived.

Cherry froze and I moved in front of one of the wine refrigerators, as though I could hide the evidence of Finn's collection from them.

"We didn't know there was wine here, we swear!" Cherry shouted.

Tatum dismissed her with a flick of her hand. "You're such a bad liar, Cher. How did you get through your teen years?"

"Um, I didn't lie?" Cherry seemed confused.

Sarah laughed and shared a look with Tatum that told me that somehow my smartest and most rule-abiding sisters did things I didn't know about in their teen years. I'd unpack that one later. "Sorry you got stuck buying wine."

Now it was Sarah's turn for a dismissive wave. "Oh, please. We saw right through that, so we went to the wine bar on Euclid and had a glass each, then we came back here."

"You knew Finn had a wine cellar and you pretended to run an errand because I said so? Why?" Cherry asked.

Tatum laughed. "Is that what he's calling his scary basement now? There are spiders in here, you know. And yes I knew. Where do you think I got the wine I just pretended to gift him?" She pointed at one of the refrigerators which had two obvious empty bottle spaces. "Grabbed it before we left."

Becca was standing in the middle of the room looking confused. It might have been the longest I'd seen her go without talking. "What am I missing? You two went on a fake wine run?" she asked.

Tatum nodded. "I knew Cherry wanted to pounce on Isla for info about Tom, but Sarah said she didn't want it to be a whole thing, so we took off for a few."

"What I said was that I didn't want to discuss it at all." I was looking at Sarah when I said it. She had the sense to look contrite.

Becca took a seat in the one chair and pointed her finger at me. "You should've broken up with him two months ago."

"That's what I said." Cherry high-fived Becca.

While my sisters discussed me behind my back, literally, I looked at the bottles in the fridge, hoping to find one with a screw top. Weren't more and more wineries foregoing corks?

Finally, on a shelf near the bottom, I spied one with a metal cap and took it out. Twisting off the cap, I held the bottle up as though in a toast. "Cheers." I unscrewed the top and took a swig. "To not discussing my love life."

Becca took the bottle from me and threw down a gulp. "To finding a better guy who appreciates how amazing you are."

"And who doesn't cheat," Cherry said, grabbing the bottle.

I nodded. "Goes without saying, but yeah, I'll drink to it anyway." I grabbed the bottle back from Cherry.

"I'm already half-drunk, but I'm getting in on this," Tatum said, putting out her hand for the bottle. "To better than average sex."

"Oh God, yes. That should've been the first toast," I said, looking at Sarah, who I assumed would want her turn.

She nodded and hoisted the bottle over her head.

"To being the mistress of your own destiny, and to hell with Tom's mistress. Cheers." She took a double swig and passed the bottle back to me.

"If we weren't all related, this would be pretty gross," I said, wondering how much of the remaining wine in the bottle was really just backwash. "What the hell." I drank some more.

Cherry put her arm around Sarah. "I agree with you, sister.

Good toast. You can do anything you want to do. If you're ready to be in a relationship, there's an internet full of guys who will jump at the chance."

I shook my head. "Ugh, I don't want to date the internet."

"Or don't date. Build your bakery empire and have babies on your own. You can totally do that. You'd be an awesome mom," Sarah said.

"Yikes, where did that come from?" I grabbed the wine back because all their pro-Isla energy was starting to freak me out. "Not sure I'm ready for all that."

"Oh, come on. You talk to your bread starters like they're human. You're so ready." Tatum sounded drunk. Or crazy.

"I talk to them because they're living things and all living things need love."

"You know who you should talk to, Blake's sister, Sydney. She just had a baby two months ago and she's doing it on her own," Becca said.

"Thanks, but no thanks. I'll talk to her when the baby's applying to college. I can relate to that."

From upstairs, we heard more feet pounding around. A moment later, Finn and Annie appeared on the basement stairs.

Annie took in the sight of us passing around the bottle of wine and didn't hesitate before extending her hand. Becca handed it to her and she took a sip.

"You all are crazy," Finn said. "But I love you, and there's dinner upstairs unless you'd rather eat in here."

Annie took another swig and shook her head. "Nope, not eating in here. There's only one chair down here. Come on, people, get your butts upstairs. You're gonna love the fried garlic. Let's go." Obediently, we followed her up the stairs.

Finn brought up the rear and when I walked past him, he leaned in and whispered, "I agree with everything they said. It's your life. Make it good."

I hugged him. For only one brother, he did the work of ten.

CHAPTER 11

 wen

I GOT UP EARLY on Friday for my drive to Healdsburg. Actually, that's not exactly true. Getting up early implies that I slept, which I did not.

After eating pie with Isla, kissing Isla, texting Isla, recalling every sigh from Isla, I was finding it hard to think about anything else.

I'd gone to my meetings on Thursday and buzzed around like I was in the throes of a manic episode, but my newfound energy was all because of her.

Then, instead of sleeping, I'd spent the night looking at architectural drawings, binging a reality show about guerrilla wilderness survival techniques, and thinking about whether to cancel my meetings on Friday and lurk at the bakery all day instead.

I couldn't get her out of my head, despite an irritating rational voice telling me to stop. I would have been smart to listen.

The problem was that I didn't want to stop. It was like a dam had been leveled with a wrecking ball, and now the water poured through unhindered. And I was a man who'd spent a year dehydrated in a drought.

I couldn't pretend I was a guy with a crush when now I was the guy who couldn't have enough of her.

No one was rebuilding that dam.

And despite my previous denial, which mainly came in the form of lying to myself about why I hung out at the bakery so often—I'm picky about my bread, I like walking two miles every morning for a wheat product, I'm a creature of habit—the truth was that I'd always been coming to see her.

But now, I'd kissed her, so there was no point in denying any of it. And I didn't want to wait until Sunday to see her again.

As soon as I got off the treadmill, I'd righted the ship and decided I was going to my meetings . . . right after stopping by the bakery to say hello. I could claim that I needed a little sourdough to carry me through until Sunday. Nothing weird about a quick errand on the way to Healdsburg—in the opposite direction.

Apparently, lack of sleep made me honest and extremely stubborn. So I went full kitchen Romeo.

Knowing how much she liked apple pie, I searched out a simple recipe that used a pre-made crust and threw together an apple breakfast pie with the ingredients I had on hand.

It didn't go very well.

I'm not a baker, and the crust kept crumbling before I could lay the whole thing into the pie tin. It was actually a blessing to be up to my wrists in hot apples that weren't behaving—it gave me something to focus on besides how bad I had it for her.

In order to make it up north for the meeting on time, I needed to hit the bakery earlier than my usual, and I wondered if Isla would be busy in the back. Normally, all the bread was in the ovens by the time I arrived and she was filling the cases in front.

Yes, I knew her morning routine. Because I was a complete and total Isla junkie.

I had the pies in the oven by four and was out the door by five. I wouldn't have time to double back to my house to grab my work stuff, so I shoved everything in the car. The drive took five minutes, but parking took an extra ten. Then I walked six blocks to the bakery in pure blackness and fog, carrying a small portfolio in case Isla was busy and I needed to occupy myself at a table. I also brought the pie.

When I peeked through the leaded windows of the cafe, I decided it was all worth it. Isla stood on a stool with her back to me, her long, lean runner's legs flexed as she stood on her toes to load baguettes into the baskets on the back shelves.

Before knocking, I waited until Isla had finished so I didn't startle her into falling off the ladder. As it was, I was pretty sure I scared the shit out of her when I tapped on the glass.

When she realized it was me, she looked relieved and came to unlock the door.

"Hey, I thought you were out of town." Her hair was twisted up and pinned on top of her head with a clip. I'd seen her hair like that so many times, but this time I had a deep urge to pull the clip out and run my fingers through the strands.

"I was. I mean, I am. I'm going. But I was up super early and realized I had time to swing by, so I figured, why mess with a compulsive habit?" I needed her to work with me here. Suddenly, all the days in the past when I'd come uninvited felt different from this day when it seemed like I needed her permission to show up.

She smiled. "Well, it's nice to see your face. Thanks again for the other night. It was good to get out. If you hadn't shown up, I'd be nursing a two-day hangover right about now."

"Ah, well I'm glad I saved you from yourself."

Then it got awkward. I looked at her and she looked at me and her smile shifted to a half-smile as she looked away. I watched her eyes go to the floor, then to the window next to me. I knew she couldn't see through the glass because it was light in the cafe and dark outside, yet she stared out as though there was something fascinating beyond the window.

"Um, so . . . thanks for letting me in early. I know it's not my usual time."

She nodded and bit her lip. "It's just . . . I just put the bread in the ovens. Nothing will be ready for an hour."

"No worries. I'm only here for a sec." I held up the portfolio as if to provide proof that I had pressing activities elsewhere.

Isla nodded but she wasn't making eye contact. She backed away a couple feet. "Anyway . . . I should really get back. But you're welcome to sit for a bit if you want. I have coffee made." She turned back toward the kitchen and started to walk away.

"Wait." I wasn't sure what to follow up with, but at least it got her to stop. She turned around and looked at me expectantly. "Um, is everything okay? I mean, is it still cool that I stop in early or did me kissing you make it awkward?" Might as well own it. If she was going to be weird with me or kick me out of the place, I'd just as soon know about it.

She smiled. "I thought I kissed you."

"Oh . . . you kissed me good." But her smile faded, so I went to where she was standing in the middle of the café floor amid the bistro tables that had yet to have their salt and pepper grinders set up. "Isla, talk to me. Is it about that? Because we can just chalk it up to beer-fueled, post-breakup madness and never speak of it again."

She inhaled and her shoulders lifted with the weight she seemed to be carrying. When she exhaled, I saw a partial smile creep over her face. "It's not that . . ." Her eyes searched my face as if she was deciding whether to tell me more. "Okay, lest you think I'm a train wreck who not only gets publicly cheated on but also is losing a grip on my business . . ."

Using hand gestures that made me want to wrap her in my

arms for a moment of stillness, Isla went on to explain that some of her exclusive restaurant contracts were in jeopardy and an unknown competitor was trying to swoop in and cut deals on the locations she'd chosen for future bakery cafés.

"And you have no idea who it is?" I asked.

She shrugged. "Some outfit named Flour Artisan. Not a bad name. Cute, actually, except that they're trying to put me under." She was getting worked up, gesturing wildly in that way I was starting to love.

"Never heard of it."

"Me neither. I haven't dug too deeply, but I intend to find out who they are. This is not going to be the end of my business or even the end of my relationships with restaurants. Whoever this is just lit a fire under me and I'm going to prevail regardless. I won't stop for some small-fry baker who thinks I can be undercut with crappy bread."

"Hear, hear. Good attitude," I said, suddenly remembering that I was holding a brown paper bag containing my apple turnovers, which had started to coat the bag with butter stains. "Oh, I brought these for you." I handed over the bag. She unrolled the top and peeked inside, then pushed her nose in and took a deep inhale.

"Did you bake these? They're still warm." Her expression told me she was impressed, so I nodded.

"I couldn't sleep so I made apple mini-pie turnover bites. Not sure that's even a thing but it worked for my skill set. Really there should be ice cream . . ."

She put a hand to her chest and looked so touched that again I wanted to wrap her in my arms, pull her into my chest, and lay my cheek against her hair. I only resisted because I still wasn't entirely sure where we stood.

"Are you kidding? Owen, that is so sweet." She swept behind the cafe counter and grabbed plates and utensils. "I'm eating this before it cools down, and I hope you're planning to join me."

We sat at one of the bistro tables—not the one where I usually hung out—and she grabbed her cup of coffee and plated the turnovers. When she dug in and took her first bite, her eyes closed and I felt like I'd earned a James Beard award.

"This is really good, Owen. If you learn to bake sourdough, you may put me out of business."

She ate the other half of the mini-pie. "You're not going out of business," I said.

Isla swallowed and her face fell. I could see how much the issue with her competitor was weighing on her mind.

I forked the last bit of my pie and offered it to her. "Is this a sympathy bite? Do you think I'm Don Quixote trying to fight a battle without knowing what I've gotten myself into?" She was looking off to the side as if she was afraid to see the truth in my eyes.

I put the forkful down and guided her face back to look at me. "Why would you say that? I think you're amazing. From what I've seen, you can face down anyone, but no one can do it alone. You need some people in your camp, is all." I was about three seconds from offering myself up to aid in whatever she needed when she nodded.

"I do have some help. My sister Sarah helps me with all the financials and she's brilliant, so I can put her on the case. If I need to make a counteroffer on rent at the locations I've scouted, I will. I just need her to run the numbers and figure out what I can afford."

"Is she an accountant? Business manager? It's nice that you can keep it in the family."

"Actually, she's a physicist. She teaches at Berkeley." She described her with pride.

"You have a physicist doing your taxes?" I probably didn't do a great job of hiding my surprise. It was honorable that she wanted to work with her sister, and I briefly wondered what it would have been like to grow up with five siblings with different talents.

I felt a bit envious of the bond that was obvious every time she mentioned one of them.

"When you put it that way, it sounds ridiculous, but she's crazy smart. She knows numbers."

She moved to where the coffee urn sat on a counter just inside the kitchen door and poured me a cup. Then she went to the mini-fridge under the cafe counter and took out a carton of soy milk.

She was distracted. I never drank soy before, and she knew it, but I wasn't going to quibble.

By the time she came back, she seemed to notice the soy milk for the first time and looked at me apologetically. I grabbed it out of her hand before she could turn back to get me something else.

"It's fine. Thank you for the coffee. Listen, I'm sure your physicist sister will use slow positrons to direct the gravitational force away from your business and nuke your competitors, but will you allow me to help you please?"

"How do you know about slow positrons?" I loved how she could get distracted by a tangent like it was more important than the conversation.

"Doesn't everybody?" That earned me a smile. "Listen, I know you don't need a hundred opinions on how to beat your competitor, but maybe I can help. I've been in the hotel business for a while now and I know a thing or two about ruthless competition for prime locations. All I'm saying is that if you'd like to talk the business stuff through sometime, I'm here. As a friend who likes you and who's a good listener."

I was doing my best to stay in my lane and not make suggestive comments about how I was also prepared to help her get over her ex starting immediately on her office couch. Didn't seem appropriate.

Checking the time, I realized I needed to hustle to make the one-hour drive north to get to my meeting on time, so I took a last gulp of coffee and stood up.

Leaning over to kiss her on the cheek, I also extended my hand. "I'll see you on Sunday and I'll come with all my business smarts," I said, tapping my temple.

"Deal." She reached out and we shook. "So what's in Healdsburg anyway?" she asked.

"I have a hotel there and we just hired new management and acquired a small winery next door, so I need to make sure everything looks as good in real life as it did in my head."

I felt grateful to earn a smile. "I hope it does. Okay, well, drink some wine for me while you're there."

"Aw, I don't drink alone. Next time I go, you'll have to come with me." The words were out of my mouth before I could reel them back in. I didn't wait for a response. Better not to give her an opportunity to shoot me down.

I hightailed it out of there, resisting the draw of her lips—I was pretty sure they had their own gravity.

I wanted her to believe I understood that she needed time to sort out her life without feeling pressure from me.

Besides, I had a legitimate reason to spend more time with her and that made me happy. As happy as a friend could be.

CHAPTER 12

sla

IF I HADN'T BEEN MIRED in worry about my business being under attack, I might have missed seeing Owen while he was out of town.

That's a lie. I still missed seeing him.

I told myself it didn't mean anything when I didn't hear from him all day, especially since he'd gone out of his way to stop by before he left.

But I felt the void.

He'd said he had meetings and I didn't expect him to stop what he was doing to send me cute emojis, but it didn't stop me from thinking about him constantly. It was a good thing, I decided, because for the moment, seeing his smile in my mind was the only thing preventing me from going into a full depression over the assault by the mysterious Flour Artisan.

A rebound relationship wasn't a good idea. My emotional

state was in flux, and it had potential to derail my work—like right now when I was thinking about him.

Stop it. Focus.

There was still time to nip this competitor assault in the bud, even if I didn't know who was gunning for my restaurant contracts. I needed to make the rounds and be sure that my goodwill with all the chefs and owners I'd worked with for years was still the thing that drove our relationships. There was more to business than money.

I started setting up quick meetings with my restaurant friends and occasionally dipped into distracted territory by checking for texts.

My team was fully capable of baking the hundreds of loaves we'd need to get into the hands of eight restaurant chefs for their evening menus, so I left the bakery and brought two dozen rounds of sourdough boule to James Brinkley in person.

He was owner of Bastille, a French gastronomy mecca in North Berkeley, and the first chef to invite me to make bread for his five-star restaurant. We'd been friends for over ten years. If anyone could help me come up with a plan for convincing the other restaurants not to jump ship, it was him.

"I need you to level with me, Jamie." I waited in the kitchen while he hauled a box of produce from the walk-in fridge.

He wore his gray checked chef pants and a white T-shirt over his broad chest and thick tattooed arms. A red bandana covered his head, but his auburn close-clipped beard revealed his hair color. He was an oak tree of a man with a huge heart and an instinct for food, which made him a legend in foodie circles.

We stood in the kitchen while he prepped for the dinner service. "Sorry I have to multitask while we talk," he said.

"Are you kidding? Multitasking is my love language." I was fascinated by how quickly he could dice a bell pepper, which he planned to turn into some kind of salsa. "So, how many times have they come knocking?" I still couldn't believe someone was trying to get James to dump me.

"Twice. Once about a month ago and again yesterday. The first time, it was more exploratory. Yesterday was pretty aggressive. The way they talked about it, it was like they were telling me instead of asking me." He started chopping leeks and scooping the tiny circles into a metal bin.

"And they didn't say anything about Flour Artisan that would give you an idea who they are or where they're from?"

"No, the guy who called yesterday was cagy about that, but he all but told me the company had a big corporate backer, as in they've got money to burn trying to take over your contracts, even if they're working at a loss. And I pushed 'em on that, told them there was no way to deliver what they were proposing at those prices. They don't seem to care. They just want the business. Have you pissed anyone off in the bread community lately?"

I almost laughed but I was too worried. "We bakers are a happy bunch generally. Besides, this doesn't sound like some small artisanal baker, despite the charming name they've given themselves."

My phone pinged with a text but I ignored it.

"I wish I had better news for you. I'm not gonna lie, this concerns me, Isla. Most of us put farm to table and local provenance above price, but if someone's coming after you like this, you need to watch your back. And from what I gleaned from their sales pitch, it's someone who knows a lot about your specific operation and is trying to replicate it on the cheap."

"How much do they know?"

He grabbed another bunch of leeks from the walk-in and started washing them in the big metal sink. "Details about your specific breads, the flours, the way your recipes have changed over time. Did you have an employee leave to start a new shop, something like that?"

"No, no one." A niggling little thought pushed its way to the surface and I tried to shove it away before it could take root, but the bugger was stubborn. There was one person I could think of who'd always taken a great interest in all the details of my bread and who'd asked me a lot of questions. I'd answered them all.

I had to steady myself against the dishwashing station behind me because I suddenly felt nauseous. I couldn't breathe. "Jamie, can I grab a glass of water?"

He looked up from the leeks. "Sure. Are you okay? You look a little pale."

No, I wasn't okay. Not if I'd been wrong about Owen and his reasons for hanging out in the shop. "Did you get a name from the person who called you? By any chance was it Owen Miller?"

I hated saying the words but I knew I'd hate myself even more if I didn't ask and later found out that he'd been playing me.

Jamie didn't look up from his prep, but he was shaking his head. "Naw, not him. I know Owen. I was in the running to open a restaurant at one of his hotels. Didn't get the gig, and I still liked him afterward, which is saying something. Owen is a good guy."

"You're sure. It wasn't him or anyone who works with him?" I had to know, even it was something I didn't want to know. And I really wanted it not to be true.

Jamie ground some pepper onto the leeks and pushed them aside. "I couldn't say if it was his people, but why's a hotel guy gonna try to sell me bread? It doesn't make sense. And that's not how he goes about doing business. I'm telling you, you wanna bark up a different tree."

He was right. Owen trying to sabotage me didn't make sense. But I was losing my mind and grasping at anything, not trusting myself to make good judgments about people.

Jamie dismissed the idea as crazy. "It's big and corporate, that was the gist I got, which was why I said no. Twice."

"Appreciate it."

We'd been working together since he opened his modern

French restaurant, and when he opened two more restaurants in Oakland and Menlo Park, he insisted I bake for those restaurants too. "It's a prestige thing, Isla," he'd said at the time. "My customers expect me to have the best food and that includes your bread. I wouldn't presume to bake it myself or buy it from anyone who doesn't have your standards."

"Thanks for being loyal." He moved to a different prep area where he started pulling oils and spices from a shelf and taking out mixing bowls in several sizes.

My phone pinged again and I felt a little surge of hope that it was Owen, but I didn't check it. My social life could wait.

Jamie shook his head. "It's not loyalty—I mean, it is—but it's about quality, Isla, and you're the best in the business. I hope you find these sons of bitches and put them in their place. They've got nothing on you and I'm not the only one who thinks it."

I reached around his thick frame and hugged him while he held the olive oil at arm's length so it wouldn't get on my clothes. "Thank you."

I hoped he was right. It would help if I could put a face to the competition though, so I'd know whose ass to kick.

I STOPPED for chicken tacos at a food truck on the way back to my car, thinking some more about what was looking less like healthy competition and more like an attack.

It made sense that if I'd had success, someone was going to come along to challenge my spot in the food chain, but it seemed so sudden and so thorough.

Then again, there were other bakeries all over the Bay Area. Who was to say they hadn't been undercut as well? I only had my own perspective and experience. Maybe it wasn't personal.

When the food truck owner handed me the small paper dish with my twin tacos, I took the opportunity to check out her setup through the window. The kitchen in that roving restaurant was impressive.

"Is this your business?" I asked.

"All mine. Try not to fall in a faint at the glory," she said, spreading her arms wide and coming to lean on the shelf between us. I smiled at her and sized her up as being about my age, maybe a little older.

She had her brown hair piled on top of her head and she wore a bright cotton scarf wrapped around her neck, reminding me of Cherry's sense of style. I loved that she took the time for accessories even though she was working the grill inside a taco truck all day.

"I love it. Nothing better than a portable business, right?"

She nodded. "Truth. If I get tired of one location or the people don't treat me right, I just re-permit and park somewhere new."

"Cheers to that." I raised my taco in a toast and she lifted a plastic water bottle.

"Enjoy the food. And if you're still hungry, try the tofu with mole. I do a decent vegan business but I'm still experimenting so you can have it on the house."

Taking a bite of a taco, I hummed my approval as the tender chicken juices dribbled down my chin. "You make a good taco," I said through my mouthful of food. It was really delicious and I found it hard to believe she could make food that good in the back of a truck.

She gave me a little salute and nodded to a customer who'd walked up behind me. I scooted out of the way and finally checked my texts.

There were a couple from Tom demanding that I call him. I deleted those. When I saw a few from Owen, my ridiculous heart swelled with happiness.

The first one was a photo of bright green grape vines taken up close against an azure sky dotted with puffs of clouds that looked like popcorn. He'd typed, "Stop and smell the rosé."

There was a second photo of him hugging a shaggy golden retriever in a vineyard that seemed to go on for miles. That one was captioned "Everything happens for a Riesling."

I typed him a text.

Me: Looks gorgeous there. And you are very punny.

The dots started jumping on my phone immediately and it made my pulse race.

Owen: I'm just one glass of wine away from typing really inappropriate things to you.

Me: Really? Day drinking? I thought you had meetings.

Owen: Kidding. No drinking. But not kidding about typing inappropriate things. I make 'pour decisions' when I'm not with you.

This was escalating fast. I had to be the adult in the room or we'd be sexting by dinner.

Me: Are you sure you're not drunk?

Owen: Positive. How are you? Are you facing down the corporate raiders?

Me: Ugh, not really. Bread company is coming for me like the devil. Wtf, did I murder puppies in a prior life? Karma hates me right now.

He didn't respond right away and I second-guessed telling him real stuff via text. Maybe he just wanted to play. Well, too bad, because this was my life. If he wanted to be a part of it, he'd have to deal.

The bubbles were back. He was typing.

Owen: Fuckers. You and me, Sunday, we're working on your business plan. Being up here has given me some new ideas that might work for you too.

I didn't know what he had planned or whether he knew enough about my business to be helpful, but seeing those words gave me hope, and I needed hope.

Me: You've got yourself a date.

Owen: Not gonna dissect that one. I'm just going to interpret it how I want. I'm looking forward to our date.

Me: Me too.

Owen: And to be clear, if I wasn't stuck up here for meetings, I'd be there in a prosecco.

Me: Where are you getting these?

Owen: Maybe I am drunk. That, or I'm at a novelty T-shirt shop.

Me: I like you either way.

Owen: Aw, Isla, that makes me happy to hear. And just so you know, the feeling's mutual.

That made me laugh. He was good at that—making me laugh or smile more than most people. I couldn't control the flood of warmth in my chest or the dumb grin on my face.

What am I doing?

With Tom bugging me with messages and this new threat from Flour Artisan, whoever that was, I was in no place where I should be texting cute guys and thinking about them around the clock. I'd just gotten out of a relationship two days ago, for crying out loud.

I reaffirmed my commitment to keep Owen firmly in the friend zone so he didn't get the wrong idea. No late-night kissing that would leave me tired and ill-equipped to save my business before it was too far gone to save.

He'd understand. We could look at business plans and have coffee like normal friends. We'd already talked about how the other night was just a rebound thing.

It didn't feel great to think about pushing him away, but I was a big girl—I could make difficult choices and stick to them. We were friends and with a little effort, I could discourage the flirting and put myself back on solid ground so I could focus.

With that decided, I did the only thing I could at that point and went back for a tofu mole taco. I insisted on paying for it— from one small business owner to another.

CHAPTER 13

wen

ISLA WAS right that no normal people get up at five on a Sunday morning, and that included me. But that was before I knew she'd be working early and before I'd waited two days to see her again.

After trying not to admit that I'd pretty much spent whatever hours I wasn't working on Friday and Saturday thinking about Isla, I gave up on lying to myself.

For the past year, I harbored what seemed like a harmless crush that kept bringing me back day after day. I figured eventually it would pass when some other woman grabbed my attention or I found a bakery closer to work. Now I didn't see either of those things happening.

After one night, a landscape in Healdsburg that normally took my breath away had looked like a sorry backdrop. All I could think about was how much prettier the royal blue sky and sun dappled acres of vineyards would be if she was standing in front of them.

I couldn't get her out of my head. I wanted to make her smile.

In an effort to do that, I'd bought her a multicolored pile of T-shirts with wine-related sayings, some of which I'd borrowed for my texts to her. Late last night, I placed them in a neat stack by the back door where I knew she'd see them first thing this morning. I'd say that I did it without thinking because I'm the kind of guy who acts first and apologizes later.

But I am not.

I think. And sometimes overthink. It's a supposed character flaw that has saved my hide in business more than once, so eventually I decided that overthinking was not a flaw at all.

Case in point, the boutique hotel I'm in the middle of opening. Initially, my investment group loved the idea of the hotel being an eco-friendly spa in Napa Valley where we could take advantage of wine tasting tours and seasonal traffic that made it an obvious vacation destination.

I almost went with the plan. But while meeting with everyone on our Healdsburg staff, a few things occurred to me that I was currently sorting out while running on the treadmill at rooster hour.

Yes, the weather in San Francisco made for some really nice outdoor jogs. But I hated the hills. Hated them with the fervor of an angry rhino. Running uphill sucked, and running downhill just made me nervous because I was always pretty sure another uphill was just around the bend. In San Francisco, it usually was.

In the case of the Napa hotel, something had been bothering me. It just didn't feel like the right location for one of our hotels. Napa was great and it had the benefit of international name recognition—the wine region exported to restaurants everywhere in the world, so it wasn't a reach for travelers to want to visit.

Maybe that was the problem, I thought, as I cranked up the speed a little faster. I couldn't hear the sound of my own breathing over the music blaring from my headphones, which gave me the mistaken idea that I wasn't panting as loudly as I probably was.

Ergo, I believed I was in better shape than I probably am. I'm not above a little illusion in the name of a workout.

There were already several known boutique hotels owned by big hotel groups in Napa. I believed ours could compete with them, but why? The wine region spread far and wide from the Russian River Valley and Sonoma all the way to Healdsburg.

There were great wineries that weren't on the typical Napa tasting path and my new hotel could help boost them up and give us a way to distinguish ourselves.

But that had been done too. Just trying to be different wasn't enough. There was still something I was missing, and I cranked up the speed one more time to wake my brain up and get the neurons to fire.

It was probably backward logic because the faster I went, the more oxygen and blood went to my heart and lungs and legs, leaving my brain shit out of luck, but somehow a lonely neuron did the heavy lifting anyway.

The airport.

Napa wasn't particularly close to an airport and a lot of visitors flew into Oakland and drove an hour to the destination. I envisioned a map of the area I knew so well that it might as well have been tattooed on my brain.

The Sonoma Airport, also known as the Charles Schulz Airport because the Snoopy cartoonist had lived in Santa Rosa for thirty years, was only a short car ride between Sonoma and the wine region I should be serving with a new hotel.

No one should be wine tasting and driving. But people had their cars with them because they'd driven up from Oakland, and now they had to hop in an Uber or go wine tasting. There was too much transportation involved.

I slowed the pace a little bit to allow my lungs to catch up to my thoughts and tried to figure out what angle I could take in

Sonoma besides the obvious convenience of not having an airport commute. I had to figure out the wine tasting route that would make the hotel destination a slam dunk.

That's when I glanced at my lonely spin bike that had been sitting in a corner, waiting for me to get excited about riding it. I still wasn't excited, but the bike gave me an idea.

Most people probably wouldn't want to ride thirty miles to taste wine, but if we offered electric bikes along with regular tasting tours by air-conditioned van, we could hit lots of different parts of the market and do something that wasn't happening in Napa.

Once I'd landed on a solution, the idea of building in Napa seemed so ludicrous I was almost embarrassed I'd considered it for so long.

Score one for overthinking.

The same logic could also probably help Isla as she tried to fend off her competition. I'd learned a few things about that as well, thanks to my lawyers and their computer skills, and I was eager to sit down with her.

Yeah, sitting is definitely the goal.

I showered and hoofed it two miles through the streets to her shop, where I saw Isla standing near the bakery case writing things on a clipboard. I knocked and she waved before coming over and unlocking the door.

"Coffee's made. I'll grab you a cup," she said like she always did. After bringing it back and depositing it on the table by the window with a carton of milk, she went back to whatever she was computing on the clipboard.

I didn't want to interrupt her if she was counting or calculating so I poured milk in my coffee and sipped it while she worked. There was nothing abnormal about the morning because I usually just sat and observed while she went about opening the bakery.

But today, I wanted affirmation that she wanted me there, and I wasn't getting it.

In fact, the silence in the room started to feel aggressive.

Yes, we'd had the just-friends discussion, and I'd done my best to ignore it and flirt with her shamelessly, but she had a lot going on, so maybe I needed to dial it back to small talk. I didn't like it, but I had to respect it.

"How's your morning going?" I asked as I did every time I came to the bakery.

"Not bad. Ovens are full, so that's good. You?" she asked, not looking up from her clipboard. She worked her way from one end of the display case to the other, making more notes. Normally, at times like this we'd talk. I'd ask her about bread and she couldn't tell me enough.

"Tell me about the bread. You try the new flour this morning? You said you had a new blend."

Finally, she looked up. "Right. The maple rye blend. I tried it on Friday but the jury's still out. I'm not sure it's bad, but maybe I just can't get used to it."

"If you need a second opinion, I'm here for you," I said.

That earned me a smile.

"We didn't save any of it from the Friday experiment but maybe I'll make some today or tomorrow."

"Great. Happy to be your bread guinea pig." Normally, it was fun to talk about things like maple rye grain. Now it felt like a giant bag of flour covering the elephant in the room. She was avoiding me and I hated it.

"Thank you, sir." I almost saw a glimmer of the more laid-back Isla I'd gotten a peek at on Wednesday before it disappeared.

Then she went back to the kitchen and came back with two trays of lemon squares. Camille was responsible for baking the pastries, but Isla always set up the front cases herself. Not that it was crazy for her to do it—it was her place and she probably knew best how she liked everything to look.

Still, having juggled multiple hotels for a while now, I knew it was impossible for an owner to retain that kind of control over every aspect.

The effort and the hours became too grueling, and with no partners or executive managers to share the burden, it often led to burnout. I'd seen it firsthand, yet it wasn't my place to tell her what to do. Especially if she wasn't even going to talk to me.

I caught her eye while she was arranging the pastries and smiled. She returned my smile, then ducked back down and worked.

Drinking my coffee, I leafed through a newspaper from the shelf where they were available for customers.

After thirty minutes, the cases had been filled and the front of the shop looked the way it always did when they opened their doors. I could tell without even looking at the time that it was nearly seven, and even on a Sunday that meant people would begin showing up in an endless stream. The cashier, Kim, arrived and started her morning ritual.

Every so often, a baker would come out from the back with a tray full of loaves which Isla then lined up on the shelves along the back wall, where they never stayed for long once the place opened for business.

At first, I only saw two bakers alternating bringing out the bread, but then a third appeared with baguettes and more of the oblong loaves.

She had three bakers.

Instead of being busier than usual, she should have had time to chat.

Wow. She'd completely shut down. She was avoiding me, plain and simple, and even though she'd let me in the door, she might as well have slammed it in my face.

"Isla," I said the next time she appeared from the back.

"Yes."

"You have a free moment, maybe?" I was asking in order to be polite, but I wasn't asking. I tipped my head at the baker who'd brought another tray of bread out, and she immediately knew what I was insinuating.

She wiped her hands on the apron she was wearing and untied it at the back before pulling it over her head and hanging it on a hook by the door to the kitchen.

She was wearing the pink 'It's wine o'clock somewhere' shirt I'd left her.

She hadn't shoved it on over whatever she was wearing before. She'd changed into it and knotted it at the back because it was a size large. It didn't fit and she wore it anyway, which gave me a tiny shred of hope.

"Nice shirt," I said. I couldn't help the smirk.

"Thanks. Someone I like a lot gave it to me." She gave me the benefit of a smile.

I nodded. "Pink is your color." She blushed and turned away, checking the bakery cases once more. They were perfect.

"I'm on a break for a bit. I've got my cell if there's a catastrophe," she told Kim, who had one long braid that hung down her back and she always wore blue eye shadow, no matter what color clothes she had on.

Isla gestured to me to follow her out the door, but not before she grabbed a to-go cup for my coffee and carefully poured it and added milk before handing it to me.

"Thanks," I said.

"Can't shortchange you on your coffee, can I?"

"Well, considering I never pay for it and you own the place, you can do pretty much whatever you want."

She smirked and pulled the door closed as we moved out to the sidewalk. The warmth of the bakery made the morning chill outside that much more noticeable, and Isla was only wearing the T-shirt.

"You're gonna freeze. Do you have a jacket?" I asked.

"I don't think we'll be that long. I can handle it."

Oh. Okay.

So this was not going to go my way. This was where she'd tell me the other night had been a mistake and I should forget it ever happened. I didn't know if I had much of an argument to the contrary, but I felt like I should at least have the option of a rebuttal, so I quickly thought of a list of reasons why she shouldn't send me packing.

"Here's the thing, Owen. I don't want anything to be awkward, and I have a business to run." She looked me dead in the eye and there was none of the mischief or fondness I saw the other night. There wasn't even the normal friendliness.

"Okay. Works for me. I don't feel awkward at all." It was sarcasm but she didn't react.

"I'm happy for you," she said, putting a hand on her hip. "Unfortunately, I can't say the same for myself."

"Why do you feel awkward?"

"Really? You have to ask that?"

"Um, unfortunately, yes. I do."

It was awkward because she was making it awkward.

We had banter. We had chemistry, I was certain of that. I'd offered to help her with work, and she seemed to have forgotten all about that plan.

She hesitated, and I prepared myself for whatever wrath was about to spew forth. Whatever it was, I probably deserved it, given that I was still clueless about what insensitive thing I'd done to piss her off.

Isla blinked slowly and looked at the sky as though my very existence was trying her patience.

"Okay, I feel awkward because I've been thinking about you since I saw you on Friday," she said with an expression that looked like she'd just admitted to having the plague. Or worrying that I had the plague. Either way, it didn't look hopeful.

"Is that . . . I take it that's a bad thing, where you're concerned? Because I've been thinking about you too—constantly, in fact—I can't stop thinking about you. I've been waiting until this morning so I could come in just so I could look at you again. You're more beautiful than I remembered, if that's possible. Anyway, I'd really like to ask you out on a real date if that's something you think you might like to do, and then maybe all the awkwardness will be replaced by something really, really good."

She looked at me with a disappointed expression that soon turned to confusion and finally settled on disappointment. She shook her head.

"The reason I've been thinking about you is that I really could use your help in figuring out how to save my business, which I'm embarrassed to admit is a bit of a disaster right now. After being good at what I do for the last seven years, I'm losing my grip. I missed all the signs. I'm out of my depth and it doesn't feel good."

Oh.

She was right.

This was awkward.

CHAPTER 14

sla

I KNEW I was hurling a knife into Owen's main artery with my words, and the worst part was that they weren't even true.

Sure, I'd been thinking about what he'd said about my business. But when I'd thought of his words, they came with a very vivid picture of other things that I wanted from him and none of them involved bakery advice.

As I stood there, I fought an internal battle because a huge part of me wanted to relent and sink into the warmth of Owen's chest. Oh, that magnificent chest that clearly didn't come from working at a computer and ordering hotel supplies. His job seemed to leave him ample time for the gym.

Or rugby practice. Or water polo.

I wanted to kiss him.

A brief scenario went through my mind where I let the bakers and Kim hold down the fort at the shop for a few hours—hell, why not the whole day?—and I took Owen back to my house and we finished what we started the other night.

He felt safe and comforting when suddenly my baking haven felt like it was under attack. But it wasn't fair to make him the rebound guy. Tom was still leaving me phone messages saying we needed to talk. I didn't intend to speak to him again ever, but he was far from gone from my life.

I still felt entangled.

"Okay, is there any chance you weren't listening before when I said what I did?" he asked. He was smiling but I could see it was a stiff cover for what was probably embarrassment.

"Owen . . . I'm sorry, I—"

He held up his hands. "No, no. You have no reason to apologize. I'm the one who got the wrong impression. And you're right. This is your place of business. It's your career. I really don't want this to be weird, although I'm afraid the ship may have sailed there, so I'll tell you what—I'll take a little break from coming by the shop, which should stop the blood flow from this gash wound of awkward I've just opened up."

"But that's not what I'm saying."

"I know you're not. Because you're a kind person and you're nice to your customers. And that's what I am—a customer. So why don't you give me a week or a month or six to get my bread fix someplace else and you can focus on your business, which, by the way, I don't believe is a disaster. It just needs tweaking and I'm sure you can figure out how to do that if you don't have the distraction of some dude who lurks at a table every day and says awkward—"

I grabbed his face and kissed him. It was the only way to stop his torrent of self-deprecating words, which were making me feel worse about lying to him.

Plus, I'd been dying to kiss him for ten minutes.

His lips were stiff at first, probably because I'd surprised him, but he caught on rather quickly. His mouth softened against mine and he moved with certainty, reaching for my hand that was hanging by my side and intertwining our fingers.

His other hand came to my cheek, which he lightly caressed while his lips gently took over the kiss. It didn't take long before I was dizzy with his woodsy, citrusy scent, and the impossibility that kissing him could feel this good.

He pulled back a couple inches and looked at me.

"But you said—"

"I lied," I said breathlessly.

"Okay. I love that." He cupped my face with both hands and moved them from my jaw to the sides of my face and slid them into my hair. We were still standing a few doors down from the bakery, which was probably open for business by now, but I didn't care. My entire staff could be standing on the sidewalk watching us and I'd just give them raises and tell them to throw out all the bread.

We turned until my back was against the closed door of some retail store that sold only wool children's hats for a reason I'd never understood.

But I loved the place now because they wouldn't be open for hours, and the cool of the glass door felt nice against my back because the rest of me was on fire.

It was early morning, and I couldn't blame the beer or the romance of a night out for how much I wanted this man. He pressed harder against me and I could feel the stiffness in his pants, which made me pull him in closer.

I was not a PDA kind of person, but I finally understood the mentality of people who were—I wanted to kiss Owen and grind against him more than I cared what people around might think. And my eyes were closed, so I couldn't see anyone anyway.

Owen's lips moved down my neck and across my throat, licking and sucking lightly while my hands roamed his back and moved to where I knew his abs were enticingly within reach under his shirt.

"We should probably . . . go someplace else." His voice was a low growl near my ear and it just made me want him with more insane lust.

I moaned at the feel of his breath against my ear and ran my hands under his shirt. Ah, the abs, the chest . . . but no, he was pulling away, backing out of my reach, straightening his pants.

My head spun, still breathless with desire and I couldn't focus on what he was saying, but I was pretty sure I didn't want to hear it if it meant we had to stop.

Then I started to become aware of my other senses—the sounds of people chatting as they walked past us on the sidewalk, the smell of the machine brewing espresso at the bakery, the depth of Owen's eyes as he looked at me.

"Hmm? I didn't hear what you said," I looked down and realized he was holding both of my hands, probably to keep them from ripping his shirt off his body. Smart man.

"Not that I'm at all against continuing in this vein, but maybe we should go up to that office upstairs. Or my house. Because I'm not about to grope you in front of your place of business."

"No?"

"Hard no."

"Okay. Good that you have standards," I said.

Clearly, I didn't when it came to him.

But that wasn't reason enough to make bad decisions like blowing off work and leaving my team to handle the place at a moment's notice. Things were already feeling precarious at work.

What if the ovens broke or the dough didn't rise or the thermostat went on the fritz and the place was too hot to keep the lemon squares and fruit tarts from melting?

What if I trusted my staff to take care of the place in my absence and they succeeded?

What if Flour Artisan chose this moment when I'd lost myself in lust to make a full court press?

Then again, it was Sunday and my staff had it handled. It was what they'd done yesterday and every other time when it was my day off. It was what I'd trained them to do, and they did it well.

So really, there was no reason I couldn't tell them I'd be back after the lunch rush and spend some time sorting through what Owen and I were doing—after what would surely be mind-altering sex. However . . .

I felt nervous.

Am I afraid of liking him when he's clearly a friend distracting me from a breakup? Um, yes.

I'd basically lost my mind just standing in his presence on a city street. Who knew what I was capable of if we were alone in the office upstairs? Someone needed to make the smart decisions and I didn't trust my emotions to do the job.

My rational side had to work overtime.

"How far away do you live?" I asked because the rational brain had left the building.

He pointed in a few directions like he was drawing a map with his finger. "Hayes Valley."

"You live in Hayes Valley? That's like a thirty-minute walk from here. I thought you said this was your neighborhood bakery."

"It is."

"But there's a Mandala Bakery right on Hayes."

He leveled me with a stare. "Really? Mandala? You think so little of me that you imagine I'd eat their bread? You make the best bread in the neighborhood. You make the best bread in any neighborhood."

I couldn't help smiling at that. "I do make the best bread in the neighborhood," I said. And I liked that he expanded the neighborhood to include Hayes Valley. "Hey, we're practically neighbors, by the way. I live on Steiner near the park."

"No. You live in one of the Painted Ladies? Tell me it's true." The Painted Ladies were a historic row of Victorians painted in different colors with balconies, porches and pitched roofs. They were a popular spot for tourist photos, but I never skipped an opportunity to walk past them.

"No, but I live near them. For a hot minute I thought I might have been able to buy one, but it didn't happen. I'll tell you that story later."

Somehow I realized we were walking in the direction of our neighborhoods and had already left the vicinity of the bakery. I quickly fired off a couple texts to Camille and my head baker, letting them know I'd be back in a few hours.

They responded immediately, telling me they had everything under control.

I was kind of in shock.

"What's up?" Owen asked. I'd stopped walking and was staring at my phone.

"I've never done that before, walked out and just . . . left everything in the hands of other people on a day when I'd planned to be there."

"Competent people?"

"Very competent."

"That's great. Why have you never done it before?" We started walking again and Owen grabbed my hand. The gesture shot a blaze of heat over my skin. It struck me how natural it felt to walk with him hand in hand.

"I . . . don't know. It's not like I don't have days off or hours when I leave for meetings. They're in charge when I'm not there, but it's always scheduled, and everyone knows ahead of time what's happening."

"But you're okay with this." There was a reason I sometimes spoke in statements instead of questions. I had analyzed it and I found that it got people to agree with me more often.

~~I She~~ hesitated answering while ~~she~~ thought. "I guess I am. Wow. Who knew?"

He brought my hand to his chest and covered it with his other hand. "I think it's good. From what I can see, you work your ass off. You have skilled people who can do their jobs if you let them. Part of the job of a good manager is to let your employees rise to the challenge of taking on more responsibility. They can't do that if you're always there watching out for them. Besides, you're going to need to let them take over when you open your new locations."

"True. If there are new locations." I was enjoying the temporary reprieve from thinking about how to save my expansion plans, but there was no escaping it.

We rounded the bend and came smack into a line of people outside the new epicurean grocery store I'd been hating on since it arrived. I jumped back like it was a cockroach, fearing the bad juju would rub off.

"Ew."

"Have you been in here?" Owen asked.

I sneered. "Are you kidding? You're the one who comes in and throws their bread in the trash every day."

"I was doing that to make a point. But their produce is good, and their cheese selection is actually one of the better ones I've found." He was edging closer to the line of people, his expression optimistic.

I backed away warily. "You're not suggesting we go in, are you?" It felt like I'd be crossing a line, entering enemy territory.

He gently guided me to the back of the line. "For research purposes only. I want you to see what they do well and where they fail. Owners who know their brand like they have a degree in it—they have it nailed. Frozen baked goods—fail!"

"Ah, so this is the beginning of the Owen Miller business boot camp? Tell me, sensei, what is their brand?"

"It will all become clear, grasshopper, when we enter the magic realm."

I reluctantly took a step closer to him, which meant I was closer to the front door. The line was moving quickly and soon we were inside. "Okay," I said, my back practically plastered to the wall while I took in the way the interior was organized into food stalls.

I couldn't say I hated it.

Owen laughed and pulled me gently away from the wall and we walked around the store, while he pointed out where he thought they'd cut corners. "They shouldn't be selling flowers here. Not their core competency and there's nothing different about what they're doing. Same with desserts. They're taking some generic cake and trying to fancy it up with a little glitter and vanilla beans. Better to partner with a really good patisserie and offer a boutique experience."

"I hear what you're saying, but in that case, they'd just be a collection of imports from other shops."

"Ding, ding, ding. Exactly. That's their brand. That's what they should do. Offer the best chocolate mousse and lava cake in the city from Bern's. Offer the best bread in the city from your bakery."

I blushed. "Come on." I'd worked hard at my reputation in San Francisco but it was really nice to hear someone else acknowledge it, especially someone who seemed to spend a lot of time thinking about food.

"Stop. You know it is. You should approach them and offer to sell to them. They carry your bread, your brand gets exposure to these hipsters who can't walk the two blocks to your shop, everybody wins." He gestured around at the patrons with a sneer, which turned into a smile when he looked at me.

"But I'm right down the street. If people want my bread, they'll come to my shop."

"Not if they're in a hurry and can only go to one place and they also need tomatoes and . . ." He picked up a carton of something white. "Coconut milk yogurt." He made a face. "Don't be afraid of being near other bread sellers. Just be better."

"You're making it sound easier than I think it is."

"No, you're making it sound hard. Stop. It. I can help you.

Later." He leaned in and kissed me. "Now before I take you on top of their perfect grapefruit display, let's buy some perfect produce and a few ingredients and go back to whoever's house is closest so I can kiss you for real."

And as if to prove how different that might be from regular kissing, he pulled me in and claimed my mouth with his. A couple dizzying moments later, he let me go. "And after that, I'm going to make you breakfast. Good?"

I nodded because I was incapable of forming words.

So good.

sla

AFTER A FEW BLOCKS, I'd worked myself into a full panic. I'd never played hooky from work, and now I felt guilty. I was also nervous because I'd basically just agreed to go back to Owen's house where we would kiss.

And make out. And have sex, probably more than once.

Did I want that?

Hell yeah.

Was it a good idea?

Absolutely not. Plus, the fact that we'd pretty much agreed on that plan back when we were kissing in front of the bakery made it even more awkward, like a booty call in broad daylight followed by a mile-long walk to analyze all the fun out of everything.

I was good at that.

"What's wrong?" Owen asked after we'd walked a few blocks in silence.

"Nothing. Why?" I wasn't going to tell him that my brain was on fire.

"Because you haven't said anything in ten minutes. And you look like you're walking to your execution. Are you having second thoughts?" he asked.

"No, of course not. I'm good." I smiled stiffly in an effort to show I was really mellow and cheerful, but he wasn't biting.

"Liar." He punched me lightly on the arm and I grudgingly stopped and looked at him. The easy blue of his eyes was focused on me, and it was hard not to relax. "I completely respect your need to take things slow, all evidence to the contrary. And I know we're just friends. This isn't a date, despite what I might be tempted to call it."

"Owen—"

He tented his fingers and rested his chin on top. "I want to help you figure out your growth avenues, if you'll let me, so let's go hang out in my living room—on separate couches—and do that. And I'll cook you breakfast as promised. No assumptions about anything else happening beyond that. Okay?"

I wasn't sure I wanted his 'no assumptions,' but I'd deal with that later. "Yes. Thank you. I don't know why I'm so skittish."

"I do. The baby you've been growing and tending for years is under attack, and you don't know how to defend it. You just got out of a relationship and you probably have some soul-searching to do. I have rebound written all over me—do you think I'm not aware of that?"

"And you're okay with it?"

He shrugged. "Mostly. Maybe. Not sure. So that's why we should just hang out and talk shop. It's neutral territory for both of us, and no decisions have to be made right here on Dolores Street."

I had to look up at the sign to even realize we were on Dolores. "Weren't we on Guerrero a second ago?"

"No. We turned off Guerrero a while back. See, I knew you were off in the clouds."

I leaned on a planter outside of a hardware store. "Sorry. It's like I'm an animal who's been removed from her customary habitat. I always work at the bakery on Sundays. I'm a little freaked out to be roaming free in the world."

The expression on his face turned horribly guilty. "Then you should go back. I don't want you to be freaked out." He turned in the opposite direction, fully prepared to walk me back to work.

I put a hand out to stop him. "No, are you kidding? Look at this gorgeous day. I'm glad to be out on a Sunday. Really. I just need a little time to adjust, that's all."

He looked to me for reassurance, his expression still wary. "You sure?"

"Absolutely. But can we stop and get some really good coffee on the way because the stuff I make for the employees is crap."

"Hey, that's the stuff you feed me every day."

"I know. I'd have thought you'd stop coming by now, but it seems I can't get rid of you."

"Guess I'm just stubborn that way. Were you really trying to get rid of me?"

I batted my eyes with a flirty smile. "Maybe. Maybe not."

"Oh, you're in trouble now," he said right before he poked me in the ribs which tickled like crazy. He scooted to get away from my efforts to swat him.

I lunged for him, but he was quick, jogging backward down the street until I caught up with him. Then he turned and raced away. Of course I chased him to no avail—never been a sprinter and I know when I'm outclassed.

When I came around expecting to see him up the block, he grabbed me around the waist and pulled me in to where he stood hiding. I squealed in his arms, so he held me tighter and kissed my neck. Then my cheek. Then my lips.

133

Pulling away, he said, "What's your poison, a latte or a flat white?"

It took a second for my brain to catch up to what he was saying when I was all about his lips. Then I looked up.

He'd led me right to a coffee place.

~

WHEN WE GOT to Owen's apartment, there was a package waiting on his doorstep in a manila envelope. He scooped it off the straw doormat that said, "hope you brought wine."

"Is this a souvenir from your 'business trip' as well?" I asked.

"Yes, and why the air quotes?" He shuttled me inside and I took in a series of black and white photographs of city buildings at night. Most were of the San Francisco skyline.

"I'm just feeling like you had an awful lot of time for souvenir shopping and I'm wondering if it was a boondoggle."

"It was a real business trip, but I'm always up for a boondoggle. I told you, we should go. You'll like it. And we could consider it 'research' for your new locations. Maybe you'll open a Victorine up there."

"I don't even want to know what those air quotes mean."

He grinned, still holding the envelope as he ushered me to a round zinc-topped table by a huge bay window with a perfect view of the water.

"I got some information for you," he said, opening the envelope and handing me the papers, which turned out to be corporate filings showing that Flour Artisan was a cute-sounding artisanal bread label that would soon be unveiled by the huge baking company Centinela Bread.

I was grateful for the information.

But also shocked. And terrified.

"Centinela Bread is trying to put me out of business?" I

deflated at the thought. It was like one tiny ant holding a bread-crumb against a national wheat field Goliath.

Centinela Bread had loaves in every supermarket in the country and even though the company had started as one Los Angeles-based bread company, it had quickly sold out and gone corporate, raking in a huge payday. I'd been told more than a few times I could do the same thing if I ever wanted to, but the quality would be instantly compromised and I could never imagine compromising the integrity of what we made by hand.

"Who gave you this?" I asked, praying it hadn't been dropped on his doorstep by the mob.

"My lawyer messengered it over. Nothing against physicists, but they don't typically carry the big guns that Silicon Valley lawyers do, and my guys are ruthless. Like I said, I've had to fend off big corporate types, and these assholes get the job done. I hope you don't mind that I called in a favor."

I'd never had anyone call in a favor for me and I wasn't sure how I felt about it. "I'm not used to it, but I don't think I mind."

Did I mind? Did he believe I was so outclassed that I couldn't fight my own battles?

Was I so outclassed I didn't even know it?

He reached for my hand which sat on the table. "Hey. I apolo-gize for overstepping. In no way did I do it because I thought you couldn't take care of things yourself. I was just trying to be help-ful, and I'll call these guys off right now if I've offended you in any way."

He held up his phone, like he was ready to tell the lawyers to cease and desist.

I shook my head. "No, no. I really do appreciate it. It's just hard for me not to see it as a failing on my part. I rarely use lawyers. I have boilerplate contracts that have always worked for me and there's never been a need for anything more, but maybe I should call them."

"Maybe. Or you could use my guys. Like I said, they're ruthless when they need to be."

"I think I need ruthless."

"Great. Done." A couple texts later, his guys offered to meet with me that week.

No sooner did I exhale than my phone started ringing. It was Tom.

"Do you need to get that?" Owen asked.

"No. I'm good." I don't know why I didn't tell him it was Tom, but after all the kissing we'd done, it felt like a betrayal to be communicating with my ex, even if Owen and I were just friends.

Besides, I didn't want to answer the phone. Tom and I were over, and I knew he understood that. I couldn't have been clearer when I told him to go to hell.

The first time he called on Friday, I ignored it and let it go to voicemail. He left his usual gruff message, "Hello Isla, it's Tom. Please return when you're able. Take care."

When we'd first started dating, his tone struck me as odd. Later, it felt charming in a stiff, corporate sort of way. I didn't respond to his message, which led to him leaving three more. I ignored those, just as I planned to delete whatever he said this time.

I was no longer charmed.

～

An hour later, I stared at a collection of maps of the Bay Area, which Owen had marked up with red circles, yellow squares, and green triangles. I felt like I was back in preschool, and I was as confused as a toddler who just wants the red ball and is forced to look at numbers instead.

Owen and I had gone through all my expansion plans and he'd summarily rejected half of what I thought were good locations. Those were the red circles.

He'd added new ones that made no sense. Those were green. Some were near other bakeries, and others were in places I'd never heard of. I had a moment of panic that maybe he was crazy.

"I'm not sure what you're seeing that I'm not," I said.

"Not yet, but you will." He seemed so certain and I had no idea why.

We were sitting in his living room—on separate couches, as promised—and he was standing in front of me holding a dry erase pen. I was distracted, looking at his furniture instead. I liked the way he'd decorated using all vintage pieces that would have been at home in this San Francisco walkup a hundred years earlier.

He had a purple velvet settee and twin grey high-backed chairs flanking an oval French wood coffee table. One wall had tall casement windows with a phenomenal view of the bay, and another wall had two large abstract paintings in gilt frames.

None of the furnishings or décor seemed like the taste a guy in his thirties would have, unless he'd traveled the world and shipped back antiques from flea markets and cool period finds from tiny shops.

The other rooms that he'd toured me through—the kitchen and a study—also had vintage touches. There wasn't a sterile piece of what I'd come to think of as "guy modern" furniture in sight. Tom's house was the exact opposite. Everything had been chosen by his designer to resemble a Dwell magazine spread and he took up residence there like a guest who didn't want to disturb anything.

I could tell that Owen lived in his place. The books on the floor-to-ceiling shelves had creases in their spines from being read. A large mirror mounted above the fireplace reflected the light coming through the window. Everything had a purpose and was arranged with thought.

Who is this guy?

Apparently, he was the kind of guy who'd roll a whiteboard—

yup, a freaking whiteboard—in from his office so he could draw on a hanging map of California. We spent the next half hour drinking the remains of our coffee while Owen tried to convince me to look away from the locations I'd selected so carefully.

"So you're telling me I didn't pick good places?"

"Not at all. I'm asking you why you picked these particular locations to expand your business, and you haven't given me a good answer," he said, tapping the whiteboard like an impatient teacher. He reminded me of Sarah.

I had better answers than what I'd told him. I'd done research. This wasn't some willy-nilly decision made by a flighty baker who didn't know anything about the local markets. It was a well thought-out plan.

I'd only recently become flighty in the face of a man I couldn't stop picturing naked, and now I couldn't remember anything about my original business idea.

Think, Isla. Focus.

"I picked the locations because I studied the map and looked at where existing bakeries are and tried to make sure there was no competition nearby."

He nodded. "That's smart. It's the beginning. But . . . it's like that grocery store near your shop. Their bread can't touch yours, so who cares if they're nearby? If anything, by being in the neighborhood, together you start to create a food hub and other places follow. Like the cheese shop next to the coffee place on Dolores. Then the customers see the area as a destination. So that's one strategy, and that gives you a lot more locations because who cares if there are other bakeries around? Your stuff's better."

"I think you're biased, but I get what you're saying. What about the ones that look like they're in the back alley of an industrial area?"

"Don't dockworkers at the Port of Oakland deserve a top-quality café and bakery? There's nothing within miles, and there are tons of union-salaried workers who'd like a good lunch and bread to take home to their families. The area isn't cute or fancy, but that's how DUMBO started in Brooklyn and now it's trendy."

I nodded. He didn't sound crazy. He sounded like he had a degree in something I knew nothing about and I felt embarrassed.

"You're right. This all makes sense. I should be thinking this way."

"Or you should be working with better people. Who did your business plan?"

I pointed to myself. "Me. And Sarah ran the numbers. I know, my physicist accountant and the fermentation queen. But we make a good team. We do our homework."

He was shaking his head, and I felt like he was judging me for being some kind of neophyte who didn't belong in the business world.

But that's not what his eyes said. They were filled with respect and a little bit of . . . wonder?

"You're telling me you did your whole expansion business plan yourself? You and your sister. You didn't hire out?"

I shrugged. "I know these markets intimately. I've been selling to restaurants all over the area for years. I grew up in Oakland. If I can't figure this out, there's something wrong with me."

I hadn't meant to say it like that. But I believed it, even if it didn't sound flattering.

As I was trying to backpedal and figure out how to say it differently so I didn't sound so self-critical, Owen dropped his marker on the floor and pulled me into his arms. His lips were on mine in seconds, his tongue working against mine in soft, sultry strokes.

I let the conversation go, intoxicated by how he made me feel.

The heat consumed me, and his hands moved up my arms and over my shoulders to where they cupped my face. Owen stared into my eyes, melding my feral desire with his own.

My brains scrambled. I couldn't be calm and collected around him. Not when I was forgetting to breathe.

So I wrapped my arms around his waist and ran my hands up his back, feeling the planes of his taut muscles. I wanted to run my fingers over every ridge and valley, then lick his skin until I knew every secret seductive spot.

"Isla..." he murmured against my lips.

He pulled me in harder and his lips met mine with more fire and intensity. This was not a junior varsity kiss. This was an A-game kiss that made me sigh and sink against his body, wanting more of him, needing all of him.

He drew back and studied my face, his eyes placid like the blue summer skies they reminded me of.

"There's nothing wrong with you. Not a single goddamned thing. You can't say things like that about yourself. Even if you've made a mistake here or there—it's just part of it. You are so talented." He kissed my nose. "And gifted." He kissed my cheek. "And insanely gorgeous . . ."

He kissed the sensitive skin below my ear and continued with a row of kisses across my neck.

His hot dusting of breath made me shiver and yearn for more.

Heat crawled over my skin and I pressed harder against him, needing more contact, wanting to erase any space between us.

"I need you closer..." I whispered.

I suddenly didn't care about my business plan or how many bakeries I opened before the end of the year. The only goal was getting more of Owen's skin against mine, even though I could already tell it wouldn't be enough.

He tried to ease my rushed pace, running his hand through my hair.

Luxuriously, he kissed my neck and gently sucked a spot above my collarbone. It felt so good, so perfect—this, whatever he wanted to give.

"C'mere." Owen lifted me up and I wrapped my legs around his waist, ducking my head to kiss the side of his neck.

His skin smelled like the woods and lemons and I couldn't stop myself from licking a trail to his jaw and biting the delicious stubble.

Then I couldn't stop myself from moaning as I moved to press his erection hard against my center and circle slowly.

"No other woman could get me so hot talking about business plans," he said, nuzzling my neck. Laughing, I let my head drop back and closed my eyes.

He took advantage of my exposed neck to plant a row of kisses under my jaw and down toward my collarbone where he nipped at the skin.

"Oh, you're gonna make me come, just like that," I moaned.

"Ah, love, we're just getting started."

How had I watched him sit at his table for over a year and not realized that this—this—was waiting for me if I'd just stopped my normal morning routine for a minute and noticed him, talked to him, begged him to bring me back to his house and do this?

When I leaned back a few inches to drown myself in the blue of his eyes again, he smiled and tilted his head, observing me with a smirk.

"I'm sorry. I know I'm getting us off track and we have work to do . . ."

"Never apologize for distracting me that," I said, surprised at how breathless I sounded.

"Never?"

I shook my head and found his lips again. It was madness how much I wanted his mouth on every inch of my skin. As long as we were both on the same page about our fling status, nothing was off limits.

That's clearly what it was, right? That's why it felt so good and I felt so free.

If I felt like we were in the tentative new days of a potential relationship, I'd be more self-conscious of every beat, every kiss, deciphering its meaning.

Was he the right guy to be dating at almost thirty-five?

Would my next relationship be the forever one?

Of course I knew that was too much pressure to put on the early days of dating. But I always thought about it a little. Maybe that's why nothing had ever worked out before.

But right now . . . who the hell cared?

I was caught up in feeling. I was going on adrenaline and lust and sensation and it was better than anything I'd ever experienced in my life.

He didn't waste any more time near the whiteboard. Keeping his arms around me and my legs around him, he walked us down the hall toward his bedroom.

The hardwood floor creaked under his feet and he was careful to guard me from bumping into the walls of the narrow hallway, where I noticed another row of framed black and white photographs but didn't register any of the images inside the frames.

When he turned to go through the first doorway, I looked over my shoulder at the fluffy white duvet cover over the king-sized bed before he flopped me down on top of it. "You make your bed," I said. "That's cute."

"It's cute?" He climbed onto the bed and straddled my legs. "Like baby animals cute?"

"Like good housekeeping cute. I like that you're not a slob." I reached up, grabbed the hem of his shirt and pushed it up, revealing those honed, sculpted abs that had been on my mind for days.

He smirked. "I don't like getting into an unmade bed at night, so . . ."

I stopped him by running my tongue down the length of his abs and teasing the skin beneath his waistband. "I'm not thinking about housekeeping anymore."

"Excellent." He brushed a few strands of hair off my forehead as his eyes moved over my face.

His hands cupped my cheeks while his eyes settled on my lips. His eyes were playful.

"I think we need to mess up these covers," he said, stroking my cheek with his thumb.

He bent down with the barest hint of a kiss. It was just a brush of his lips and it lit every one of my nerve endings on fire.

"Yes, please . . ." My voice sounded breathless.

I wanted more. I reached for his face and held it tight, delving in for a deeper kiss, a swipe of his tongue, and more of his mouth moving against mine.

This was everything I'd never felt for a year when I was with Tom, but after realizing that important truth, I scrubbed Tom from my mind and put all my focus on the present. Because being with Owen overwhelmed my senses and pretty much made thinking impossible.

His gaze trailed over me like he was trying to decide which part of me to have for dessert.

He moved his hands beneath the hem of my T-shirt and lifted it over my head. I hadn't planned on having anyone see my bra, which was plain beige with a lace edge, but I was too consumed by him to care what he thought of it.

Owen dipped down and kissed my breast over the thin silk fabric, his hand cupping and massaging my other breast. A quiet sigh escaped my lips as my nipples hardened and he rolled his thumbs over them. I quivered under his touch.

"Owen . . ." It was a whisper and a command and a plea.

There had been men in my life, but this was different. Maybe it was the unfettered joy of not having to worry about a relationship or where it was headed. Every touch felt so good.

I reached around and unclasped my bra. Too much fabric, not enough of his glorious tongue. He watched me toss it to the floor, and his eyes roamed from my face to my breasts.

"You're beautiful and I don't think you even know it. Which is so fucking sexy."

He ran a single finger along the slope of my cheek, along my jaw and down to where he traced the contours of each breast. All the while his gaze made me feel appreciated in a way I needed. Then his warm lips lowered onto my skin, his tongue circling one nipple before he took it in his mouth.

To hell with my bakery plans and my ex.

As he worked my very average sized breasts and hummed in appreciation, Owen nudged me toward seeing myself through his eyes and what I saw made me irrationally happy.

I reached for him and pushed his shirt up over his head, practically gasping when I saw the carved muscles of his abs. "Holy crap, are you a professional athlete also?"

He smirked. "I have to do something to work off all your bread."

"You're ridiculous. And freaking hot."

It was a sin how gorgeous this man's chest was and I felt a desperate need to have my hands on it. And my tongue.

I gripped his strong shoulders, appreciating every swell and sinew of his muscle tone.

My hands continued their tour of his chest his defined abs, appreciating the hell out of whatever workout he did to get them. The V of muscles directed my eyes and my hands down to where they wanted to go next.

But he lifted me up before I got any farther and

I straddled his lap, my legs wrapped tight, the heat of our bare skin melting us against each other. I circled my arms around him and held him closer, feeling his throbbing erection pressed hard against me.

"Tell me something, Isla…" he whispered in my ear, following with a lingering kiss.

"I'll tell you anything." It was mind control, pure and simple. If

I was in charge of state secrets, national security would be totally blown.

"If I were to slide your panties down your legs, would I find you wet for me?"

If I hadn't been already, the growl of his voice vibrating against my skin would have clinched it. "Yes," I said on a sigh. "Take them off, please."

"Soon," he whispered, making the heat pool at my center and my body throb in anticipation.

Digging my fingers into the muscles of his shoulders, I relished the feeling of him pressed against me, his length hard against my center as he ground his hips lightly. Then harder.

Until I was desperate for more and he knew it.

Owen's hands were in my hair and his mouth worked over mine. I bit his bottom lip and he kissed me harder. Our tongues wrapped and tangled and stroked.

"This is . . . please . . . I want you . . ." I breathed, unsure if my garbled thoughts were making sense.

He smiled and dropped a gentle kiss on my forehead, then my nose. Finally, my lips. "You've got me. I want to do things to your body that will make you sore for days . . . I want to taste you . . . Tell me you want that."

I nodded like a victim of zombie mind control. He could do whatever he wanted. I officially relinquished the reins.

Laying me back down on the bed, Owen slid the very unsexy baggy pants down my hips and stared appreciatively at the slightly sexier beige panties that coincidentally matched my bra.

Finally, karma had done me a solid when I rummaged through my drawers that morning.

Hooking his finger in the waistband, he slid them down. His eyes were fixed on mine, watching my reaction to him and my anticipation of what he planned to do.

Then his gaze shifted down to the final part of my body he'd revealed. I saw the storm build in his eyes before he moved farther down the bed to where he settled between my legs.

"Oh, baby," he said, gently opening my legs to the sides. "You are gorgeous."

He kissed the inside of my knee, lingering there until I thought I'd melt out of my skin. Only then did he begin moving slowly along my inner thigh with more light kisses that made my toes curl, torturing me in the most sublime of ways.

I grabbed fistfuls of the comforter in my hands. Then I pushed my hands in his hair as my head tipped back.

One finger circled my entrance. Slowly, painstakingly. Until I just about died from the pleasure of his touch.

Then he moved farther away and I nearly whimpered at the loss of him.

"Patience, grasshopper." He returned with another string of kisses that ended at the top of my inner thigh.

Then finally, *finally*, he placed one soft, searing hot kiss to my center.

Now I was moaning because the feel of one kiss was so intense I almost couldn't take it.

His tongue circled and roamed, tasting and worshipping me in a way that left me breathless and quivering. He slid a single finger inside, while continuing the assault with his tongue. Circling, building, sucking on the most sensitive part of me, until I started to lose the line between us.

I'd sign over all of my decision making to him and let him take me wherever and however he wanted.

"Come for me, Isla."

He didn't have to ask twice.

I was already there, riding the pleasure wave higher and higher. I felt waves of hazy heat rolling and cascading through my body. Nothing made sense except the feeling of him and wanting it to last forever.

I silently cursed every man I'd ever met before him for hindering my path to him.

He was the destination.

"Owen . . . oh my God."

"Yeah?" He looked a little smug. As he should. He also looked ready for more.

"Oh yeah." I made quick work of unfastening his belt buckle and pushing his pants down. Okay, what the hell—the boxers should go too. He didn't seem troubled by my haste.

Then . . . wow. He was magnificent and thick and hard. I loved how determined he looked when he wanted me.

His eyes dilated as I ran a finger down his length and back up, circling the tip. They stayed locked on mine as I wrapped my hand around his shaft and stroked.

"I'm not gonna make it for long if you keep doing that . . ." His voice was husky and strained.

I smiled. "You'll make it. I have faith in you."

He leaned to the bedside table drawer and quickly grabbed a condom, which he unwrapped and handed to me. "Would you like to?"

I nodded. I liked it very much, the feel of him jumping at my touch as I rolled the condom on. "Thanks for having faith in me," he said.

I thought he was responding to what I'd just said, but a part of me wondered if he had a deeper meaning. Then I didn't have the wherewithal to think much of anything because he was sliding inside me, inch by incredible inch.

Staring into his eyes, I saw the pleasure splay across his features when he started to move—slowly at first, circling his hips and hitting all the pleasure spots.

I was already starting to build again.

Every shift in position felt better than the last. Every movement brought me more pleasure. Everything fit.

My nails raked over his back as we moved in perfect rhythm. I felt myself crest a higher peak than where I'd been just minutes before.

How did he do this to me? It was unreal.

My core was contracting around him as though screaming for more. And he gave it to me.

My orgasm unfolded like a lightning bolt, lifting me higher, but he found ways to push me higher still. Then I was careening off a cliff at warp speed, falling into a beautiful abyss, and his body was following right behind.

I crested the peak and felt his final thrusts.

In his eyes, I saw the same amazement I felt.

It was like we had to double check with each other—that was pretty fucking incredible, right?

Yes. Yes, it was.

CHAPTER 16

 sla

FOR THE NEXT FEW DAYS, I avoided thinking about whether it was a good idea to have phenomenal sex with my new friend Owen.

Lying in his bed with his arm draped across my chest and my leg looped over his, there was no question that it was a very good idea. But there was also no question that I wasn't in a position to be dating.

So the new us—whatever we decided we were—had to be casual.

We had to agree.

I didn't want him to invest in me and get hurt because I had no idea what I wanted or what I could give. In the aftermath of Tom, I needed to take time to become whole again.

And I needed to be honest with Owen about what that meant.

The warmth of his body felt so good tangled with mine and I didn't want to ruin the moment. Maybe the *just friends* talk could wait.

The midday sun peeking between two buildings had the effect of casting long bright beams across the white of Owen's bed and the couch I hadn't noticed at the foot of the bed. Once I noticed it, I was distracted by thoughts of how to incorporate it into another round of what had turned out to be the kind of sex I'd only read about in romance novels.

I must have stiffened because Owen rolled onto his side and cupped his hand around my cheek. It was something I'd noticed that he did—when he was reacting to something I'd said, he'd caress my cheek. It was such a sweet and lovely gesture and I didn't dare say anything lest he feel self-conscious and stop doing it.

He leaned on one elbow and studied my face. "What's up?"

I smiled at him. "Nothing. I'm good."

"Liar. What?"

I loved that he could tell just from a subtle shift in my body that something had changed. I wasn't used to someone who knew me that well, and it was a little shocking that he knew me so well so quickly.

"Ugh, it's crazy, right? That I could be so completely lost and transported by you one minute, but then reality shoved its stupid nose under the tent and now I'm thinking again."

"I'm going to focus on the part where you were transported."

"You should. That was a very good part. You have many talents."

He smiled and kissed me, and I wanted to get lost in him again. It seemed to be the only way to stop me from thinking about everything else going on in my life.

I rolled to face him and kissed him more deeply, searching for his tongue and savoring the taste of him again.

Owen pulled back and kissed me lightly before tilting his forehead against mine. "Talk to me, Isla."

"I'd rather kiss you."

He lifted my hand to his lips and kissed it. "That works for me as well, but it's also avoidance. C'mon. We're friends, you should tell me what's on your mind. That's what friends do."

He was right and I had to appreciate that he was being a friend even if it meant we had to talk instead of kiss.

"I'm kind of a mess," I said.

"Hardly."

"Well, I've lost my mind, you know that, right? It's barely a week since I broke up with Tom. In that span of time, I've gone from being in a dead-end relationship to round-the-clock sex. My work life is falling apart, my sisters are pushing artificial insemination on me, and my emotions are all over the map."

"All normal. Although I didn't know about the insemination part. We should talk about that."

"I'm not doing it."

"Good because I'd be offended if you didn't at least consider me. As a friend, I'm there for you."

Is he serious?

I cocked an eyebrow at him. "You're kidding, right? You want to go from being my friend to my baby daddy?"

"You really like titles, huh?" He shrugged as though the idea wasn't as crazy as it clearly was. "I'm just saying if you needed me..."

I shook my head. I couldn't add more crazy ideas to the ones I'd finally put to rest. "No. Not having a kid unless it's for the right reasons. It's a non-issue, end of discussion."

"What were your wrong reasons?" Owen fixed his eyes on mine, and his thoughtful gaze made me feel like he'd listen without judgement.

He was interested, not scandalized.

I looked away for a moment, but he guided my chin back so I was looking at him again. "The wrong reason would be that my ovaries are getting tired of firing off practice rounds and maybe, at thirty-four, I should get on with it."

"Do you want to have kids?" His gaze remained steady and I

couldn't tell what he was thinking.

I nodded. "I do. Just not right now and not necessarily by myself." I shook my head. "It's not happening. I don't know why I brought it up."

My hand was curled around Owen's shoulder and I moved it down his arm until I clasped his hand and intertwined our fingers. "I like that we're friends. I like hanging out with you."

He squeezed my hand. "I like hanging out with you too. And I don't think you're a mess."

"So you're good with the friends-with-benefits thing we've got going here?"

"Another title."

I looked at him to see if he seemed offended. His expression was controlled.

"I think I need the title. I like knowing that we're both on the same page," I said.

He nodded and rolled onto his back. "Okay, then that's what we'll call it."

An almost imperceptible flash of something shifted his expression—whether it was sadness, annoyance, or a fleck of dust in his eye, I couldn't be sure—and then it was gone.

I continued watching him to see if it would reappear, but his face was unreadable, still bearing the contented look he'd had since I walked in the door.

"Yes, we're on the same page. I wasn't under the mistaken impression we were suddenly dating. Don't worry."

But I did worry.

He was so nice. I didn't want him to get hurt if I was working out my relationship aftermath at his expense.

Owen seemed fine with everything that had happened between us so far, so maybe I needed to relax. Rebound sex or friends with benefits or whatever this temporary thing was, it was supposed to be fun.

No analysis necessary. That was the point.

I inhaled deeply and moved to rest my head on his chest, but he let go of my hand and slid to the edge of the bed where he'd thrown his pants. He reached down and retrieved my clothes from the floor and put them on the bed near me.

His eyes were bright when he turned to me, smiling. "You distracted me a bit from the next real estate lesson I had planned for you. In the best possible way." He put his elbows on the bed and leaned in to scoop me into his arms. He kissed my lips and set my feet gently on the floor. "Should we give it another go, friend?" he asked.

"Sure." I nodded and pulled my pile of clothes against my chest. He made quick work of getting dressed and walked to the doorway.

"Take your time. I'll make us some coffee."

"I believe I was promised unhealthy snack food when you lured me here," I called after him.

He stuck his head back through the doorway with a wink. "I always keep my promises. By the way, when's the next day you have time off from the shop?"

"Next Thursday afternoon. Or Friday. Why?"

"Will you hold those dates for me? Field trip. More research. Trust me."

"Sure." I watched him go and heard him humming a Roxy Music song we'd been listening to earlier. When I looked down at my clothes, I was suddenly aware that I'd been frozen there naked and I should get dressed.

Was I crazy to think he'd jumped out of bed abruptly? Did I make him uncomfortable with my friends-with-benefits comments?

I couldn't imagine too many guys who'd balk at the arrangement, and he'd hardly been complaining.

That led me to conclude that Owen was fine.

He was fine.

The bigger question was . . . was I?

CHAPTER 17

wen

WE WERE SITTING on a patch of grass in Alamo Square Park near the Painted Ladies down the block from Isla's house. The area was shaded by tall Monterey cypress trees, each with multiple trunks soaring up into the late afternoon sky.

Isla had homework in the watercolor painting class she was taking, and we decided to turn it into a date. Only we still weren't calling it that.

I marveled at how she had time to fit a painting class in with everything else in her busy schedule, but I liked that she made time for hobbies.

Work wasn't everything.

I needed more hobbies in my life. Which was why I agreed to come to the park and paint with her, even though I'd never shown a scrap of talent for painting in my thirty-five years.

To counter the idea that this was a homework outing and not

a date, I brought food, a plaid picnic blanket, and a bottle of wine we could surreptitiously drink out of red plastic cups.

What can I say? I'm stubborn.

"Isla . . ." I was watching her paint. In theory, I was painting too, but I knew next to nothing about watercolor painting, so I was really just watching her paint.

"Yes?" She didn't take her eyes off the paper in front of her. She'd shown me how we had to tape the watercolor paper to the stiff pieces of wood that sat on our laps to prevent the pages from curling when they got wet. Then we painted the paper with water before we started to take the coating off the paper so it would absorb the colors better.

I'd only drawn a few brown sticks that were ostensibly supposed to represent the cypress trunks.

She had a whole landscape going with the Painted Ladies in the background, each a different bright hue. It made no sense that she thought she lacked artistic talent. Her painting was beautiful.

"Any chance you want to take a break and eat?"

"Eat?" She said it like she didn't understand the meaning of the word.

I laughed. "Yeah. I brought food." I held up the bag, which she seemed to notice for the first time.

"Oh, wow. You're amazing." She put her brush down and turned to me, hopeful. "I forgot to eat breakfast. Bad habit. So . . . yeah, I'm hungry."

I wasn't surprised she'd skipped breakfast. I'd noticed that despite working around food all day long, she sometimes forgot to eat.

Hence, I supplied food when I got the chance.

When I started taking the items I'd bought out of the bag, a grin spread across her face. "You remembered I like Ruffles?"

"No weak potato chips here. Check. And you said sour

gummies, not regular, if I recall." Of course, I recalled. Nothing she did or said was lost on me. I tried to rationalize that I was just a good listener, but the truth was I was falling hard for her.

I spread the rest of the snacks on the blanket. Isla nodded approvingly at the Greek yogurt parfaits, the cheese selection, and the seeded crackers.

When I pulled out the wine, she actually blushed. "What if we get caught?"

Looking around, I saw no evidence of anyone who'd care if we were drinking wine from plastic cups. I shrugged. "Then I'll happily share a jail cell with you."

The wine had a twist-off cap and I poured a good amount into each of our cups. "To great art and days off from work."

"Days off from work are key. Although technically, this isn't a day off since I worked all morning," she said, digging into the potato chips.

She dipped her brush into the water, which had become pretty muddy since she'd started painting. My water, on the other hand, was pristine. She assessed my brown lines. "Are you done painting?"

"I'm not sure. Can you tell what this is?"

She looked up at the tall trees and gestured to the trunks. "But they're missing the tops and maybe some details around them." She waved a hand at the landscape.

I shrugged. "I'm feeling pretty good that you could tell I painted tree trunks. I may stop."

"You can't stop. At least do the foliage. Or the grass. Something."

"Fine. I'll keep going." I dipped my brush in the water and swept it around in the green paint, adding a little black to it to make it darker like the cypress greens, but the paint never made it onto my paper. I was more interested in watching her.

Squinting into the sun, she took her wine cup with her and

stood up to get a better angle on the houses. When she sat back down, she dipped her brush in the yellow paint and mixed it with enough water that it was very faint.

"You're good at this," I told her. "Maybe I'm more of an art patron than an artist."

Laughing, she pointed at my paper. "Quit avoiding. Paint some leaves."

"Yes, dear." She smirked and I dipped my brush in the green paint I'd mixed and swirled it on the page. I had to admit, it made my stick trees look better.

The truth was, I possessed some artistic skill, just not this kind. I had an ability to create and envision things that didn't exist, but I generally needed someone else to put those ideas on paper.

Isla stopped painting and put her brush in the water jar. Her hazel eyes looked brownish gray today, and I would never get tired of waiting to see what color they'd be with the changing light.

Leaning back on her elbows, Isla closed her eyes and let the sun warm her face.

"You're beautiful," I said. She didn't open her eyes, but her lips turned up into a smile.

"You're sweet."

"Not sweet, just calling it like I see it. To hell with the damned trees—if I were a better artist, I'd paint you. That would be artwork worth hanging on any wall."

She reached for my hand and interlaced our fingers without opening her eyes. Just knew where it was.

"C'mere," I said, moving my paints and paper away and pulling her toward me.

I leaned back on the blanket. She shifted so her head was resting on my chest, her honey-colored hair splayed out around her.

I ran my fingers through the strands and tried to imagine a scenario where I'd be happier. I couldn't think of a single one.

That's when I knew I was in trouble.

sla

I TILTED MY SEAT BACK, took my hair out of the clip, and opened my window. It already felt like a vacation and we hadn't even left the city.

"You could not have suggested this at a better time," I told Owen as we drove north on Highway 101 toward the western corner of the wine country.

I hadn't slept well for the past few nights worrying about some new aggressive moves Bread Artisan had made in the past few days. Their only objective seemed to be to squeeze me until I gave up. I wasn't going to do that, but the stress of mounting a defense was starting to get to me.

"I could tell. You sounded tense," Owen said, reaching for my hand and rubbing the back of it with his thumb.

"I did? You didn't even hear my voice. How can a person sound tense via text?"

He smiled. "I know you better than you think."

Maybe he did. I liked the idea that it was true.

Owen drove with one hand on the steering wheel and the other on the stick shift of his navy blue Porsche coupe. We hadn't had occasion to drive anywhere together so I'd had no idea what kind of car he owned. But for some reason, the sexy sports car surprised me when he pulled up to my house.

What did you expect? Lots of people drive nice cars.

Tom had driven two. He alternated between his Tesla sedan and a Maserati SUV he used to drive up to ski in Tahoe. Apparently, the Tesla didn't do well in freezing cold weather and he didn't want to deal with finding Superchargers in the mountains. At least, that's how he'd explained it.

He also had a Vespa which I never saw him ride, and a very expensive road bike. He never rode that either.

I looked at Owen, trying to identify if he really felt comfortable behind the wheel of such an expensive car. He was so laid back, and his hoodie sweatshirts and plain button-downs made me think of him as a guy who'd drive a Honda Accord, not something whose tawny leather interior had me surreptitiously stroking the seat.

"You okay?" he asked. I realized I'd been silent for the last few minutes.

"Yeah. Sorry. I'm just . . . tired, I guess." It wasn't a lie. The hum of the motor and the bright warm sunlight filtering through the windshield were making me feel calm and sleepy.

He reached over and stroked my cheek. "Take a nap for a few. I'll listen to a podcast."

"I can't be that kind of passenger."

"What kind? The tired kind?"

I sighed and sat up a little higher in the bucket seat, trying to wake myself up. "No, bad road trip company. I won't do that to you."

His eyes crinkled behind his sunglasses when he smiled.

"Trust me, I make this drive all the time alone. I'm fine zoning out if you want to sleep."

"Nah, I want to hear your podcast. What kind of stuff do you listen to?" I wasn't going to pass up a chance to dig below the surface of Owen Miller when I had the opportunity. His podcast tastes might give me a new window into his brain.

He swiped across a few apps on the phone that was mounted on his dashboard until a radio voice came through the car speakers announcing the beginning of My Favorite Murder.

"You listen to murder podcasts?" I was surprised. He seemed so mild⋅mannered, not that he needed to be a killer himself to be interested in them.

He shrugged and paused the podcast. "I listen to a bunch of stuff. There are some good ones on the founders of companies and how stuff works. How about you?"

"I listen to music when I run, and other than that, I don't have long spans of time to listen to stuff."

"Not while you're baking?"

I considered the question and realized I needed to explain my approach to bread in a way that sounded logical to someone other than me.

"I don't like to be distracted when I'm working with the dough. I feel like it requires all my senses even though it probably doesn't. Truthfully, I could bake just by feel and smell, but I have this weird idea that there's a sound to good dough and baking dough, even though there probably isn't."

He turned to look at me before gluing his eyes back on the road. "Why do you think there isn't a sound component? It sounds reasonable to me," he said.

I was suddenly overwhelmed by how much I liked him. "I appreciate you, Owen. You always take what I say at face value, even if it sounds crazy."

"Don't you mean half⋅baked?" He rolled his eyes and grinned.

I laughed. He was so easy. Spending time with him never felt like work.

Getting dressed to the nines with men I used to date so we could jet set to five-star dinners with investors and their wives was never appealing to me. I did it because it was part of being a couple with the men I chose and I was a team player.

But now . . . this . . . I didn't feel like I had to sell anyone on anything. I could be myself, and better than that, I could be with a guy who I liked for being himself.

It almost felt like the perfect relationship, even though I knew it wasn't one. Owen didn't seem to want anything more than the casual hanging out—with off-the-charts benefits—and I wasn't going to rock the boat.

"So, do you come up here a lot?" I asked.

"About once a week. There's always a reason to come to one of the properties, but it's usually meetings. I had a girlfriend once who lived in Napa so that commute was interesting."

"Was she an earthy organic wine maker? A peasant produce picker?"

He cast me a side eye. "She was in marketing. Why?"

I shrugged. "Just curious what kind of women you date."

"Only extremely beautiful and talented bread wenches."

"Ah, but we're not dating, remember?"

"Right. We're friends. I do remember."

I wrestled to get my hoodie sweatshirt off without taking off my seatbelt. Not easy. He smirked at my struggle. "You okay there?"

"Yeah. All good. Okay, so an ex in Napa, interesting. You seem like the kind of person who's friends with your exes."

"No. I'm not that kind of person at all."

I quirked an eyebrow. "Really? You're so easygoing, I'd think you'd find a way to remember the good times and put a happy spin on the end of a relationship."

"Eh, if someone's done with me, I have a hard time finding it in me to keep something going."

"I guess that makes sense." It was less fun talking about his ex-girlfriends than I thought, so I decided to shut up.

Once I'd gone back into my head and started staring out the window, Owen started the podcast. I heard a vague description of a man who intended to rob a wealthy friend before his plans went awry.

Owen shifted gears, and the car sped up as traffic dissipated on the road ahead. For the first time in a week, I started to relax. This was great—sitting next to a good friend, listening to a guy with a funny voice talk about murders. It was the perfect escape.

CHAPTER 19

wen

I DEFIED anyone to have a bad day wine tasting. If one glass of wine wasn't great, the next one would be better. If the sun went behind a heavy cloud, there was always a local restaurant with a great wine list and food raised and grown nearby.

There was always another picture-perfect vista, a mountaintop winery, a cool old wine cave, and seventeen more wines to taste.

The climate was perfect for growing grapes, which meant it was hotter in the Napa Valley than in the surrounding areas with miles and miles of vineyards, rolling hills, and mostly blue skies.

We spent the first part of our day in Sonoma, where I toured Isla through the new property I'd managed to get a realtor to show us on last-minute notice.

The plot of land was a partially cleared empty parcel situated right near the Russian River. It was the perfect spot for a romantic escape with wineries nearby, and importantly, the Sonoma County Airport for easy transportation.

"The fire took out most of the structures, except for what's left of that one," the realtor told us as we walked the property.

She looked to be in her mid-fifties and had blond hair sprayed into stiff bangs over her forehead and a high ponytail in the back. She wore a purple pantsuit and low-heeled shoes that were more suited to a political debate stage than the middle of a field. She pointed at a dilapidated dark brown hull of burned wood in the distance.

"That was part of the cask storage and fermentation house. The good thing is you can start fresh without having to do a lot of demo."

"True," I said. I'd happily forego the cost of demolition, and the property was big.

Beyond the property we could see miles of planted vineyards, the green leaves on the vines snaking around stakes and trellises and providing a backdrop of lush green.

"I have another showing at noon," the realtor told us, looking at her phone.

It was already a quarter to twelve. We'd only been there for a half hour and I really wanted to walk the rest of the grounds.

"Oh. I was hoping for a little more time to get a feel for the property, see how the light changes later in the day. Can we come back?" I asked.

I was also curious about the structure and interested in how it had survived the fire.

She scrolled the screen on her phone and shook her head. "I'm booked this afternoon. But it's not like you're going to rob the place. If you put the padlock on the gate when you leave, you can stay as long as you like."

"Great. Thank you. We won't be long," I said.

"Stay," she said, shrugging. Then she shook our hands and tottered off toward the driveway where she'd parked her car.

I looked at Isla. "What do you think? Can you picture a new, healthy vineyard with bungalows spread throughout the property and maybe a food garden over in this area and a lavender field over here with an indoor-outdoor spa?"

I was pointing in all directions and Isla was laughing at me. "What?"

"You have vision. It's awesome. I'm not sure I see it all laid out the way you do because I'm distracted by the weeds and the dead tree stumps, but I can see that it could be something special. I think people will be really happy to get away from everything here."

She held her hand against her forehead to block the direct rays of the sun as she gazed out over the acreage.

I grabbed her hand without thinking about whether it was something friends with benefits—or whatever she'd decided we were—were supposed to do. "I'll race you to that broken down shack over there. I'm dying to see what's inside."

"You think some wine survived the fire?"

"I hadn't thought of that, but here's hoping . . . ready, set—"

I never got to 'go' because Isla pulled her hand from my grip and took off running.

Hell, she was fast. Her long legs chewed up the landscape and I struggled for a minute to keep up with her. Then my own speed kicked in and I blazed past her, feeling my lungs sucking air as I went—the structure was at least a few hundred yards away and I'd never been a sprinter.

I looked over my shoulder at Isla and saw she was grinning and dropping her pace a little. I slowed to a jog and she closed the space between us.

"It's farther than it looked," she said. Both of us were slightly winded from the sprint. The building was also a lot larger than it had seemed from where we'd first taken in its hulking shape.

The property was thirty acres of mostly-flat land butting up against a low hill with a manmade lake on the other side. We'd covered about half the field and still had a decent distance ahead of us.

We walked the rest of the way because we'd basically been given the keys to the kingdom—what was the rush?

"Wow," Isla said as soon as she stepped through the doorway of what we expected to be a burned-out old building. It was anything but.

The only thing that seemed to have been damaged in the fire was the wooden double door that led into the space. Even that had only taken a modest beating. The two doors were charred but still hanging from their hinges and heralding the entrance.

The entire interior, though a little smoke-stained, was intact.

"I had no idea this was here. The realtor didn't mention it, which is nuts. It's the best thing about the whole property," I said in disbelief.

The bright sun appeared to be muscling its way through the doorway to prove that the interior was sound. The floors were a warm beige stone and the walls were the kind of rough plaster that looked like an underground crypt.

"Look at this. Is it all stone inside?" Isla asked as we stepped into the room and took in the domed ceilings and high arched entryways made from rows of red brick. The walls took a forty-five degree turn at the tops to continue up and meet in a triangle at the ceiling.

"Looks like it. Do you feel how much cooler it is in here? That must've been great for wine storage." Isla was moving through the front tasting room to where wooden barrels sat stacked two-high on metal racks against the walls of a storage area.

At the far end, I could barely make out the shape of a large stone fireplace. Wrought iron sconces flanked a mantel with big pillar candles on top.

All of it had survived, while the entire exterior landscape had burned to ash.

"It's magical," she said. Light from a high stained-glass

window cast a pink and purple light on the floor in the tasting area. I could imagine groups standing in the warm glow of light and sipping wine.

"No wonder it withstood the fire. Most of this wouldn't ever burn," I said, marveling at what felt like a lost civilization. I could picture the winemakers checking the casks and leading tours. We made our way through the space, which had still-standing metal wine casks and a lot of the original equipment. "We've got to keep this whole thing. If it's restored, maybe it can still be used for winemaking onsite."

"I didn't know you were planning on making wine." Isla ran her hand over the cool stone of the interior wall. "This whole place is gorgeous. I love that it's here. Like a memory of what came before. You can build something completely new but have this nod to the old."

She was right. There was no way I'd tear down any of it. She was also right that I hadn't planned on making wine. There were enough wineries doing it well and they didn't need one more amateur coming in and trying his hand.

"I never planned on making wine, but look at this. It begs to be used. Maybe I can make a deal with a small wine label and let them use the space in exchange for being our exclusive supplier."

"Or better yet, you can have a rotating list of winemakers use it. Kind of speaks to your whole boutique idea—feature different local wines and keep changing it up so people will keep coming back to taste whatever's new."

I grabbed Isla so abruptly that she squealed. "That's brilliant. It's completely the vision I've been going for."

I didn't let her go.

She turned around in my arms. "Yeah?"

I nodded. "Absolutely. I hadn't been thinking of it like that, but with this wine cave, it's perfect. It's exactly the kind of history I want to infuse into each of my projects."

I loosened my grip a little when I felt her pull away. My heart lurched into my throat as I realized that the spontaneous gestures were all mine. She was still an expert at maintaining boundaries.

The friend zone was smacking me hard and I needed to pay attention or risk alienating her entirely.

Still, she didn't seem put off that I'd grabbed her—her face held a radiant smile. "Learned from the master. All the things you said made me reevaluate how I'd been thinking about expanding. I was going for the easy, low-hanging fruit instead of thinking a little harder about how to do things differently—and better."

That made me feel like a gazillion bucks. "I'm glad it was helpful," I said.

What I wanted to tell her was that she should have her bread in the restaurants at every one of my hotel properties, but I had to tread carefully. If she found out that I'd already been running numbers and thinking about how her business might work in conjunction with mine, she'd probably freak out.

And I was having too much fun with her.

I didn't want to ruin it by letting her know I'd been wondering if I could get her to supply bread to this new hotel long before the two of us ever had a real conversation.

And way before we'd come up with our strange definition of friendship, which still didn't sit entirely right with me.

The last thing I needed was for her to think I had designs on anything having to do with her business, especially now that she was mired in worry over a competitor she couldn't get to back off.

Better to keep quiet and show her a good time for the next twenty-four hours.

"C'mon, let's check out the rooms over here," I said. I led her to the opposite side of the tasting room, where another part of the cave had pressing equipment and more barrels.

The place was incredible.

Isla sat on one of the upturned wine barrels while I continued to poke around. "Let me know if you find a bread oven and I'll

169

come running." When she spoke, her voice echoed throughout the room.

"Would be easy enough to put one in," I said with the same echo back to her. I kept walking until I found a second room with an old crystal chandelier hanging from the arched stone ceiling. I called Isla to come check it out. "Look. My guess was there was a dining room set up in here at one time, maybe for exclusive entertaining. Do you see the size of the chandelier?"

Her eyes widened. "It's massive." She leaned against the wall and looked up toward another high window, the only source of light in the room. But there were more candles on tall iron holders with curled metal leaves winding around the stems.

"This is the first time in my life I've wished I was a smoker, so I'd have matches in my pocket," I said. "Note to self, Owen Miller: always come prepared."

She laughed. "Did you know that I didn't know your name for the longest time?" She said it like it was a mammoth confession and she expected me to be insulted.

"What do you mean? When I first started coming to the bakery?"

She took a deep breath. "Yes. We'd talked and you'd told me your name, but then I forgot. Then after seeing you the next few times, I couldn't come out and ask you after pretending I knew. So for months, I hoped it would somehow come up in conversation—not that there was any organic reason for you to suddenly blurt out your name—which is why it never came up."

"But you called me Owen when we first started talking the morning you saw all that crap on social media about Tom."

She nodded. "Yes. I knew before then because I finally asked Kim to look at your credit card and tell me. I was embarrassed that you kept coming in and asking all these questions about bread making and I'd forgotten your name . . . can you forgive me?"

She was adorable. But I wasn't about to pass up an opportunity to get something I wanted. "Hmm, that's pretty insulting. I'm not sure I can forgive you. Not without some groveling . . ."

Grinning, she moved closer to me and wrapped her arms around my neck. "Please, Owen. Once I knew your name it stuck. And now, I'll never forget it . . ."

"Nope, I don't feel quite seen. I may need some actual begging." I grabbed her ass and gave it a squeeze. She yelped and pressed closer. Our lips were inches away from each other and I could have happily closed the distance, but I wanted to see what she'd do.

Her lips were on mine before I could give anything else much thought.

She kissed me hard and I gave back just as hard. When she withdrew, we were both breathless and her cheeks were flushed pink.

"Please . . . I do want to make it up to you and I have an idea."

There was no music, but she started dancing through the room, spinning to music that apparently only she could hear. Dancing over to me, she took my hand and I wrapped an arm around her waist so we could properly Fred and Ginger around the room.

As we danced, she looked around the cool, dark wine cave as if trying to find inspiration. I was onboard with whatever that amounted to. "You know, I've always kind of had this fantasy about being taken in a barn by a cowboy . . ."

I couldn't stop the smile from taking over my entire face. "I hate to be the one to tell you this isn't a barn. And I ain't a cowboy . . ."

But I was hardly going to let that make a difference if she wanted a fantasy.

She waved a hand. "Semantics. Fine. Take me in the wine cave until I don't know my own name."

"Darlin', done."

She led me from the front area of the original tasting room

where shards of light shone through high windows onto the dusty floor. We wove between old casks positioned under high arched ceilings with balustrades criss-crossing overhead.

"How about here?" She was leaning against an old metal barrel and looking straight into my eyes.

"No way am I saying no to you anywhere." I lifted her up, pressing her hard against the curved side of a metal vessel. She wrapped her legs around my waist and bent her mouth to my ear.

"Whatcha wanna do, big guy?" she whispered, her breath warming my skin and reducing my options to one.

"I wanna make you come in a wine cave." I wanted to make her scream so loud that the winemakers in the next country would stop and say a prayer for their harvests. I wanted to fuck her so badly that I'd have given away the whole property if it meant I could have my way with her in the wine room for another two hours.

I wanted this. I wanted her.

I tried not to let myself acknowledge that what I really wanted was much more than two hours in a wine cave. I tried not to think about how it was temporary because we were just friends.

In that moment, none of it mattered because she was mine.

Her hands were in my hair, and her breasts pressed so hard against my chest that I had chills. The combination of her hard nipples and her wild eyes brought me back to the present with sudden urgency.

We went from zero to a million in seconds, just like every time I was with her.

Lifting her higher, I sat her on the flat top of a large barrel and she yanked me closer. Our lips fused and our tongues danced.

It wasn't polite or gentle. It was a need to consume each other. It was all lust.

I pulled the thin sweater over her head, revealing the luscious full cups of her pink lace bra. She smirked. "I remember you liked me in pink."

Then her lips were hot on my neck, sucking so hard I was sure I'd be walking into work with a hickey, but I didn't give a shit.

"I love you in pink." I popped the button on her jeans, revealing panties that matched.

She wriggled out of them, pulling at my shirt at the same time, so I whipped it over my head and her hands went straight to my chest.

"You are so goddamn sexy, it's dangerous," I whispered, knowing my breath near her ear made her crazy.

She returned the gesture by sweeping her tongue down the side of my neck, hopping off the wine barrel, and continuing her assault down my chest and over my abs, sucking and licking and nipping at me with her teeth.

She looked up at me and smiled. In that moment, I knew I was done for.

Her fingers reached to unbuckle my pants and I groaned in anticipation of whatever she wanted to do.

Then her lips were back on my skin, sucking hard and kissing my abs lower until she slid down my pants and her tongue ran lightly over the head of my cock. A tease.

"C'mere, cowboy," she said with a grin, looking up at me with her mouth wrapped around the tip. There was no more beautiful sight than her lips around me, enjoying the fact that she owned me right now.

Her hand wrapped around the shaft and she moved slowly as her mouth closed around me, taking deep and sucking lightly. Teasing again.

Then taking me all the way, sucking me to the back of her throat, her tongue running down the length of my pulsing erection.

My hands fisted in her hair, feeling the build of my release. I wasn't going to last long, not when she hummed against my skin and sucked me even harder. When her hand went between my legs and she stroked my balls, I lost my fucking mind.

I didn't want to come like this, not if she didn't want it. I'd pull out and try to wrangle enough brain cells to put on a condom.

"I'm close... let's—"

"No," she said, refusing to relinquish an inch. "Come on, cowboy. Show me what you've got," she said between luxurious licks and strokes.

That's all it took. I'd passed the point of no return and surrendered to her mouth, gripping her and filling her throat. I pulsed and thrusted. I moaned her name and fell completely under her spell.

Right then I knew three things.

She was going to kill me with those lips, I was going to fall madly for her, and there was nothing I could do to stop it.

CHAPTER 20

*J*sla

WE SPENT a good long time living out my barn fantasy, and the reality exceeded my wildest expectations.

What the wine cave was missing in hay bales it more than made up for in beautiful spaces with natural light making everything look magical.

After we'd clicked the padlock on the gate to the property, I'd assumed we'd make the drive back down to San Francisco, maybe stopping on the way home for dinner.

Owen had other plans.

"You said you're not opening the bakery in the morning, correct?" he asked.

"Right. I should stop in around noon and get everything prepped for the week, but I have no morning plans. Why?"

He was looking ahead at the miles of vines at the adjacent property so I couldn't get a direct look at his face, but even from the side I could see his eyes sparkling with mischief.

"No reason. And you didn't make any plans for later tonight?"

"No, I'm free all evening. Why? Is there another property you want to check out?"

He nodded. "There is. Are you game for a little adventure?"

He unlocked the car doors with his clicker, but he still came around to the passenger side and swung the door open for me.

"Always. You had me at merlot." I was quoting one of the T-shirts he'd brought me. They were adorable and even though he wasn't looking directly at me, I could see his smile from the side.

Any adventure with him sounded great. I'd been burning the candle down to a nub and hadn't taken time off in months. It was starting to catch up with me.

Driving around and looking at empty fields—and multiple orgasms in the wine cave—sure beat spending another day looking over spreadsheets and trying to figure out how to beat back Centinela Bread.

When Owen closed his door and started the ignition, I leaned over and kissed him on the cheek. "Thank you."

"For what? I should be thanking you for your brilliant ideas and for spending your free time tromping through dead vineyards."

"You've thanked me plenty, rest assured." I smirked at him, remembering exactly how attentive he'd been. "I'm thanking you for getting me out of my bubble. I needed a break, and I didn't even realize it."

He smiled. "I'm so pleased to hear you say so." He backed the car up and put it in gear. I was starting to appreciate the speed and handling of the Porsche as we left a cloud of dust behind and zoomed along the wine route.

The late afternoon sun bounced off the rows of winding grapevines and I marveled at how I could feel like I was on a faraway vacation just by getting an hour outside the city.

"I used to do this all the time when I was younger, just take off and drive north. We used to go wine tasting or bring our bikes up and ride. It's hilly up near Calistoga but this area is fun to just go. Oh well, that was a long time ago," I said.

When I looked over at Owen I noticed he was chuckling. I elbowed him in the ribs. "Ow."

"Why are you laughing at me?"

"I'm not, I swear. It's just, the way you talk about the olden days or whatever, it makes it sound like you think you're a hundred. You're thirty-four. You haven't missed the baby window. You're not a geriatric bread widow. Your life is good. You have so many more days ahead of you to drive up here and ride your bike around."

He was right. I sounded ridiculous. "Yeah, for sure. I don't know what's gotten into me lately."

"I do. Or at least, I'll venture a guess if you won't elbow me again if I'm wrong."

"Can't make any promises." I readied my elbows.

He smiled and stared out at the road ahead without speaking. "You're just letting things get to you, is all," he said quietly.

I was glad he didn't feel the need to be specific.

"No elbows for that. And you're correct."

"Can I venture another guess?"

"You don't have to ask. I'm not going to hurt you. I like you too much." He had no idea how true that last part was. I did like him too much and I had a feeling it would be my undoing.

"Okay. I also think you're someone who's always succeeded at everything you've ever tried to do. If I were to guess, captain of the track team, MVP or some damn thing? Winner of whatever awards they gave at your school for being responsible and motivated and purposeful? Opened your first bakery and succeeded within a year so you wrote a cookbook and that led to a second one along with several awards and accolades as you dominated the San Francisco restaurant scene."

"Someone else has been Googling, sounds like. And what's your point?"

"You haven't failed. Ever. And it scares the shit out of you that you might do it now. But I'm gonna tell you two things. First, if you fail here or there, who gives a shit? Dust yourself off and keep going. Figure out how to bounce back and move on. Run up the next hill, bake the next loaf and keep going. But second . . ."

He turned and looked at me. I had no choice but to return his gaze. His hand went to my cheek and I was a little nervous we were going to career off the road, but thankfully the roads in Napa are pretty straight.

So I stared back and let myself float away in his eyes.

"You're not going to fail. You're in this horserace until the last lap and there are lots of ways it could go. Consider all your options, figure out how to pivot. People love you way too much to watch you fail. I think you've called time of death prematurely. Sorry for the jumble of metaphors."

He was right, and on my good days I believed most of it, but I wasn't going to lie—it was nice to hear it from someone else.

I never used to doubt myself or my abilities, but it was mainly because I'd achieved success. It was a drug, and I didn't realize the haze it had kept me in, always wanting more. It had also blunted the reality that not everything was going to go my way.

"Thanks for that. You're right. I'm overreacting." I reached over and put my hand on Owen's thigh. He immediately put his own hand on top of mine.

"I didn't say that at all. Every reaction is valid, and you're lucky that you've done well in life. I was merely saying you need to cut yourself some slack now and again."

The rest of the drive was lovely after that. I didn't feel the need to defend my life choices and I finally felt relaxed enough that I did eventually close my eyes.

But I kept my hand on his leg and as I was drifting off, I was aware that he didn't move his hand from mine.

~

"Okay, sleepyhead, we're here." Owen brought my hand to his lips and I opened my eyes to a bright yellow sun resting atop the trellises of grapevines. The vineyard in front of us soared as far as I could see into the distance.

It was beautiful, but then, everything in the wine country looked like this—endless hanging grapes on endless vines. I kicked myself for not having made the trip in years.

Why wasn't I considering opening a Victorine here?

It would give me an excuse to come more often. I was finally starting to understand why Owen opened hotels where he did. Why not create excuses to visit beautiful places?

"Where is here? Because it looks an awful lot like a vineyard and I can't tell them apart." I watched Owen pop his door open, and before I could grab my purse from the floor and get out, he'd opened the door on my side.

"M'lady, come with me," he said, extending his hand to help me out of the car. Unnecessary, because I'd never needed help exiting a vehicle before, but so sweet. When I got out, I noticed to our right a two-story wood and glass structure with a large front porch.

It looked at home amid the grapevines, so much so that the trellises abutted the building and bunches of hanging green grapes framed the sides.

Looking up, I noticed living gardens on the roof of the first story and wild expanses of succulents, pink roses, and lavender bushes spanning out from the building in both directions. The whole tableau had the effect of making the building feel like it was part of the landscape.

We walked up the steps of the building to the porch where Owen grabbed two filled champagne flutes and handed one to me.

"It's sparkling wine. Champagne only comes from that region of France so anything from here with bubbles is sparkling wine. I'm probably telling you something you already know."

"Tell me more," I said while raising my glass to clink against his.

"To life," he said.

We each drank a sip, and I was surprised at how cold the sparkling wine was, given that it seemed to have been sitting out on the silver tray on the porch. There was no signage to indicate we were at a bed and breakfast or some other landmark. The porch looked like the front of a house—a phenomenal wine country fantasy house.

"Tell me where we are and how you know about this place." I sat in one of the twin Adirondack chairs on the porch and took another sip of the wine.

A person could get used to this life.

"We're in Calistoga and it's one of our properties. We've had a lot of trouble finding the right person to run it, so I'm going to have to spend a few minutes meeting with our new general manager and see if he's the guy we need, but then we're free to run among the vineyards and drink all the wine."

"That sounds amazing. And I'll sit right here and start on the wine if you need to go talk to your guy."

"Ha. I don't have to meet with him for an hour. I figured I'd give you a tour of the property first, but the rest of the day is yours. You can take a nap, have a two-hour spa treatment, go for a run, whatever you want."

I couldn't wipe the grin off my face. "You're talking to a girl who hasn't had a spa day in, um, I don't know, five years . . ."

"Done. Spa it is. I'll get you the menu and you can see what you want to do."

I put a hand out to stop him. "Wait. Don't go to the desk or wherever. All that can wait. Just . . . hang with me here for a bit."

He cocked his head and stood in front of me. "I plan to. I was just going to grab the spa menu off the table in the room. Cool?"

I nodded and he turned the doorknob, at which point I realized the porch led to a well-appointed living room with an overstuffed sofa, a writing desk, and two leather chairs, and that was just what I could see peeking through the doorway.

I'd assumed we were sitting in front of the main reception building for the whole place.

When Owen came out with a small booklet, I looked at him agog. "Is this one of the rooms? As in, we're staying in this house here in the middle of a gorgeous vineyard?"

He nodded. I stood and threw my arms around his neck and jumped so my legs were wrapped around his waist. "Ah, this is the reaction I hoped for," he said, tipping my face up and kissing me lightly on the lips. "I'll admit I was a tiny bit worried I'd tell you that I planned for us to stay here tonight and you'd think it was a violation of our friendship code."

I shook my head. "It's amazing. And now I have to see the rest of the room even though I said I wanted to sit on these chairs forever." I released my legs from around his waist and slid them down his body, not taking a step backward.

My arms still encircled his neck and I felt no urge to let go, so I tipped my lips up again to kiss him before we checked out the room.

"Calling this a room was a bit of a misnomer," I said when we'd walked through the living room and past the full kitchen. "This is nicer than my house."

Owen laughed. "That's the point. It's supposed to be a life upgrade. Why would you want to go on vacation and sleep in a more uncomfortable bed than what you have at home and look at a worse view?" He said this as he walked me up a set of stairs, past a yoga meditation room, and straight through the master suite and onto a sweeping balcony with a one-hundred-eighty degree view of vineyards and gardens.

The entire length of the teak wood railing had hanging planter boxes blooming with purple and white flowers that blended with the landscape in front of us.

The sun was hanging low in the sky, but the spring days were getting longer and we still had a few hours before it would set.

"I don't know what I want to do more—sit back here, sit on the front porch, go to the spa, jog in the vineyards . . ."

He was right. The whole point of getting away was to improve upon life at home and he'd accomplished that.

"You can do all of it. Here, sit." He motioned me to a lounge chair where a thick terrycloth towel had already been laid out and a tall glass bottle of water chilled in a silver bucket.

While I kicked off my shoes and settled back on the lounge chair, Owen went back for our champagne glasses and reappeared with them as well as a bottle, which he used to top off our glasses before sitting down. "Okay, you have exactly fifteen minutes to relax here before we're due for a relaxing walk in the vineyard for six minutes on the way to a relaxing spa session."

I laughed. "Sounds like my kind of relaxing—on a schedule."

"Why doesn't that shock me? I'm kidding about the time limits. The only thing required of you is that you do whatever you want until you decide to do something else. I do ask, however, that you have dinner with me at some point, and if you want to do a striptease on the eight-hundred thread count sheets, I certainly won't call foul."

"Sounds like a perfect evening."

He eyed me hungrily and I loved the wolfish gleam in his eye. So much so that I debated hoisting myself from the comfort of the chair to test out the sheets immediately.

Then I panicked. "Oh. I don't have anything to wear to dinner. Or a toothbrush, for that matter."

He directed my gaze behind us to where an overnight bag— my overnight bag—sat on a luggage rack at the foot of the bed. "How did you—?"

"Sarah. She packed it for you."

"You called Sarah? Did you track her down at her campus number?"

He looked from me to the vineyard and grimaced as though he'd done something wrong. "Actually, she called me." I still didn't see why that would make him look so guilty. I also couldn't imagine why Sarah would call him.

"What did she want?"

"She didn't tell you." That must have seemed clear from the confused look I was giving him because he explained. "She wanted me to assure her that I had nothing to do with Centinela Bread—no ownership stake, no advisory role, no connection whatsoever to the company—because you mentioned to her that Centinela seemed to know specifics about your business plan, things you'd told me."

"Oh. That." Honestly, I'd put the whole thing to bed once Jamie had said that Owen hadn't been the one he'd talked to. Mostly. I had told Sarah, maybe as a safety valve in case my growing affection for Owen made me completely blind to everything going on around me. It seemed like a growing risk.

I was a little bit impressed with my non-confrontational sister. "I told you she looked out for me. But I hope you know I wasn't worried. I told her as much."

He exhaled and picked up my hand, rubbing his thumb over my knuckles. When he met my eyes, there was hurt that I didn't expect. "Why didn't you tell me? Why didn't you ask me if I had any connection to Centinela? I could have set you straight in a heartbeat."

"I didn't really think you were part of it." Okay, I couldn't lie. "Fine, I considered it for a few minutes, but then I decided it didn't make sense. You can't fit a hotel in a bakery space."

His slight look of hurt turned to a mixture of hurt and anger. "Wait, the only reason you decided I had nothing to do with it was that it didn't make sense? What about the fact that you know me? Don't you know I'd never—and I mean this wholeheartedly, never—do anything to hurt you or jeopardize your business? You *know* me."

I turned to face him, to reassure him, but he'd turned in on himself and had his arms folded across his chest. "Owen . . ." I reached a hand for him but he moved away. "I do know those things. I do know you."

"Do you?"

I nodded. "Owen, look at me . . ."

He didn't. He stared out at the field and I wondered if I'd blown everything. He was right—I should have been able to make the call about his involvement based on my gut instinct about him, but I couldn't. So I had to own it.

"Owen . . . here's the thing . . . you're right. I wasn't ready to know those things about you," I said.

It was the most honest I'd probably ever been because I knew it was liable to end the friendship I had with him and I had to tell the truth anyway.

He looked at me. "I'm listening." His expression was blank, but at least the disappointment was gone.

"I like you—a lot—and I was worried that my . . . affection for you was clouding my judgement."

"That's what's supposed to happen." He picked up his glass and drained it before filling it again. He didn't top mine off even though I'd finished about a third of it. "You should trust me. Have I given you any reason not to?"

"No. And I told you, the reason I never said anything was because I wasn't worried."

"Because I can't fit a boutique hotel into a bakery space."

"At first. Maybe that was the proof my head needed to trust that my heart was right about you. And I'm sorry if that's hurtful, but this has all made me crazy and worried and I'm not going to stop watching my back."

I got ready to take my overnight bag and haul it back to San Francisco in an Uber because Owen still looked hurt and angry. It didn't seem like he was going to get past my mistrust, and I didn't have any other ways to make it seem okay.

Owen unfolded his arms and scooted closer to me, and then leaned forward so our foreheads were touching. "Say that part again about how your heart was right about me." I couldn't see his face from the close angle but I was pretty sure he was smiling.

"My heart really likes you. So much."

He nodded. "Then I don't give a shit about the rest. Okay? My heart likes you too." He brought his hands to my face and tilted it so our lips aligned.

His hands pushed into my hair and he kissed me slowly, with languid intensity. It was a completely different tone and pace from how we'd practically attacked each other in the wine cave.

I felt the swirls of desire unfold and pool in my chest. I scooted my lounger closer, the dragging sound of the legs on the wooden slats standing in for the groan building with me.

In one sweep, Owen lifted me onto his own chair so I was straddling his lap. Our bodies pressed tighter, our tongues tangled, and our hands roamed everywhere.

It was becoming harder and harder for me to convince myself that I could continue to be just friends with Owen without wanting more. Even after only a couple weeks, my heart had assumed full control.

CHAPTER 21

wen

It was the middle of my Tuesday morning staff meeting when I got a call from a number I didn't recognize. There was always some robocalling marketer or PAC solicitor calling from a city where I knew no one.

But this was different—hang-ups from the same number—and it had been happening more and more.

I almost clicked it off and let it go to voicemail, where the caller would probably not leave a message and I'd have three seconds of dead air before the line went dead.

Or I could answer and hear some breathing on the other end before the caller would similarly hang up. I was starting to feel like this mystery caller and I had a sort of relationship after several weeks of this nonsense. Maybe it was someone lonely—or a kid with access to an unlimited calling plan—and it helped to know there was someone on the other end of the line.

I wondered if the caller was working up the nerve to say

something. As long as there was a human on the other end of the line, I'd keep answering.

And because I suspected I'd get another heavy breathing hang-up, I leaned down, away from the others at the conference table, and said, "Hello?"

There was the usual pause, and I readied myself to hang up as soon as the line went dead.

But it didn't.

I heard breathing, then a cough. Someone was definitely there.

I got up so quickly, my chair went spinning around behind me, and I didn't bother to excuse myself before showing the glass door to the conference room open and walking into the hallway.

"Who is this?" I was holding the phone with both hands. It's not like I thought someone was going to tell me I'd won a sweepstakes contest or something, so I couldn't figure out why I felt so nervous.

There was a scratchy sound on the other end of the line, then a quiet woman's voice began speaking. "Owen, it's Jen. Can we talk?"

Jen. My sister. I hadn't spoken to her in five years.

My heart started pounding, and without thinking, I was moving down the hallway and out of the building. My forehead broke out in a cold sweat and I felt light-headed. As soon as I reached the front of the building, I leaned against the outer wall and inhaled a deep breath.

"What's up Jen?" I asked. I knew it wasn't particularly friendly, but I didn't care. This was the first time she hadn't hung up, and I just wanted to know why she was calling and get on with my life.

"Owen, I just wanted to tell you...you're an uncle." Her voice squeaked at the end and I could tell she was happy, and she wanted me to be happy.

But I was having trouble feeling anything.

"Congratulations." My voice was strained. A part of me felt

wistful that I wasn't there to meet my new niece or nephew. *Is it weird that she hasn't said which?* But the other part of me wanted this phone call over.

I was in a full•body cold sweat. She was talking again and I only heard part of it. "...so if you ever want to come out."

"Are you asking me to come visit you?"

"If you want...we'd love to see you."

"Jen, since you left for college, how many times have you come back to San Francisco to see me?"

She didn't speak, but I heard her breathing with such labored difficulty that I wondered if she'd started smoking. Maybe she had emphysema and this would be the last opportunity to see her. No, she'd have said that if it was true.

Finally, "None. I haven't been back. You know I had my reasons."

"No, Jen, I don't know. All I know is that you didn't care enough to buy a single plane ticket. Or hell, to get in the car when you were in grad school in Seattle—which I fucking paid for."

"I know, Owen. I should have. There were always things that got in the way." Her voice sounded strained. Why the hell did she call? She had to know she wasn't going to get a warm reception. That's probably why she'd hung up so many times, working up the nerve.

"Why are you calling me now? Are you okay? Is Jim okay?" I couldn't help the parenting instinct I'd had for her since I was sixteen.

Her voice brightened a little. "He's good. We're good. I just wanted to share the news. You're an uncle," she said again.

"Okay, well, I'm glad you're okay. Tell me the name of my niece or nephew. I'll send a gift."

"You don't need to do that. That's not why I..."

"Jen, I'm sending a goddamned gift. Just tell me if it's a boy or a girl."

She hesitated, then probably gave up trying to get me to change my icy response to her. That wasn't going to change. "It's a girl. Lila."

"That's a pretty name." My voice still sounded stiff. If I didn't know myself, I'd say it sounded like I was going to burst into tears at any moment.

Get a grip, Owen. She left and never looked back. You don't owe her anything.

"Jen, I'm in the middle of a meeting, so maybe...maybe we can talk another time." I said the words even though I didn't mean them.

"Sure." She sounded hurt. What did she expect? "Call me whenever, okay?"

I hung up the phone and wiped the sweat off my forehead. Still reeling from the strangeness of the call, I tried to refocus my mind on work before I reached the conference room.

Looking down at my phone, I debated blocking her number so I wouldn't have to deal with another ambush again.

Instead, I entered it into my contacts list and went back to my meeting.

CHAPTER 22

sla

OVER THE NEXT WEEK, I started to rely on Owen's presence in my life, even as I reminded myself that he wasn't my boyfriend.

He was my sounding board when I looked at other options for where I could expand Victorine if Centinela Bread was dead set on outbidding me on the locations I'd already scouted. I just had to hope the behemoth company wouldn't stay on my heels and challenge me everywhere I tried to go.

I came to rely on his comforting presence, his whip-smart brain, and his gorgeous body to make me happy, even on days when I got more bad news about my restaurant clients deciding to cancel their contracts to buy bread from me.

He made me feel like I could weather the storm.

So I decided it wasn't too much of a risk to invite him to a family dinner night. My sisters and I had made rules about guests —specifically boyfriends—mainly because a few of us had had particularly bad luck after introducing someone we were dating to the rest of the pack.

But those relationships probably had issues to begin with that had nothing to do with my family.

At least that's what I told myself when I invited Owen to come over. That, and the fact that he wasn't my boyfriend. There was nothing to break up.

Besides, I really wanted my sisters to know him. He'd been so good to me in the past few weeks, and thanks to Owen, I was happier than I'd been in a long time.

"Is it time to talk about it?" Cherry asked me on our hike through the North Berkeley hills to Finn and Annie's house. She'd agreed to the two-mile walk despite a big hill we'd reach in the second half.

Cherry was always up for exercise as long as it didn't feel like a workout. She preferred competitive sports for fun, hikes and walks where she was distracted by conversation, and anything that kept her out of a gym.

For the moment, we were still buried amid tall trees that flanked the homes on Walnut Avenue, having just walked through Live Oak Park, one of my favorite nooks in North Berkeley. It was a little out of the way if we were intent on a direct route between Cherry's house and Finn's, but the whole point of walking was to deviate from the direct route.

I also planned to have us walk through the Berkeley Rose Garden on Euclid if we had time. "Maybe Finn can terrace his hillside with roses once he's done with that wraparound porch. What do you think?" I asked.

"I'm not letting you change the subject," Cherry said quietly, her breathing steady. She spent three mornings a week with a rowing club that competed locally and was in phenomenal shape.

Eh, maybe we'd skip the rose garden if it meant she'd have less time for an interrogation.

"I think I already did," I said, walking a little faster. "I changed it to the subject of Finn's porch. Let's talk about that some more."

She picked up her pace to keep up with me. "You're impossible. I'm just trying to help you do things the kinder, gentler way."

"What's that supposed to mean?"

"By talking to me. I could be telling you to go see a therapist, but the gentle way is to have a relaxed conversation while we walk up a hill. Are we stopping at the rose garden?" she asked, shifting the bottle of wine she'd brought from one hand to the other.

Only Cherry would think nothing of carrying a wine bottle for two miles without putting it in a tote bag. She also thought nothing of doing the walk in cute boots with a two-inch heel and a cashmere scarf wound around her neck and trailing down her back. She looked fashionable no matter what she was doing, and she'd been that way since birth.

I, on the other hand, was not too proud to wear an old pair of Chucks for our slog up the hill. At least I wouldn't get blisters.

I tried to change the subject again. "Cher, those jeans are cute. Have I seen them before?" She was wearing a loose-fitting pair of jeans rolled at the bottom.

She cast me a side-eye. "That's a funny question. Wouldn't you know if you'd seen them before better than I would?"

"Okay, Ms. Literal. I don't think I've seen those before. Are they new?" I asked, enunciating my words for distinct clarity. She could be as big a pain in the ass as she wanted, as long as she wasn't trying to force me to talk about personal stuff I preferred to leave buried.

"They are new. From a very expensive shop that had no business charging as much as they did for 'boyfriend jeans' that probably did originate in some dude's closet, though I'd prefer not to think of it. That's what happens when you don't have a boyfriend to give you his old stuff. You get reamed at retail."

"Eh, I've never had a boyfriend give me his old jeans. Boyfriend jeans are a myth."

We arrived at the rose garden, and I stopped to take in the sweeping expanse of greenery and roses budding in terraced rows heading down the hill before us. The upper level had a terraced overhang crawling with vining roses, and beneath each concentric half-circle of planter boxes, a path allowed for viewing and smelling each variety.

"Finn *should* plant roses," Cherry conceded.

I walked down the path amid the tender blooms, completely ignoring the fact that I'd wanted to speed our walk. The flowers were too pretty to skip.

Cherry checked the time and plunked down on a bench. "We're early. That's what you get for race-walking up the damn hill. Now I have you captive for the conversation you don't want to have." She patted the seat next to her.

I could have walked away and pretended to be super interested in the Queen Elizabeth roses I knew were nestled in the lower tier of the garden, but Cherry was probably right. I had to talk to someone, she knew my history with Tom, and she'd also been the first one to suggest he might have something up his sleeve with all his attempts to reach out.

"You need to stop avoiding Tom or you'll never be done with him," she said.

She was right.

I'd finally listened to Tom's messages. He wasn't asking to get back together. He was asking to help me. "He's offering me funding so I can fend off Centinela Bread. If there's anything I know Tom can do, it's raise ridiculous sums of money."

He made it sound painless and easy to win back all the locations by matching or exceeding Centinela's rent offers. It seemed crazy to get into a bidding war with a giant company, but Tom assured me that he knew how to handle a behemoth like Centinela.

I actually felt relief at the idea of handing off the whole thing to him and moving on with my plans to expand.

"How does he even know about Centinela? Did you tell him?"

"No, but it's Tom. He makes it his business to know about who's raising money, who's making acquisitions. Plus, he's been hovering and trying to find his way back into my good graces, which won't happen. Still, I have half a mind to take his money purely out of revenge."

"True, but then you'd be in bed with Tom."

I glared at her. "Hardly."

"Sorry, I just mean, do you want that entanglement? Isn't there another way to raise the money?"

"Not that I've come up with. But I'm still looking."

"Keep looking."

"Wow, hate Tom much?"

She rolled her eyes. "After what he did to you, yes. The last thing I want to see is you back in a relationship with him."

"I'm not gonna date him."

"It doesn't matter. It's still an entanglement. He'll be in your business, not just your bed, but your business that you worked your tail off to build. Do you really want that? You'll never get rid of him. You don't need that guy, regardless of what he might think."

She was right, of course. I didn't want Tom anywhere near my business, but I was starting to run out of options. "No, I don't want that. But sometimes it's not about what I want. It's about what's best."

"I know." She spoke quietly and turned to look at me. "I know you live a lot of your life logically, doing what you think you should do. I remember being a kid and watching you bake, and I don't mean once you'd won the science fair and started really baking. I'm talking about when you discovered the Mixmaster mom had hidden in the back of the cabinet and started making cookies loaded with M&M's and doused in colored sugar sprinkles. Your cookies were messy and gleeful and gorgeous. You were messy too. Total slob."

"I remember. I'd use one bowl to beat eggs and all the measuring cups and a sifter for the flour, which ended up everywhere. I hadn't learned the magic of cleaning up as I went."

She laughed. "Don't I know it. You were so bossy. If any of us wanted to eat whatever you'd made, you forced us to do all your dishes."

I held up an admonishing finger. "Hey, that's the sign of a good kitchen steward. There's no free lunch." I inhaled a deep breath. There was no escaping the beauty of where we sat, no matter what direction the conversation went.

"Whatever. I was eight. And you had me scrubbing mixing bowls for permission to eat a cookie."

I felt a little bit proud of my bossiness. "Yeah, I did love baking back then. It was different."

"Right? Because it was for fun. It wasn't a business." She stopped speaking abruptly and looked at me like she wanted to say more, but she turned back toward the water and said nothing.

I nodded. "I know what you're saying. But I do still love it. It's just that I realized in order to make a living doing something I love, I had to deal with what I think of as market forces. Think of Tom as a market force."

She rolled her eyes and smacked my shoulder. "You've been drinking Finn's econ nerd Kool-Aid."

"Oh, please. You work for a startup. You know that in order to make a business profitable, it can't just be the whim of the creator. I have to run the business with customers in mind. Always. I can't just bake cookies with crazy sprinkles all day long because they're fun."

"You could though . . . I'd eat them and so would lots of other people."

The way she was talking reminded me of Owen. He had the same near-blind optimism about my potential, and some of the time I had a hard time seeing what he saw. But I did appreciate the effort he made to see it. It was what made my heart surge with joy just by thinking about him.

Cherry looked at me and smiled. "Owen?"

"Yeah. How'd you know?"

"I know what love looks like, and it's that. Your face."

It was crazy. We'd only been spending time together for a few weeks, but Cherry was right.

I was falling in love with the guy. And falling without a net.

CHAPTER 23

 sla

OWEN HAD BEEN at the new Sonoma property all day and was planning to meet me at Finn and Annie's house on his drive back to the city.

Annie, my four sisters, and I were sitting around Finn's kitchen table with three open bottles of wine, two reds, and a white. Finn had gotten stuck in a faculty meeting on campus and wasn't going to make it back in time to cook. Annie had offered to make the whole dinner herself, but we immediately voted her down.

"Pizza and wine make a perfect dinner," Becca said. She dialed Zachary's on Solano. It was close by, and they delivered.

"If I'd known, we could have picked it up," I said. We'd passed right by Solano. Cherry looked at me like I was nuts. "What?" I asked.

"You'd have made me carry four pizzas up the hill for two miles?"

I shrugged. "You didn't mind carrying wine for two miles in heels."

"That's different. It's wine."

I saw her point. Delivery it would be. "Are you really thinking we need four pizzas for seven people?" I asked the group. Zachary's pizzas were stuffed deep dish Chicago style pies with layers of toppings, a second layer of dough and seasoned crushed tomatoes on top. We'd all grown up eating it, and Annie claimed it was one of the reasons she convinced Finn to move back to the Bay Area from Los Angeles.

Becca rolled her eyes. "Yes, we're ordering four. And now I'm thinking we need five. Are you making some kind of point, Island?" That was her nickname for me. When we were kids, it embarrassed me, but now I kind of loved that she still used it.

"Fine, whatever. Get five. But I defy you to eat more than two pieces. That stuff's filling. We'll have at least two whole pies left over."

"Exactly my plan," Becca said. "Blake will be jealous that we Zacharied without him, so I promised I'd bring some back."

We ordered an assortment of pizzas and Tatum topped off everyone's wine glasses. Then Sarah and Cherry went with Annie to see what other wines we might want to pilfer from Finn's collection before he got home. The rest of us stayed in the kitchen.

"Wow, this could be dangerous on a hot day in the shade. I could drink a lot of it without realizing it," Tatum said. I couldn't imagine her doing that because she was a slave to her job in Silicon Valley, but I was happy to hear she was imagining a time when it might happen.

I leaned back in my chair and sipped what turned out to be a sauvignon blanc that tasted like grapefruit. "I wasn't expecting that taste. But if my time in the wine country taught me anything, it's that I don't know anything about wine."

"You know enough to drink it from a wineglass instead of a tumbler with a straw. That's sufficient knowledge where I'm concerned," Becca said.

I lifted my glass in her direction.

There was a faint knock at the front door, but it was loud enough to get my attention. "Oh, that must be Owen."

"Wait, you're letting him come to a family dinner? Have you learned nothing? You know it's the kiss of death to a boyfriend," Becca said. Bringing Blake to dinner at my house when they were first dating almost ended their relationship.

I waved her off. "I don't believe in curses, and besides, we're not officially dating, so the curse doesn't apply."

"Suit yourself," Becca said, but she looked wary. "And why aren't you officially dating?" she yelled after me.

"Because it's only been three weeks since Tom," Sarah yelled to her on her way back upstairs.

Tatum followed me to the door. "I wanna meet him first. Is that cool?" She was following me regardless, which was typical of my sisters.

"Sure. He's a good guy. You'll like him."

I opened the door and took in the sight of Owen in a pair of low-slung dark jeans with a belt and a button-up white shirt over a grey T-shirt. His hair was slicked back, and he wore aviator sunglasses. I unconsciously felt my heart sink at not being able to see his pretty eyes. But I was so happy to see the rest of him.

He smiled when he saw me and pulled me in for a hug and a quick kiss on the lips. Then he looked over my shoulder at Tatum.

"This is my youngest sister, Tatum," I told Owen.

"The rest of the sibs will monopolize you so I wanted to get in my own hello first," she said.

After letting Tatum take in the full glory of his smile, I handed off Owen's proffered chocolate mousse so she could put it in the fridge. Then I stepped out onto the porch and closed the door behind us.

"Hey." I hugged him and gave him the kiss I'd longed for all day. It only make me hungry for more, so I wistfully looked in the direction of his car, contemplating an escape.

"Are you going to invite me in? Not that I'm opposed to doing this for a lot longer." His hand glided along my jaw, cupping my face as he bent to kiss me again.

When he finally pulled away, his eyes went to the front door, which I made no move to open. Then he looked at me.

"So…?" he asked.

All I could think of was the earlier comments about the curse. It was insane. There was nothing to it. Right?

"Okay, full disclosure… My sisters seem to think there's some kind of family curse that will rear up with you being here. The family dinner has led to some breakups."

He cast his eyes down so I couldn't read into them. When he looked up, his expression was serious. "Do you believe in it, this curse?"

"Not really. It's kind of a joke, mostly, but I like you too much to take a chance."

His eyes softened and he bit his lip, nodding. "Then we shouldn't risk it." He looked like he wanted to say more, but he pressed his lips together and watched me.

I couldn't hide my shock. "Really? One mention of a curse and you fold? I had no idea you were that superstitious."

He shrugged. "Not superstitious, just practical. I want to meet your sisters, but not at what sounds like great personal risk." His eyes danced with amusement.

"Okay, forget I said anything. There's no curse. It's ridiculous. In fact, the real thing you should be worried about is spending two hours with my sisters. They can be a bit much."

He laughed. "I'm all in for that, curse or no curse. I want to meet these hellions of whom you speak. I bet they'll behave."

"They most definitely will not, but you've been warned. All legal recourse is null and void."

He nodded. "I'm good with that." When I kissed him this time, it wasn't quick. I knew my sisters were inside gossiping about us, but I didn't care.

The truth was I wanted him to meet all my siblings so they could tell me I was right in pushing right through all the friendship barriers and starting a real relationship with him, even if it did begin right on the heels of my breakup.

I wanted to tell the whole world how I felt about Owen Miller. Even if I still hadn't figured out how to tell him.

I ushered him in, and my sisters were on him like concert groupies. They practically hoisted him over their heads and carried him through the house.

You'd think they'd never met a male before from the way they were chatting him up about his hotels and his favorite kind of bread.

When I caught his eye to make sure he didn't feel assaulted, he flashed me an ok sign and kept on talking with them, asking about Becca's job, Sarah's interest in welding, Cherry's love of fashion, and Annie's legal cases.

I couldn't remember the last time one of us asked Annie about her legal cases. Bad sisters. Tatum hung out on the outskirts of the conversation like she often did, and Owen even managed to draw her in.

Soon the pizza came, and the feeding frenzy that my sisters had focused on Owen was shifted to the food, so I finally had a chance to get near him. Finn was a little formal and always insisted we eat in the kitchen, but since he wasn't around, we moved to the living room, which had a back deck with a view of the hills.

Owen and I shared an oversized stuffed chair, and we shared a single plate of pizza. I caught Becca's approving eye and she winked.

Once my sisters had stuffed their faces with pizza, they piled on Owen again with questions.

"So Isla says you have one sister," Cherry was working the cork from a bottle of wine unsuccessfully but wouldn't let anyone help her.

"Yup, just one." Without asking, Owen reached over and held his hand out for the bottle. She passed it to him without argument and he pulled the cork free.

"Thanks. I'll bet this motley crew makes you glad you don't have more."

He smiled and shook his head. "You guys are great."

Cherry started asking more questions about his sister, where she lived, what she did for a living. Sometimes she had a crappy radar for when to stop talking and this was one of those times. I could see Owen getting more and more uncomfortable with her questions, which was odd since he'd never done that with me, no matter what I'd asked him.

Then again, except for the first night we went out, we didn't talk about his sister.

"Hey Cher, come help me pick out another bottle from downstairs, will you? I don't know how to pick reds."

"Sure thing." She followed me out of the kitchen, and I hoped no one else would feel the need to interrogate Owen about his family. I knew he wouldn't want to talk about his parents.

When we got downstairs, I smacked her shoulder. "Do you have to run an inquisition for gosh sakes? You were making him uncomfortable."

"I was? Yikes. Sorry."

"Just stop doing it."

"Does he not, like, get along with his family?"

"They get along fine but not everyone wants to answer a million questions. Some people just want to eat dinner."

"Well, he shouldn't have come here, then."

She searched around the bottles, grabbed one that I wasn't even sure was red, and jogged back up the stairs. I didn't care which wine she picked as long as she left Owen alone.

Then again, more wine was never the answer to reining in my sisters. I sped upstairs to run interference.

CHAPTER 24

wen

"Sorry about my family. I should have warned you they're nosy and intrusive," Isla said when we got in my car.

"I have to tell you something," I blurted out. It felt wrong to let her keep thinking my sister and I had a great relationship, even if she wouldn't be able to relate. And based on the close relationship I'd just witnessed with her family, our siblings were polished red apples to sickly pale oranges.

She looked up. "Uh oh, that sounds like a confession. Did you eat the bread before it cooled? I knew it."

"Well, yes, if I'm confessing things, then you ought to know that I've never—and I say this with full confidence—never waited for your bread to cool. I eat it on the way home while it's still hot." I looked at her to gauge her reaction.

I wasn't sure if her bread instructions were really a polite guideline or whether she expected mere hungry mortals like me to obey them.

She smiled. "I had a feeling. Don't sweat it."

"You should take it as a compliment. It's that good. And I lack willpower, apparently."

She nodded, satisfied that the bread thing was my only confession. I needed to plow ahead and tell her the rest.

Other than the first night we hung out together, I'd never mentioned my family to her again. My sister lived far away and my sad little story about being left behind was far in the past, so there was no reason to revisit it. Except that it wasn't in the past.

"I have another confession besides the bread." I watched the easy smile fade from her face.

"Okay . . ." she said warily.

"It's about my sister."

Her expression clouded with concern, her body stiffened, and her eyes shot to mine. I loved that she was as invested in my family as she was in hers, even without knowing anything about Jen. "What about her? Is she okay?"

"She's fine. It's just that when I first told you about her, I probably gave you the impression we were close. Or at least cordial."

She looked confused. "Yeah. You're not?"

I told her about Jen, about how she'd left for college in Washington state, and how I'd moved an hour west of our hometown to San Francisco, fully expecting her to join me. "We were the only family we had. I got a two-bedroom house with a yard because she'd adopted a cat during her senior year. But instead of moving back to California, she moved to Vermont with her boyfriend. They're married—eloped. She never came back, never visited—just left it all behind."

"She left you behind," Isla said, nodding. "I'm sorry. After all you did for her, that must've hurt."

"It was gradual. At first, we talked a lot and she'd promise to come out. Then she'd come up with excuses and a year would go by. Then two. Finally, I stopped inviting her. Then I stopped returning her calls, figuring if she couldn't come out one time to see me, that said a lot. My little sister's married to a guy I've never even met."

Isla moved over the stick shift, which took some flexibility, and made her way to me until she was sitting sideways in my lap. Then she wrapped her arms around me.

The gesture was so much more than an attempt to use her body to distract me from thinking too much. She was giving me all of herself, her beautiful figure that melded perfectly with mine, her big, wide-open heart, and her acceptance of whatever weird, dark detail I flung at her about my past.

Her finger traced the side of my cheek. "I'm so sorry. I mean, I'm sure she had her reasons—maybe it was too painful to come back to the place where your parents basically abandoned you, but still . . . she was really lucky you were there for her and that's not a very nice way of saying so."

"Thanks for that." It was the most basic response but I was out of practice.

"Do you think..." She bit her lip and I knew she was worried about offending me with whatever she wanted to say.

"What? Tell me." I brushed back a tendril of hair that had fallen in her eyes and cupped her cheek.

She leaned into my palm. "Just that...do you think maybe you sort of left her behind too, once she didn't do what you expected? I'm not excusing what she did, just asking."

I shrugged. I didn't know anymore. "It feels like a long time ago. That's why it's easier sometimes to pretend it's not important."

Her hazel eyes looked green tonight as they focused serenely on mine. Our faces were inches apart, but it didn't feel like a kissing moment, even though staring into her eyes made me feel even closer than when I was inside her.

Her voice was quiet when she spoke. "It is important. You

should tell me these things. I want to know them. I want to know everything."

Because she had no reason to lie, I believed her. She wanted to know everything I wanted to tell her, and that forced the last bit of wall I'd built around my heart to cave.

I love her.

I wanted to say it, but something held me back.

Maybe it was the growing concern that she didn't feel the same way—would never feel the same way.

"I guess maybe I didn't expect you to stick around once you got to know me better." I sounded as insecure as I felt when I revealed things about my family, but it was the truth and I wanted her to have it.

Her face cracked into a huge smile. "Why? That's exactly when I started to really like you—once I saw that you had quirks and depth."

Her smile made me smile. "Really? With all my many talents and abilities, that's what you like about me?"

She brought out the best side of me, the part that felt free to share everything I'd buried. I should tell her.

I love her.

She had my heart and there was no point in denying it.

She nodded. "Just so you know . . . I'm not running. I'm not going anywhere. You've got me as a friend whether you like it or not."

The word was a glass shard in my gut. Friend. Friendship. Friends with benefits. I was starting to get tired of all the ways she could come up with to resist having actual feelings for me. And here I was sharing things that only Rafael knew, and he'd known me for eight years.

I was still recovering from the fucking word and she was oblivious. "Of course, you do everything in a way that makes you seem like you have it all together all the time. It's inspiring." I wanted to hear her words as a compliment, but I couldn't get past what I was starting to see as an immovable line in her mind.

"I'm . . . not the man you think I am. I don't have it all together."

Because I'm losing my heart over you.

She laughed, kindness in her eyes. "I don't want to offend you, but you're exactly the man I think you are."

"I feel like I should be a little bit offended by that."

She leaned in and whispered in my ear. "No one has it together, even the people who seem like they do. Take it from one who is an utter and complete mess and I still manage to get by every day."

With her voice and her breath near my ear, she unleashed a torrent of electricity that went straight to my dick. The woman was destroying me bit by bit with her lips and her brain and her beautiful body and I didn't want to resist.

"You're the most gorgeous, talented mess I've ever seen." I lowered my lips to her throat and savored the gardenia and honey smell of her skin and its velvet softness against my lips.

I kissed my way down to her collarbone and back up again. Her hair tickled the side of my face and I brushed it to the side so I had full access to her beautiful neck.

It felt like we were a couple of teenagers in my dad's borrowed car. Although in my teen years, it was my own shitty used Corolla with the door that didn't lock and AM radio only. But it didn't matter. I'd have made out with Isla all night long in that car.

Things got hot and heavy fast as they did every damn time I was near her. For the first instance since I'd bought it, I hated my small car.

Isla seemed to realize its limitations at the same time, not to mention that we were still parked in front of her brother's house. She backed away with a satisfied hum and settled herself back in the passenger seat. "To be continued?" she asked.

"My house or yours? '/

"Whichever one's closest." She smiled.

"Maybe mine. By a block."

"I'll make the saved time worth your while." She whispered it in my ear, and I nearly aborted plan and carried her back into her brother's house—surely they had a back room we could use . . .

But no, I could be patient. Sort of.

I started the drive down the hill toward the freeway that would take us over the Bay Bridge. Isla was quiet for a while, holding my hand in her lap except for the times I had to use it for shifting gears.

I was solely focused on getting us back to my house by the most expeditious route possible when she turned in her seat to face me more squarely. I couldn't look, but I felt the heat of her eyes on me.

"So you don't talk at all, you and your sister?" she asked.

"Not in five years. Although now . . ." Yeah, there was that other part I hadn't told her. Well, might as well rip off the Band-Aid. "She's suddenly reached out. I don't know . . . maybe she wants to repair things."

"Oh. Well, that's good, maybe. Is that what you want? Can you do that?" There was no judgement in her question and I didn't know the answer to it. I shrugged.

"I don't know." It was the truth and I knew she wouldn't judge me for it. "Oh, and she had a baby. I'm an uncle."

"Seriously? That's exciting! Congratulations, Uncle O."

"Thanks."

She was silent for a moment. We both stared straight ahead through the windshield.

Do I want to see my sister?

"The truth is I miss her. I do want to see her. I just . . . it's hard. I guess I can be man enough to deal with hard things."

From the corner of my eye, I could see Isla tilt her head, considering. "You want my advice?"

"Yes. Always."

She nodded. "I think you should. Start fresh. Babies have a way of demanding that. Maybe that's why she reached out to you now."

"Maybe." There was traffic. We slowed to a stop and I looked at her.

"She's your family. Don't hold a grudge. It's like drinking poison and expecting the other person to die." She quirked her mouth into a half smile.

"Very wise."

"Isn't it? I saw it on a T-shirt."

I could not have loved her more, even if she still thought of me as a friend. So I battled Bay Area traffic and took her back to my apartment so I could demonstrate the depth of my affection. To her credit—or maybe mine—she didn't utter the friend word for the rest of the night.

wen

FLOUR COVERED every inch of the long wooden table where we were working.

Isla kept referring to it as a bench, even though all the benches I knew about allowed for a person to rest and she had me working my ass off.

We'd been at the bakery for two hours already and our dough had just finished its first rise, which made me surprisingly happy. I couldn't believe that mixing in a little bit of starter with the flour, water, and salt was all it took to make bread dough that had doubled in size all on its own.

"I'm still amazed this worked." I pointed at the baskets in front of us, where fluffy air-filled dough had just come out of the proofing drawer. An hour earlier the dough looked thick, beige, and unappetizing—and nothing like any future bread I'd want to eat. Now it looked like bread fairies had visited and sprinkled it with magical rising powers. "It even smells like bread."

I stuck my nose close to the beautiful smooth dough in the basket and inhaled. When I looked up at Isla her lips were pressed together like she was trying to stifle a laugh.

"What?" I asked.

"You're cute."

"I'm cute?" That was enough to make me ignore the dough entirely in favor of stepping behind her, dipping my nose toward her neck, and inhaling the much preferred rosemary mint of her shampoo. "*You're* cute."

I kissed the line of her jaw and ran my nose along her neck until I got to her ear. When I exhaled a breath against the tender skin there, I felt her melt against me.

The flour that coated my forearms and hands didn't stop me from pulling her close. She turned within my arms so she was facing me and put her hands at the nape of my neck.

"You are very cute. And you've been hanging out here for over a year, so I'm pretty sure you know how fermentation works to make dough rise, so I think it's sweet that you're indulging me in my lessons as though you're a newbie."

"Oh, bread lassie, don't you know I've been hanging out here and only paying attention to you? I don't know shit about fermentation, but if you'd like to teach me, I promise to be an attentive student." I had utmost respect for what she'd built as a baker, but I assumed we were both on the same page—this time in the kitchen was a big flirtation leading someplace good.

Her eyes lit up and I sensed I was in for some hot making out amid the bread ovens.

Um, no.

Isla was unstoppable, talking a mile a minute and gesturing wildly. "I love teaching people about this. It's been a while since I've had an apprentice or anyone who didn't know anything about how sourdough gets made so I want to make sure I teach you everything about feeding the starters, weighing everything in metric, grinding the salt—I'll leave nothing out."

I started to say that she didn't need to go crazy. I wasn't looking for a job at a bakery so I didn't need an encyclopedia of bread knowledge, just a few *bons mots* that would prevent me from starving if it ever came down to me, some wheat, and a bread oven.

But she was off and running and her enthusiasm was so fucking adorable I didn't have the heart to tell her to slow down.

"Let's look at these starters." She took all the jars down from where they were sleeping under burlap cloth. "They're all a little bit different because each grain of wheat is a little bit different so even if I add the same amount of flour and the same amount of water, no two starters are exactly the same. Plus—and this is the best part—as long as I feed them, they'll live forever. These starters could outlive us. In fact, these are the progeny of my original bread starters from when I opened my first bread shop seven years ago."

Her face was flushed and she looked so damned happy talking about microorganisms feeding off flour and creating their own byproducts which were the rising agents in her bread.

"When you stop and think about it, it's a little disgusting, isn't it? It's like the waste products of your starter organism are what's making the bread rise," I said.

"I don't think about it like that." She had a very serious face and I was pretty sure I'd just insulted her very core.

"Right, sure." I backpedaled.

She stared at me and I wondered if she might hit me. Then her face slowly cracked and she was grinning. "I'm kidding. Of course that's what's happening. I'm glad you get it. But one organism's waste product is another organism's va va voom."

We kept going like that, with Isla giving me what felt like a monthlong bread education in a matter of hours, all the while waiting for our next batch of dough to rise. Once it did, she showed me how to knead it properly and punch the air out. "I don't want to punch it down. I feel like all that rising time just went down the drain," I said.

"Don't worry about that. It's going to have a second chance to rise. You want to punch the air out and keep working the dough. That's how we get the gluten to really bind with the water molecules."

I looked at the blob of dough on the bench in front of me. I couldn't see any evidence of gluten binding with anything, but she was knocking hers into submission until it started to take on a glossy sheen. "You're like some kind of bread whisperer," I said.

She didn't stop what she was doing, moving from one ball of dough to the next and kneading while directing me at the same time. "You need to seal the edges. And not too much flour. You want the work surface to create tension while you're kneading. That helps build elasticity."

Watching her work, I felt the now-familiar tug at my heart that made me want to tell her everything, admit I'd been falling for her for weeks and hope that the feeling was mutual.

If I didn't push Isla, I'd regret it forever.

I had to know how she felt, and even if I didn't get the answer I wanted, at least I wouldn't labor under the delusion that we were something. It didn't have to be today—I just needed to know she thought we had potential.

Walking around every day with my heart in my throat, cringing every time she called me a friend...I couldn't take it when she'd yet to give me a sign she felt a fraction of what I'd been feeling for her since the first moment our lips connected.

And even that was a lie because I'd felt things for her long before that.

The kiss just confirmed I was right.

We were so good together, it was hard to imagine a future with anyone but her. If she rejected me, so be it. I just couldn't dangle in the wind anymore.

"Isla, I need to tell you something."

"Yes?" Her bright eyes stayed focused on the dough as she multitasked and put the perfect rounds into lined baskets so they could rise for a second time.

I was about to unburden my heart when her phone pinged on the stool where she'd left it next to her purse. I assumed she'd ignore it. We were already at the bakery, so no one was calling with a work emergency.

She glanced at it and I saw the smallest flicker of annoyance cross her face, but she put the phone down without typing a response.

Then she picked it up and read the text again and typed a quick response before nearly slamming it down on the stool. It was a little dramatic, but she'd been under a lot of stress over the assault by Centinela Bread, so I chalked it up to that.

It did have the effect of sidelining my confession, at least for the time being.

I turned back to the bench and we resumed my bread lesson, something I'd apparently earned through good behavior at some point in Calistoga.

I rolled my ball of dough closer to hers, so close that they almost touched, and she jerked hers away. "Hey, no getting handsy with the dough."

"I still want to know what I did to deserve a bread lesson from San Francisco's finest bread maker."

"Not telling," she said with a smirk.

"Foolhardy woman, if you tell me, there's a good chance I'll do it again."

She seemed to be considering it. "What good would it do if it was something you couldn't repeat here? Like if I said the spa treatments?" She was baiting me.

"Was it the spa treatments?"

She laughed. "Do you really want me to tell you the spa treatments were better than three orgasms you gave me in the governor's cottage?"

"Are you kidding? If the spa treatments at my hotel beat what I'm fairly certain was *four* orgasms before we left for home, I'm putting that on our brochure. The place will be booked for months."

She kneaded her dough with quick rolling motions that showed off her toned arms as she quickly turned the dough. It was hard to believe kneading dough could be a turn-on.

"You're funny, Bread Boy. Now focus on your dough. You need to really work it in your hands if you want a good loaf."

"Why does everything you say about baking suddenly sound sexual?" This bread lesson could go in a very different direction and I'd relinquish bread rights without complaint.

Shaking her head, she took my dough away and held it hostage behind her back. "You're not taking this seriously."

I laughed because she was taking it so seriously. "I'm sorry. You know I love and respect your work. I guess I was thinking of all the kneading as foreplay."

"You're terrible. There will be no sex in the vicinity of the bread."

Probably true. Nevertheless, I held out my hand. "Can I have my dough back? I promise not to fondle it beyond what's necessary to help it rise."

"Okay, now you're making everything sound sexual on purpose." She took a swipe at me, but I caught her hands and held them down, at the same time pulling her closer to me.

"Come on, you've never gotten a little naughty with a hot loaf?" I asked.

She struggled to get away but I held her tight. "You may have successfully ruined my baking career forever. I'm never going to be able to look at a hot loaf the same way again."

"Sorry." I kissed her. "Not sorry."

With a little burst of force, she wrenched her hands free and picked up a metal instrument with a rounded handle and a straight edge and held it up with a flourish. "This is a dough scraper. Lesson two will show you what to do with it unless you want to work up your comedy act some more."

"Oh my God, you're a bread dictator, do you realize that?" I couldn't believe what I'd gotten myself into, but I loved every minute of it. I'd also lost all track of time, but I had the sense that we'd been in the bakery for hours. "Maybe it's just the smell of fermentation, but I'm getting hungry. You?" I asked.

Isla nodded. "Yeah, I could eat. How about we get these last few into the baskets and we can go grab a bite while they're rising?"

Her phone pinged again and she looked at it . . . and seemed interested. Her expression shifted to frustration as she read the message, but at the end she laughed. She typed a response and waited. It pinged again and she responded again, smiling, before putting it down.

Staring at it as if it was a bomb that might explode, she waited again, but the phone stayed quiet.

I looked at her expectantly, wondering if she was going to fill me in on what was going on. If it was something having to do with Centinela Bread, wouldn't she tell me?

But she said nothing. Her eyes stayed fixed on the phone.

"Everything okay?" I asked. It was a little strange how she seemed to have forgotten I was standing right there. It was unlike her to be so wrapped up in something else while she was with me.

As soon as she looked at me her expression softened. "Oh, yes. Sorry about that. It's nothing, just...that was Tom, my ex."

Of all the aggravations I imagined her dealing with, Tom Stone wasn't one of them. Just hearing his name made my stomach turn. But I hadn't told Isla I'd had my own dealings with her ex, and I wasn't sure I felt like getting into that.

"What does he want?" I tried to keep my tone even, but my face felt hot.

She shook her head. "He offered to back me."

"Back you?"

"You know, give the money to outbid Centinela so I can continue with my plans." She was emotionless about it.

I about hit the roof. "Are you kidding? You can't take his money. You're not thinking about it, are you?" The guy always had an ulterior motive, and I didn't trust his reasons for wanting to help Isla.

"I mean, I don't want to have anything to do with him, but it's an option. I think I should at least consider it."

"And you think his intentions are purely magnanimous? Come on Isla, he wants you back. You see that, right? He's using his deep pockets to get back in your good graces." And her pants. Just thinking about it made me want to smack some dough around. Or his head.

"I didn't say I was taking it. I said I was thinking about it," she said.

How did she not see him for what he was? She was brilliant in all areas except for her radar about Tom.

"I can help you. Why didn't you even think to ask? Why do you still not trust that I have your best interests at heart?" I had plenty of money socked away and I wouldn't have blinked over giving her all of it.

Because that's what you do when you love a person.

The more time I spent with her, the harder it was becoming to be the only one who felt that way.

"Of course I trust you. But we've already crossed all kinds of lines and I don't want to mix money with all that. I'd hate myself if I failed and lost your money. If I lost Tom's money…I could live with that." She shrugged.

"You're not going to fail."

"Okay. You've made your point." Putting a hand on my chest, she leaned in and kissed me. "Thank you."

I nodded. Some little part of me wondered if she was telling me everything. She didn't seem as bothered by the texts now as she undid her apron and helped me off with mine.

"Shall we?" she asked, tipping her head toward the door.

Maybe my disdain for the man was making me overreact. I needed to calm down. And all the bread smells were making me hungry and therefore cranky.

I nodded. "We shall. What do you feel like eating?"

"Duh, bread." Her expression was serious, then a grin spread over her face. "Just kidding. How about poke bowls?"

"Works for me." I grabbed my jacket and hers and we headed out. I talked myself down and told myself not to get all wound up over a couple of texts. Like everything, it mostly worked. Until it didn't.

CHAPTER 26

sla

I CALLED an emergency meeting at Becca's house because Centinela Bread had just pulled out all the stops. They'd outbid me at every location I wanted and I'd lost every single one of them.

It meant that after a year of scouting locations, meeting with designers and bakers, and running numbers, I was back to square one.

So we were circling the wagons—getting the brainpower of Blake, Becca, and Sarah all in one room. After the uncomfortable conversation with Owen about Tom's offer, I decided not to include him in the family meeting. He seemed overly worked up and that wouldn't help matters.

Sarah had been up all night running numbers to see if there was any possible way for me to come up with higher bids on my own to kick Centinela out of the equation and still have the locations I wanted. She looked exhausted, sitting on the floor with folders spread out around her. She'd always preferred to work on the ground, and it didn't matter if she was sitting on plush carpet or concrete.

"Who wants coffee?" Becca asked, starting the espresso bean grinder before any of us had answered. We all put up our hands.

Becca nodded and grabbed a tall jar of gray colored liquid from the fridge and handed it to me. "What the hell's that?" I asked.

"Almond milk from this nut farmer lady at the farmer's market. I got into a conversation with her about her rescue dogs and I started telling her about the feral cats that live here and by the time we were finished talking, a half hour had gone by and she hadn't sold a thing to anyone else. I felt guilty. This is fifteen dollars' worth of guilt milk."

"That's a lot of guilt," Blake said. He'd ditched the afternoon prep for his tasting menu so he could be there to weigh in.

"Sarah, are you sure you have time to keep doing this for me? You have your teaching and your volunteer stuff," I said, knowing she'd probably worry that I was asking because she wasn't doing a good enough job.

"Are you not happy with the job I'm doing?"

And, bingo.

"I'm ecstatic but you won't let me pay you and it's becoming a lot more work than it was when you started. Once I expand it will be a ridiculous amount of accounting. There are people who do this for a living."

Over time, I'd been slowly trying to scare Sarah with how much potential work she'd have to do if she didn't let me offload some of it to a firm who did this every day and could find some economies of scale. But she wouldn't bite.

She scribbled on a blank sheet to get her ballpoint pen to work, then she went from page to page of printed numbers and marked certain ones in specific columns that had no meaning to me. There were about ten pieces of paper spread out around her, some marked in blue pen, others highlighted in yellow.

Sarah straightened the papers into a pile and tapped the edges to pull them together. "Okay, what do you want first, the good news or the bad news?"

That was easy. I never wanted bad news.

"I'll take the good."

"The good news is your numbers are solid. You've socked away enough cash to put down deposits on the new spaces you want to rent and buy the ovens and startup materials. And you can do it without involving any investors. You'll be the sole owner," Sarah said, shooting me a look—she understood.

"That's exactly what I want." Sarah knew I'd worked hard to make sure I had enough money saved to expand without having to raise money from outsiders. Including Tom...

"Can I ask why?" Blake wasn't taking an accusatory tone, but I still felt defensive.

Sarah explained. "Part of why I wanted to have Blake here for our meeting was to talk some sense into you."

"You think I'm missing sense? Is that the bad news?" I asked.

Sarah shook her head. "Hardly. But in your business, it's rare to take on the whole financial burden of expansion by yourself."

Blake accepted the coffee I handed him and nodded his agreement. "One of the benefits of succeeding is that other people want to be involved in your future endeavors. You should have no problem finding investors."

"I don't have a problem finding them. It's by choice. I don't like having to answer to a board or an investment group for my decisions. I know it increases my risk, but I'm happier with that than increasing the risk of other people."

"But you need the money," Becca said. "If not Tom, then why not Owen? You said he offered to help."

That wasn't supposed to be public knowledge, but Becca had an agenda—protecting me from financial exposure. "I can't take his money. It's...too complicated. At least with Tom, it's purely financial, and even then, I hate being indebted to investors."

"I totally respect that," Blake said, sipping from his cup.

"Thanks. It works for me—I sleep better at night."

"Yeah, see, I'm the complete opposite. If it was all my money, I wouldn't sleep at all, worrying I was one bad restaurant menu from closing my doors," he said.

"Exactly," Sarah piped in. "This is what I want Blake to convince you of—you shouldn't carry this all on your shoulders."

"Says the sister who won't let me hire an accountant so she can cut back at one of her three jobs."

Becca rolled her eyes. "Oh my God you two, it's like you're back in high school, trying to one-up each other on who's more hardcore, the cross country runner or the varsity tennis player, when both of you were up before all normal humans to work out."

I ignored her. "Okay Sarah, was that the bad news? You'd rather have me pick up some investors? Because if that's it, I'm golden. Even though I hate it, I have options."

Sarah stretched her legs out on the floor and bent over them to stretch. I was beginning to understand why she liked it on the ground—it was easier to avoid looking anyone in the eye, and there was something she wasn't telling me. "No, that's not the bad news."

"So tell me. What?"

"With what Centinela is prepared to offer to keep you from getting these spaces, you'll only be able to afford to open one new place, not four. And even then, you'll need to borrow to cover it. That's the bad news." She looked at Blake and nudged her chin forward as though it was his turn.

I was shocked. "They're offering that much?"

Blake seemed equally shocked. "Who are these people? And why do they want these spaces so badly?"

"They're really good spaces. I worked hard to find them. Everything lines up for them to be stellar businesses."

Sarah pointed to the pages on the floor. "Isla did her homework."

I threw up my hands. "That's it. I'm not going to cave to these people and I'm not paying extra money to compete with them. There are plenty of other great locations where I can do a good business. I'll just have to start over."

The thought of it drained me. I'd spent so much time on the plans I had and even though everything Owen and I had discussed made sense, the thought of going back to square one felt unbelievably daunting.

The only option that would allow me to stay on track with my current plan involved going back to Tom for funding.

I hated the idea of that.

Becca nodded like she could tell what I was thinking. "I don't want you to have to go back to him either. But maybe Blake and Sarah are right. Maybe you need investors. It would give you much more freedom and lower your personal risk. If not Tom, then someone else."

I sipped my coffee with a pain in my chest. I didn't like any of my options and I was running out of time.

CHAPTER 27

wen

I WASN'T CRAZY. Isla had been distracted ever since the dinner at her brother's house, and I didn't think it had anything to do with a curse.

At first, the change was subtle. I'd send a text and instead of responding right away, Isla might wait a few minutes.

Or a half hour.

I wrote those instances off as her being busy baking and not having her phone nearby, even though I knew exactly where she kept it, and even though a week earlier it hadn't taken her a half hour to respond.

If I'd had the clarity of hindsight, I would have heard her words for what they were—warnings that we weren't headed for a relationship.

Or rather, I heard the words and chose not to listen to them, believing that my heart knew something my brain didn't.

The undeniable connection I felt with her in those moments

when we looked at each other and couldn't tear our gazes away—those had to mean something.

Isla had to feel something.

To me, there was nothing confusing about what was happening between us, even if we'd laid ground rules and told ourselves we'd only be friends.

Things change.

People fall in love. Glorious lives of happiness ensue.

I wanted to be able to tell our grandkids about the friends experiment that quickly failed because our feelings for each other couldn't be denied.

I was deluding myself.

Raf had left a pile of resumes on my desk after meeting with candidates to run the new Sonoma location once we got it built. We were probably a year out on needing to hire anyone, but Raf was thorough and that meant starting early, vetting the best candidates over an extended period of time, and locking in the best ones with contracts months before we even had a place for them to work.

His process never bothered me. If anything, I appreciated that his zealousness had landed us the best staff in the hospitality business at each property. It didn't go unnoticed with guests and his eye for people was one of the reasons I'd made him my partner.

But right now, I didn't want to look at resumes.

My mind was stuck in an endless loop of rehashing conversations I'd had with Isla since our weekend in Calistoga. And in thinking of the recent ones, it became ultra clear that I was moving forward into relationship territory and she wasn't.

My phone buzzed. It didn't sound like the usual tone for a text or a missed call, so I checked the screen and saw it was a keyword notification. I forgot that I'd typed in Isla's name as a keyword and accepted notifications from a couple of the gossip sites that were hassling her on the day Tom Stone's photos showed up with his Swedish model girlfriend.

At the time, I'd wanted to buffer Isla's mortification and help her weather the crap flying her way, and I'd forgotten to turn the alerts off.

The new notifications informed me that Tom and the Swedish model were finished. Rumor had it that she didn't know he had a serious girlfriend during the time she was seeing him, and she didn't want to be a homewrecker.

There was speculation Tom Stone was starting up again with his celebrity chef girlfriend.

Isla.

I felt a burning pit in my stomach picturing her with Tom, not because I gave a flying fuck about Tom Stone but because Isla belonged with me. I knew it in my bones.

And there Tom was again trying to ruin things. Just like he'd done with my girlfriend all those years ago when he'd convinced her to dump me. A mere days after I turned down his overture to finance my boutique hotels into a faceless, moneymaking conglomerate, he gave Lexi the hard sell and she bought it.

Apparently, all it takes to break up a relationship is a billion dollars and a chin that can cut glass.

I couldn't believe it was happening again.

The idea of Isla cooling things with me because she was going back to that asshole made me sick, but it made sense in a poetic injustice sort of way.

Of course she'd want to rekindle something with a guy she'd already invested a year with. How had I not seen that coming?

To her credit, she'd never pretended to love me. That was all me.

My mind was still reeling with how I'd allowed myself to fall for her given everything she'd explicitly said, when my phone pinged again, this time with a text message.

Isla: *Hey, what're you up to?*

This time, I waited to respond, not because I was playing games but because I didn't know what the hell to say.

Me: Not much.

Isla: Want to come over?

Did I want to come over? Not especially, but that's because I knew it was the last time I'd see her, and I wasn't ready for that.

But I needed to do the right thing for once.

Me: Sure.

~

I SHOWED up at her door fifteen minutes later with Japanese udon bowls and my heart in my throat.

Isla wrapped her arms around me as soon as I walked in the door. She leaned into me and laid her head on my chest. "I'm so glad to see you, you have no idea."

She was right. I had no idea because I didn't believe her anymore.

Or at least, I didn't believe that she could possibly feel what I was feeling and that hurt more than thinking she was a liar.

Nonetheless, I sat on her couch while she put out orange paisley placemats that her sister Becca had sewn for her onto the table and grabbed two beers from the fridge.

"Hey, ooh, you went to the good place. Thank you!" She seemed happy with the food choice and happy to see me.

Her phone started buzzing as soon as we sat down with the food. She kept apologizing, but something seemed off in the same way it had at the bakery the other day. I couldn't help but assume it was Tom.

She seemed distracted but not upset by whatever she was reading on the screen. She also seemed a little oblivious to me, which only made me more certain I was finally seeing things clearly.

On the surface, there was nothing different about the way she was with me, other than the texting disruptions.

She'd never wanted more than my friendship with benefits. She'd told me so time and again. I'd been kidding myself all along.

Realizing my stupidity, I sat on her couch making quiet conversation about I don't even know what for ten minutes while we ate.

When she got up to use the bathroom, her damn phone started in again.

I didn't want to pry into her private messages, but I had to know who kept texting her. If I was wrong about Tom, I'd admit to my mistake and apologize. I'd calm the hell down and we'd go on the way we had been. Or some fucking thing.

So I turned over the phone and saw one new text on the lockscreen. From Tom Stone. And it confirmed that he was meeting her at the bakery after hours. Like we had done a couple days before, when baking had led to dinner, which had led to sampling our finished bread and going upstairs to make use of her newly decorated office. The pillows had been the perfect touch.

But now, she was going to do the same thing with him.

It was like a single rock toppling off a mountain, bumping along slowly in the distance but picking up a few smaller bits as it went, sending all the loose stones and dirt into motion until the entire side of a mountain caved on itself and destroyed everything in its wake.

I loved her. I fucking loved her, and she just wanted to be my friend.

She's going to go back to him. And you're a lovestruck idiot.

Who wouldn't want to be with Tom Stone? Despite the cheating and the fact that he was clearly wrong for her, she'd invested a year with him and at thirty-four, she knew what she wanted.

I'd been deluded, thinking I could go from being the rebound guy to being *the* guy. I was only making myself miserable by hanging out with her all the time and pretending we were dating. I needed to cut bait. I should have done it a long time ago.

When she came out of the bathroom, I was standing up with my jacket in my hand. She looked around the room and back at me. "Going so soon?" she asked as though I was joking around.

I pointed at her phone. "You have a text."

She looked puzzled that I was pointing it out. "Okay . . ."

"Damn guy always gets what he wants. I don't know why I'm surprised," I muttered. I fucking hated him.

"I don't know what you're talking about."

"Tom Stone. Are you getting back together with him? *And* taking his money?"

She almost looked relieved as though she could finally be honest. "Oh. No, but he's persistent. He keeps coming back with better offers."

"Right. Of course he does." I had no reason to believe the tabloids, but she wasn't giving me much reason to believe her. Going into business with him, going to bed with him—was there even a difference?

And I knew the guy. He'd want both.

Isla's sisters had talked to her about having kids. Tom had good genes even if he was a son of a bitch.

"He's just trying to be helpful," she said.

"He's not, but whatever."

Being with Isla was starting to make me sadder than I figured I'd be without her. At least if I wasn't seeing her every day, I could try to focus on other things. Like the hotel in Sonoma I'd never want to return to because it only reminded me of her. And the new property, that amazing wine cave—I'd just have my subcontractors report back to me on the progress. Maybe I'd move away from San Francisco entirely, or at least away from the neighborhood.

"Tom just might be . . . easier. I don't know what else to do," she said.

Easier? I shook my head. It wasn't worth explaining it to her. "I'm gonna go and I . . . I don't think we should see each other anymore."

The shock registered on her face and her wide eyes fixed on me. "What? What do you mean?"

"I just think our whole friends-with-benefits thing has run its course."

She was speechless. I could tell I'd surprised her, but she wasn't arguing with me. "Um . . . wow. Okay . . . sure. If that's what you want." She seemed dazed—and hurt, which wasn't my intention.

Or maybe it was.

She didn't seem to have any idea how much it pained me to hear her blithely refer to us as friends over and over again.

"It is. I think it's time to end things," I said, a sickening, tinny taste in the back of my throat when I heard the words.

She didn't make a move, didn't take a step closer to me, or beg me to change my mind. Of course not. Why would she? "Can I ask why?"

"Sure. You can ask. It's because I love you. I am so in love with you it hurts, and I can't be your rebound guy anymore. Not that you need one now." I didn't want to be mean or spiteful, so I needed to leave before I said something I'd regret.

"Wait. You're telling me you love me and breaking up with me in the same sentence? In what world does that make any sense?"

"It just does."

"Can we talk about this? You're blindsiding me. If we could just talk, figure out how we both feel . . ."

"Isla, do you love me? I'm asking you flat out. It's not a hard question." Not hard if you know the answer.

She swallowed and ran a hand through her hair. "I just . . ."

She didn't finish the sentence, just stared at me like a rabbit right before it darts into the underbrush.

"No." I shook my head. If she felt what I did, she'd know by now. "I know how I feel. It's crystal clear. But I'm tired of waiting for you to catch up. I can't do this shit anymore."

"Owen, this doesn't make sense. I feel like we're not on the same page here."

She was right. She was a smart woman.

"We're definitely not." I leaned in and kissed her because I loved her and couldn't go without kissing her goodbye.

Then I walked away.

CHAPTER 28

$\mathcal{O}$wen

Raf was a good friend.

I'd known that for the past eight years we'd worked together, but nothing speaks friendship like showing up at the apartment of a guy who's just had his heart gutted and bringing tequila and a sixpack of beer.

He gave me a bro hug-slash-pat on the back and went straight for my kitchen where he started slicing up limes. We'd had more than a few work crises over the years, and he knew his way around my place.

I didn't even bother to get up off my couch when he came in. The door was unlocked and if a fleet of unarmed flat-footed robbers had tried to ransack the place, I wouldn't have cared enough to get in their way.

Lying on my back with an arm over my eyes felt like the right way to spend the rest of my life.

In under five minutes, Raf was back in my living room with

shot glasses for the tequila, an opener for the beer, and tortilla chips in a giant orange bowl I didn't know I had.

He poured the two shots, handed me a lime, and clinked my glass. The burn of the tequila went well with my mood.

Raf uncapped a beer and looked at me. "You look terrible. Just so you know."

"Thanks. And fuck off."

He laughed. "Boy, I knew you were in love with her, but this level of wallowing tells me she really had you. I'm sorry, man."

"You and me both." I popped the cap on a beer, but he'd bought some kind of lager I hated. I winced at the taste and poured another shot instead.

He studied me and sipped his beer. "You gonna be okay?"

I shrugged because I honestly didn't know. "Maybe. No. Who knows? I'm so done. I should've walked away sooner,' maybe it wouldn't hurt so fucking much now."

"Probably. I mean, you were bound to do it eventually."

What the hell did that mean? My head whipped around to look at him. "Come again?"

"This isn't new for you, man. I hate to break it to you." Raf took a swig of his beer and looked at me calmly like he was waiting for me to solve a Dixie cup riddle. But I had no idea what in the fancy blue moon he was talking about.

"What's that supposed to mean?"

To hell with the beer—I was sticking with tequila. I poured another shot.

"You shut people out when they don't do what you want."

I rolled my eyes at his idiocy. "Give me one example of when I've done that."

He laughed. "I can give you twenty. But for starters, your sister. I know it's a huge bummer that she found a way to be happy and not have you take care of her until she's old and in a rocker, but to not talk to her for five years? Come on."

I didn't want to get into a discussion about my sister. And it was hot as shit in my apartment, so I went to shove open the casement window. The wet foggy air slapped me in the face and it felt good.

"What's your point?"

Raf laughed again and shook his head. "My point is that it was goddamn heroic of you to basically raise a kid when you were a teenager. No one's begrudging you that. Then you sent her to college, which was, again, a superhero thing to do and she's lucky to have you. But what did you expect? Did you think she was going to move in with you afterward? Would you even have wanted that?"

I took a deep breath. He was maybe ten percent right. I shook my head ever so slightly.

"It's what every parent dreams of—their kid being independent enough to leave the flock and soar off on their own—but don't you think that every damn one of them cries about their empty nest? Every one. Why should you be any different? Why should she?"

"Because I was all she had."

"And she was all you had. But you found other people, made a life. Why shouldn't she? It never sounded to me like she was trying to cut ties. She was just trying to live her life."

The anger and frustration I'd felt for the past hour was starting to dissipate a tiny bit. The tequila was helping.

"So, fine. I didn't take it well that she moved forward and never came back. That's for me and her to solve someday." I thought about my sister, how she'd reached out after being nervous and hanging up so many times. That wasn't something a person did if they were cutting ties. "Or sometime sooner, who . . . who knows?"

Thinking about Jen in addition to Isla was making it hard to breathe. I went back to the window. Maybe I could force some air into my lungs so I didn't start sobbing in front of my closest friend.

"Dude, it's gonna be okay. I know you're broken up about Isla and I didn't mean to drag your sister into it too, except by way of example. You do push people away, and maybe you're doing that now to Isla, is all I'm saying."

"Oh, I'm definitely doing that. She needs to be pushed far away so I can take a deep breath eventually again without my lungs seizing up."

I'd barely made it out the door of her house before feeling overcome with an urge to both vomit and suffocate on the last breath I'd taken. Before I'd walked a block, I was calling Raf and telling him Isla and I were through. He didn't need any more information. He just came.

It felt like my soul was dying, knowing I wasn't going to see her again. No one had ever gotten me worked up like that before.

I'd never loved anyone as much as her before either, not even close.

I went back to the couch and slumped into the pillows with my tequila. This was how I'd spend the rest of my life. Raf was sitting close to the coffee table, so I pointed at my phone. "Hand me that, will ya?"

Raf looked wary. He picked up the phone and held it close, as if I was going to wrestle him for it. As if. "No drunk dialing. I won't allow it."

"I'm not gonna call her. I want to erase her number. Delete the photos of us. Come on, give it."

He looked sympathetic. "I'm not gonna let you do that either. Let's make a deal. Give me your phone and get on with your life. Use one of the other company phones. I'll put this one in a drawer, and if you come back to me in a month with the same request, I'll delete everything for you myself. But until then . . . all I'm saying . . . life is long, you know? Just . . . drink your tequila and live to build another hotel another day. Cool?"

It seemed like a foregone conclusion he'd be deleting everything a month from now and having to use a different phone only spelled hassle for me, but I was too beaten down to argue.

"Fine. Do what you want. And in a month, give me back my goddamned phone and do what I'm asking."

He nodded and slipped the phone into his pocket. It actually felt good to be rid of it. But it was the only thing that felt good.

sla

CAMILLE and I were in new territory—specifically the get-your-boss-through-the-most-depressing-breakup-in-the-history-of-breakups territory. And Owen and I hadn't even been officially a couple.

It was completely my fault. I saw that now.

For whatever chip on his shoulder he seemed to have about Tom—I'd looked at the text and seen what must have set him off —his bigger issue was with me.

He'd flat-out asked me if I loved him and I froze. It made no sense because I did love him. There was no question in my mind. But I'd been so shocked and confused that I hadn't been able to articulate anything at all.

Every time I started to roll out my dough, I thought about the day Owen and I had spent in here making bread and I started crying. My tears would drip down and get in the dough and I'd have to throw out the batch.

"This is no good," Camille said. "You cannot be here. Your bread will be full of tears, too salty."

"I have nowhere else to be."

I still didn't understand why Owen hadn't given me a chance to talk things through with him.

"He's a guy. A man of action, not thoughts. He made a decision and he needed to do something about it," Camille said.

"I know, but I thought he knew how I felt about him. How could he just leave?"

"Did you tell him how you felt?"

I hung my head. "No, I called him my rebound guy. I told him we were friends because I thought he wanted that too."

The coffee machine began the sputtering and spewing that signaled it was finished brewing. I went into the kitchen to grab us some cups. Then we sat at one of the tables in the café. Both of us had prep to do for the day's bakes, but I appreciated that she could tell my heart wasn't in it.

"You love him," she said. It struck me as odd that she wasn't asking—she was telling me.

"It's only been a month since Tom and I broke up."

"So what?"

"So a person can't get over a relationship and fall in love with someone else so fast."

"Oh, forgive me. I didn't know there was a rule book. Please explain what else a person can and cannot do with a guy who's so obviously the perfect one."

I wanted to talk some sense into her because she was being ridiculous, but I couldn't come up with a logical argument. "I don't know. I don't know the rules."

"That's because there aren't any, so don't feel so guilty about calling him a rebound guy. That seemed logical at first, but now it's clear that's not who he is to you."

"So what should I do? Should I call him? Text him?"

"Yes and yes. Do all the things. But apologize to him to start with. You have that thing we all hope for, *un fou d'amour*, so fix your mistakes. Do it now."

~

AFTER THAT, my week got worse. Two new landlords who'd given me the go-ahead were now jumping ship for Centinela Bread. It was pure economics, they said.

It was my own fault for relying on a handshake deal and not getting everything in writing upfront, but that was how I'd always done business because trust was key. If I needed a legal document to make sure a partner followed through and there was no implicit trust, what was the point?

So I followed up with each of them in person. I took Owen's advice and pushed the idea of my reputation and the farm-to-table nature of my business. I tried not to think about him—I just pressed forward with the logic he'd presented like it was an emotionless business deal.

By the end of my meetings, I felt like I'd done a good job of convincing the landlords that it would make them look good to have my business in their spaces. It was goodwill that money couldn't buy, even big money from a competitor who'd yet to show his or her face.

They agreed not to make any bold moves yet, but they wanted to warn me they had to consider their bottom line and Centinela was willing to pay enough to make it hard to say no.

Neither one would be more specific when I tried to press them on their timelines but they indicated that no matter how much money I offered in rent, Centinela would pay more.

Both got very quiet and ended the discussion.

To add to my overall crummy mood, I hadn't gone running in three days and I missed the endorphins that had become a pale substitute for happiness without Owen. I missed his deadpan declarations that were supposed to serve as questions.

I missed looking at him. I missed his eyes.

And I couldn't tell him. He hadn't replied to any of my texts and my calls went straight to voicemail. He'd probably blocked my number. Besides, he'd made it very clear that we were done.

Mornings had always been my favorite time at the bakery. I loved the sense of renewal and the unknown—the bread would always turn out a little differently and I never knew who might stop by. But I could always count on Owen being there.

I'd never realized what a comfort it was to see him in the mornings. More than that, I loved seeing his face.

I loved him.

Ugh, that's in the past. It has to be.

I had no idea what I needed to do to get over Owen, but I really wanted to figure it out so I could get start doing it. Sitting around in the kitchen eating bread was not the answer.

I started spending a little less time at work. Of course Owen had been right—my staff had been trained to run the place without me and if I ever hoped to expand, I couldn't be everywhere at once, so I needed to start letting go.

That meant I had to quit staring at the empty table against the wall and move on.

wen

I'D ALMOST FORGOTTEN I'd put Julia on a side project that I'd been mulling as a way of offering a better experience to our hotel guests. If I'm honest, I'd also seen it as a way to work with Isla down the road, which would never happen now.

But Julia was diligent, and she sent me a text telling me she'd finished a preliminary version of the drawings.

I didn't even want to see them. What was the point?

I'd look at them eventually, but I could think of ten other things I wanted to do more urgently. Having tea in a pit of alligators, for one.

Of course Julia was the first person I saw in the hallway that day. She smiled at me in the goofy way she always did, the bashful look that Raf interpreted as her "wanting to bone me."

It was just the way she always looked. I pushed him to ask her out instead.

Raf hadn't done it yet, partly because he had a whole ritual of building up to his eventual seduction. He took her out for working lunches a few times and she started to loosen up a little bit, foregoing the usual blazers and conservative dresses for an odd variety of fashions that didn't speak to one particular style.

Today, she had on one of her strange get-ups that looked like she'd bought it at a children's clothing store in Japan. Her skirt was tiny and bright orange, and she wore it with royal blue tights and a fitted white sweater with anime characters on it. Her lips were a darker pink than usual and she'd swept her hair to one side in a giant clip.

The clip looked like it was teetering on the side of her head, about to fall down and take the pile of hair with it.

I mentally high-fived Raf for getting her to leave her comfort zone a little bit. She looked happier, and for the first time, she looked me in the eye when she spoke. "Thanks for your feedback on the designs. I put together some revisions. Want to see them?"

"Oh yeah, about that, it's not super urgent."

I saw her visibly deflate, which made me feel terrible. She'd obviously worked hard. "But I'd really like to see them," I said.

"Great. Now?" The flush rose in her cheeks.

I checked the time and realized it was coming on six at night, which was when a lot of people left if they had families to go home to or social lives to keep afloat. Julia worked traditional hours, and I was hesitant to ask her to stay late, especially when it was ridiculous to push forward with the designs.

Isla and I would probably never speak again, so what did any of it matter? I had to be some special kind of masochist to keep moving forward with concepts she'd never see, but maybe I just needed to torture myself a little bit more by seeing my vision for her bakeries come to life even if they died on the page.

Julia pushed her glasses up on her nose and shrugged at me. "I don't mind staying late if you want to work."

I felt the hollow rumble in my stomach remind me I'd skipped lunch and if we sat in my office for another hour, it would be eight before I could grab dinner. "Are you hungry? We could grab a bite and work while we eat."

Her glasses slipped down again, and she pushed them up and stared at me. Her eyes looked bigger than usual through the thick lenses and I wondered if she'd worn glasses since she was a kid. Knowing how self-conscious she was, I didn't ask. "Sure, I could eat."

"Great." I might have sounded a little too enthusiastic and I saw the shock on her face. "Sorry, I skipped lunch and as soon as I said the word dinner, my mind went to pizza. Do you eat pizza?"

Her expression said she still thought I was strange, but she nodded. "I eat pizza."

"Meet me in the lobby in ten and we'll find a place." She nodded again and went toward the cubicle where she'd been working all day.

I turned back to my office to grab my stuff. Maybe if Julia helped me finish the drawings I'd started, I could get some closure. I desperately needed to stop thinking about Isla every goddamned minute, but I wondered if I ever would.

There was no doubt I'd always love her. I'd given up the ghost on thinking I'd ever get over her, which meant I'd end up being a shitty boyfriend to the next woman I dated and probably end up alone forever.

For now, though, I'd keep myself distracted with work, even if it was work I'd started when Isla and I were still together . . . or whatever we actually were.

When I got back to the lobby, Julia was waiting for me wearing a tiny pink backpack instead of a purse and carrying a sketchpad and toolbox. She'd taken the clip out of her hair, thank God, because I wouldn't get through a conversation without staring at the clip, waiting for gravity to take over.

"There's a decent place near campus, but it'll be full of college students. Do you care?" I asked her. Pizza or not, there was almost no restaurant near the office that wouldn't be filled with Stanford kids. Sometimes their energy fueled me, so I didn't mind, but Julia was the one whose creative focus I needed, so I'd defer to her.

"Um, maybe not near campus. It'll be too loud, don't you think?"

"Okay, well, you live in the city, right? We can head toward home and find a place there."

She brightened at that. "Oh, there's a great place in the Mission that I love. Can we go there?"

"As long as they have food, I'm happy."

"Great." She told me the name, I plugged it into my GPS, and a half hour later, we were at a giant table that just happened to be a perfect size for her sketch pad and a pizza. In a fucked up twist on Murphy's Law, her go-to pizza place was on Valencia Street, just a few blocks from Isla's bakery.

My mind immediately wandered to her and wondered what she was doing.

Stop it.

When I finished my mental conversation, I found Julia looking at me expectantly.

Right, I'd called this meeting.

Julia jotted down some notes and positioned her sketchpad in a way that allowed for our plates and glasses to fit comfortably and still give her ample room to present her drawings.

"Lemme guess, you come here and work sometimes?" I asked.

She blushed and nodded. Then she got down to business, sketching a few modifications on the plans she'd already rendered. "It makes it feel less like work when I'm eating at the same time. Sometimes I have a beer." She said the last part like she was divulging the mysteries of the universe.

"Let's have some beer," I said. Or straight tequila.

We agreed on a pizza that was half Hawaiian pineapple—for her—and half tomato basil for me. She sat across the large oak table from me with her back ramrod straight like an attentive student and a pencil poised over a spiral notebook, ready to jot down any other thoughts I had about her work. I desperately needed her to relax. "Julia."

"Yes?" Her pencil edged closer to the paper.

"Put down the pencil. Let's at least wait until our beers come. Just . . . relax," I said. The concept seemed to make her nervous. "Have you and Raf been having a good time?"

She nodded.

"He's a good guy. I'm glad you like him." She nodded again. This was getting painful. "Julia, do I make you nervous or something?"

She looked down at the table. "Not nervous, but you're my boss and I'm mindful of saying the right thing."

"There isn't a right thing. Okay? I'm just making conversation. If you don't want to talk about Raf or any other dumb thing I happen to bring up, just say so. I don't subscribe to the whole boss-employee thing. We're equals. We have different skillsets but we're all just doing a job."

She nodded slowly and finally . . . finally . . . she smiled. "Okay, boss. In that case, I really like Raf, but between you and me, he's not really my type. And also . . . is he a little bit of a prude? He seems almost asexual."

While I was busy hoisting my jaw back up from the table, our waiter delivered our beers. Julia looked at me expectantly, but I wasn't even going to touch that one. Raf was probably the horniest guy I knew, and he'd laugh his ass off if he'd heard what she just said.

For the rest of dinner, I made sure we only talked about work.

CHAPTER 31

sla

IT WAS OFFICIAL—A half dozen almond croissants and a good-sized glass of absinthe proved no match for the sadness I felt without Owen.

He told you he loved you, and you said nothing.

The self-torture had been thorough. I'd run countless miles up steep hills, I'd wallowed at home with Dunkin Donuts and bad cop shows that guaranteed I wouldn't witness any kissing, and I'd talked the ear off of every one of my sisters. And my mom.

It had been almost two weeks and I didn't feel any better. The loss felt just as huge and I felt just as awful as the night he walked out. If anything, I felt worse.

I sent him a text.

Me: Hey, can we find a time to talk?

Me: If you're free sometime, maybe grab a drink?

I sounded more casual than I felt. When the friendly texts

247

didn't get a response, I threw caution to the wind. What did I have to lose by telling him what I wanted to say?

Me: Owen, I'm sorry. I hate apologizing via text but you're not giving me a choice. So . . . I'm sorry. You're more to me than just a rebound guy.

I figured that had to earn me some kind of response. Or even an emoji. I was desperate for anything. But after a day and a half, I gave up hoping that he'd respond. It only added to my mood.

Well, if he was going to ignore me anyway, there was no harm in letting him know the final damning bit of truth.

Me: Also, I love you.

I didn't feel the need to get all flowery about it. Simple was best. He didn't have to respond. He probably wouldn't. But I needed him to know.

When I got no response, as expected, I tried to move past it, even though the giant lump in my throat wouldn't budge.

Nothing good was going to happen by mulling this stuff over for another hour. I'd do better by heading home and starting a new watercolor painting. Watching the pale paint colors bleed on the page made me happy in a deep soulful way. I'd grab a photograph of a gorgeous beach I wouldn't have time to visit anytime soon and paint it. I'd been at the bakery long enough.

When I stepped outside, I found the night cooler and foggier than I'd expected, but it felt nice to walk and feel the mist on my face. Someone had parked in my usual spot behind the building again, so I'd circled the neighborhood a few times this morning and had finally found a space on one of the side streets a few blocks away.

I almost regretted that the walk wasn't longer because it felt so nice to be outside.

As I walked down Valencia, I saw a couple exit a pizza place. The woman caught my eye because she was wearing a bright orange skirt and I immediately thought it looked like something Cherry would wear.

Then I noticed the black portfolio under the arm of the guy—just like the one I'd seen under Owen's arm a few mornings when he was heading to work. My stomach dropped.

It looked like Owen, but maybe after thinking about him nonstop, everyone looked like him.

No . . . I was pretty certain it was him. The slope of his shoulder and the flick of his hair as he shook it off his forehead—if it wasn't Owen, the man across the street bore a striking resemblance.

Too striking.

He moved the same way, stood the same way.

There was no question it was him. Backing into a doorway, I felt like an unrepentant spy, but I couldn't stop watching the two of them.

From where I stood, I could tell he was laughing at something she said. She had a cute figure in her orange skirt and heeled booties, but I couldn't really see her face. Did it matter?

When she took a step closer and looked up at him, I felt a sharp pang in my chest followed by a surge of bile at the mere thought that it was Owen and that he might be on a date. And yet...I had no claim on him.

She stood on her toes and pressed her lips to his. I squinted my eyes to bring them into clearer focus but the mist in the air made it hard to see his expression.

Is he happy? Does he love her?

Rationally, I knew he probably hadn't met and fallen in love with someone in two weeks. Maybe it was just a first date.

Regardless, he'd moved on.

We were no longer in the friend zone or any zone. We were nothing.

It hurt so much I found myself pressing a hand to my chest to counter the pain, but it wasn't going away. I stood there like a lurker, watching someone else's love story unfold and wishing it were mine.

Owen didn't seem to linger or deepen the kiss, but he didn't stop her either. I was really hoping he'd pitch a fit or yell and walk away, but he didn't.

They moved a few paces down the block to where she popped the lock on her car and slid into the driver's seat. Owen leaned in before closing her door. I couldn't tell if he kissed her again, and I couldn't see her face to determine her level of cute, but so what?

He was with her and I was standing in a doorway, filled with regret.

She drove off and he turned and walked in the opposite direction of where I stood. Eventually, he turned the corner, and I was left only with a searing emptiness in my gut and a hurt so much more intense than what I'd felt seeing pictures of Tom with another woman.

After denying my feelings for Owen and defining him in the most unflattering terms, I'd pushed him to find someone who saw him as a great guy and a nice date, which he was. How come I couldn't just do that? Why did I constantly try to label what we had?

I was a drama queen, wallowing over my ex, complaining about my business, and never taking him at face value—as a date, as a relationship, as a person.

No wonder he'd grown tired of waiting around.

wen

I WASN'T GOING to lie. It felt nice to have someone desire me.

I'd been feeling so beaten down by Isla's brush-offs that when Julia turned her face up to mine, I'll admit that I considered her for a split second.

But only for a second.

Julia had been dropping not-so-subtle hints all night long about how Raf wasn't the kind of guy she was looking for and gazing at me from under her spidery lashes in a way she probably thought was cute.

I ignored all her innuendos and stayed focused on the work. She tweaked the sketches to get closer what I envisioned, and when we'd finished our pizza and beer, I paid the check and herded us out the door.

The moment her lips turned up toward mine, I froze—not because I was swept up in the moment, but because I immediately knew I didn't want to be there. I didn't want her or anyone else.

It wasn't a matter of finding someone—anyone—to substitute for what I wasn't getting from Isla. If I couldn't be with Isla, I didn't want Julia or anyone else.

I didn't care if that meant I'd spend a lifetime alone. The alternative was worse—trying to be with someone else and always comparing her to the woman I couldn't have.

But that didn't mean Julia should go wanting. I tucked her into her car and leaned down to talk to her. "Raf's a really good guy. And I guarantee you he likes all the sex. I'm just saying, maybe give him a chance."

She smiled and kissed me on the cheek. "I know he is. I was just kidding before. It's fun to get a rise out of you. Sorry if it's inappropriate, boss."

I laughed for probably the first time in over a week and it felt good. "Thanks for that."

"For what?"

"Just . . . thanks. I'll see you at work."

I watched her drive off and turned in the other direction toward my car.

At home, I made some more tweaks to the designs she'd handed off. The sketches were first-rate, and my instincts about her skill had been right. She'd turned all the wayward thoughts about what might work within the scheme of my hotels and made them beautiful architectural visions.

And I really hoped she'd take my advice about Raf. She'd be good for him.

Meanwhile, I had to decide what I wanted to do with the full architectural renderings once they were finished. Maybe I'd just roll them up and store them in a tube. I couldn't think about that right now.

When I checked my phone, I saw a slew of missed texts from

my sister. In a moment of conciliatory guilt after talking to Raf, I'd left her a message, saying maybe we could talk.

The texts were effusive and joyful. They immediately reminded me of what Jen was like as a kid, when it was just the two of us. We were always happy together because we knew we had each other—it was a vow and a choice. Maybe that was why I took it badly when she didn't come back.

Jen: Hey! Happy to hear from you. Yes, I'd love to talk.

Jen: I miss you.

Jen: I know I'm annoying, but I'm excited to talk, so call me as soon as you can.

Jen: And I know it's premature since we haven't talked yet, but I'd love to see you. Can we?

Instead of debating my words or their implied meaning, I typed my response and sent it.

Me: I'd like that. A lot.

I thought about it for another minute. Then I sent one more text.

Me: Love you, sis.

I immediately felt better.

When I scrolled through the rest of the missed calls, I found a message from my lawyer. I hadn't called him, and he never phoned unless it was urgent. He billed in five-minute increments, so any call he made had better be important.

When I listened to the message, I understood immediately why he'd reached out. He had information that definitely interested me, information Isla would want to know.

But it wasn't my job to be that guy for her anymore. She could figure it out on her own or talk to the lawyer herself or just lie in the bed she'd made.

Or maybe I'd be the bigger man and pass the info along. I couldn't decide.

Maybe if I slept on it, everything would be clear.

Work had gotten really busy now that the design phase had started on the Sonoma property. I needed to line up new contractors since my in-house team would still be finishing up work on the Bodega Bay location for the next six months. We'd be ready to break ground long before then and I had to find the right guys for the job.

The demolition team had called to check in when they saw the old building on the property. I still hadn't decided whether or not to let them knock it down. Rationally, I knew the building was a gem that would sell the hotel experience to guests, but emotionally, every time I thought of it, I pictured Isla dancing in the tasting room, and it gutted me.

Two more weeks until Raf would give me my phone back. Then I'd erase every trace of her. Maybe then I'd have the closure I needed.

CHAPTER 33

wen

I DIDN'T GO OUT to lunch very often, partly because I generally consumed so much bread on a given morning that I had no appetite until way later in the day. I also liked drinking a pressed juice at my desk and keeping my head down more than I liked spending an hour at a restaurant.

But sometimes investors or in-demand designers wanted to eat out and I couldn't say no.

I'd just come from a meeting at a trendy watering hole that served me a single scallop on a mint leaf with some raspberry coulis and charged me twenty-eight dollars for the privilege.

My landscape architect had wanted the four-course tasting menu, but I didn't have the patience for that. After I ate my scallop and assured her that all the plant configurations she'd specified for the new hotel could be worked into our budget, she was happy to let me go back to the office and finish the tasting without me.

I just wasn't in the mood. Hadn't been for three weeks and two days.

What I wanted was some real food, so I hopped in line at a food truck selling burgers and pie on the way back to my car. I noticed the Pie of the Day was apple and a nauseated pit settled in my stomach. If I could go just one day without something reminding me of Isla, it would be a cause for celebration.

"Hey, Owen, right?" The woman in front of me in line was looking up at me. She was a good foot shorter than me, but I noticed she had on Vans, so she didn't have a fighting chance at height.

I didn't recognize her right away, although something about her looked familiar. "Yeah, tell me your name again?"

"Tatum. I'm the youngest one. Isla's sister. We met at my brother's house in the hills."

She was the quietest of all the sisters and we hadn't gotten much of a chance to talk, but I remembered her as soon as she said her name. "Of course, right. I'm so sorry. It was just out of context. Do you . . . you work in Palo Alto?"

"Yeah, at Boxspring. I'm on what will surely be the only lunch break I'll get this month, so I'm celebrating with a burger."

It was almost impossible to be the sullen asshole I'd been for the past month around Tatum. She was quiet but exuded such bright energy that I found myself feeling slightly better in her presence. She reminded me a little bit of Isla.

I offered her the best smile I could muster. "Well, I hope you get out more than once in the next month, but just in case . . ." I lowered my voice to a whisper. "Get the bacon *and* the cheese."

She laughed. "I plan to." An awkward silence followed while we waited. I felt like I needed to ask the obvious.

"So how's your sister? How's Isla?" I didn't really want to talk about her but it was the right thing to do.

Tatum leveled me with a look that seemed to say I was an idiot who ought to know exactly how she was. I guess I did. I wasn't an idiot—I could connect the dots. "Right. I assume she's good? Happy with Tom, or whatever?"

Now Tatum's eyes bugged out like I was an even bigger dolt. "Isla's not with Tom. She hates him. And she's not happy. She's miserable."

I hadn't been back to the bakery, so I had no idea what was happening with her expansion plans. Maybe she was still having trouble with Centinela.

Or Tom. Or a different guy.

I shrugged. Did I need details? I felt too worn down to care or to try and put another face to a guy with his arm around Isla.

"Oh. I guess I read some rumors," I said.

She rolled her eyes. "You know who starts the rumors, don't you? Tom. He wants her back so much that he'll tell the gossip rags they're together like that will make it true."

"Okay, whatever. So, she's fine though?" I needed to know. Even if I couldn't be with her, I still cared about her. I wanted her to be okay even if I wasn't.

Tatum looked like she was getting ready to throw a punch and I had no doubt she could inflict some damage. She was petite but feisty. "No. She's a wreck. Just like you."

I didn't like hearing she was unhappy, but it did give me some small bit of satisfaction that Tom didn't get what he wanted. "So what are you gonna do about it?" Tatum asked.

"What am *I* going to do? I'm going to do nothing. I can't be her friend—been, there, done that, bought ten shirts. I wish I could be a bigger guy about it, but I'm not. I can't be her friend. It's too hard."

It was Tatum's turn to order, but when the cashier asked what she wanted, Tatum held up a finger and spun around to face me. "I don't think she's in the market for a friend, and that was never what you two were. Just talk to her. I'm no relationship expert, and I only saw you together for half a minute, but that was enough."

"Enough for what?"

"Enough to see you two are every relationship goal I didn't even know I had. She loves you. She's just really, really stubborn. And sometimes she forgets to eat."

For the first time in three weeks and two days, I smiled. "Yeah, I've noticed that." I was still digesting what she'd said and trying to square it with everything I knew to be true about Isla.

I wasn't sure if I believed the love part.

"Trust me on this. I may be the youngest, but I'm the smartest sister. She only loves you. She's in love with you and she's miserable without you. Just . . . stop wallowing and call her or something. Have a burger together. I'm sure it will all make sense from there."

The woman in the food truck was getting impatient, so Tatum whirled around to give her an order, but not before she threw her arms around me. "See you someday, future brother-in-law."

I laughed. That might have been a stretch.

But hearing her words gave me hope. I knew how I felt, and if there was half a chance Isla felt the same way . . . maybe we could get a burger.

CHAPTER 34

sla

I'D WOKEN up to my phone pinging with a text. I was used to getting the occasional question from one of my bakers when I wasn't there in the mornings, so I braced to answer some inquiry about fixing a broken flour scale or some café snafu.

But the text was from a number I didn't recognize. Not one of my bakers. It was brief.

Unknown number: Tom Stone is a shadow investor in Centinela Bread. Thought you should know.

My heart started hammering in my chest and I worried for a second that I might be having a heart attack.

Was this somebody's idea of a sick joke?

Why an anonymous text?

Is there a chance it's true?

Something about the tone of it made me think it was from Owen, but it wasn't his number and he wasn't speaking to me. Besides, what difference did it make who sent it?

I spent the rest of the morning on phone calls with the "ruthless" lawyer Owen had connected me with weeks earlier. He sent me screenshots of all the information he could find to show that Tom's venture fund was the primary backer of Centinela Bread. And Tom had invested personally. I was in shock.

He couldn't have known they were gunning for me, right? If he did, it would almost make him complicit.

Tom Stone was a cutthroat businessman, but I was still his girlfriend when this all started. At least I thought I was. Now I couldn't even recall the exact timing of everything.

"It's someone who knows an awful lot about your business. Down to dollar amounts that you spend on flour and employee pensions." Blake's words echoed as I stood in the empty café that I'd almost lost thanks to my conniving ex.

I knew Tom would meet me when I texted him. He'd figure I was planning to roll over and give him what he wanted.

Waiting for Tom to show up, I took stock of the situation I'd been blind to for countless months. Of course Tom had been working an angle, and he'd done it so well and with such finesse that I'd never seen it coming.

After all the years I'd spent dating men who were busy building their brands and their companies on the backs of smaller, less-savvy business owners who had no choice but to do their bidding when faced with Goliath, I'd have thought I'd recognize a player when I met one—when I crawled into his bed and told him details about where I was looking for potential new locations.

But Tom had been better at playing the game than anyone I'd ever met. He'd fooled me, cheated on me, and still had me thinking twice about whether I should let him bail me out. He was the true master of the game.

When he walked into the bakery, just as he had so many times before, with his confident comportment, his effortless, gorgeous appearance, and his cocky smile, I saw a different man than the one I'd known.

"There she is," he said.

It used to make me smile.

Now I wanted to throw something at him and was only disappointed that the heaviest nearby item was a raisin scone.

"I got a table for us at Mercer's at seven. They have a two-month wait but I pulled some strings." He always pulled strings, and everyone just fell in line to do his bidding. I couldn't believe I ever found that attractive.

"I'm not going to dinner with you." I was seething.

He shrugged. "Listen babe, I don't know if your flour didn't rise or what, but fine." He held his hands up as though he didn't want to argue with someone who was clearly premenstrual and crazy.

I closed my eyes and shook my head. "I just need to know—when we first started dating, had you already decided you were going to use me to get information that would help Centinela Bread run me out of business? Or did that idea occur to you one night after I'd given you a blow job?"

His face betrayed his surprise, but I wasn't sure if that was because I'd found him out or because he'd always considered 'blow job' an inelegant term. Didn't stop him from enjoying them.

"Isla. No, you don't have the correct information."

He put his hands out, pleading. His expression was hurt, as though I'd insulted his very ethical core and his sensitive feelings. He was convincing as the misunderstood gentleman.

"Your company is the principal backing investor for Centinela Bread. They've been systematically going after every location I targeted for my expansion. You knew about every one of them. Are you honestly telling me it's just a coincidence?"

"Yes. It must be." He was a thespian, I had to give him credit. Even when faced with irrefutable facts, he still kept up his act.

I rolled my eyes. "Come on, Tom. There are no coincidences in your business. You're the one who informed me of that. Again, back when we were in bed. Tell me, do you do all your manipulation on behalf of clients on your back?"

"Well, now you're just being crass."

"Please, after a year together, do me the courtesy of at least being honest. I don't care that you did it—well, I do—but I need to know what I'm up against. Is the plan to go into every market where I am until they run me out of town? Take every restaurant contract?"

He let out a deep exhale. His eyes looked vacant. It was odd for him not to have the focused determination to slay the world. "They're not interested in that. The restaurant stuff was designed to rattle you. They just want the locations."

"Fine. I can deal with that. It's fine," I said. It was business, and Centinela Bread could offer more money per square foot than I could. In a market economy, that made them the winner. I didn't need Finn's economic brilliance to understand that. I just needed to know I wasn't under attack personally.

I also needed him to say the words, admit what he'd done.

"And so we're perfectly clear, you gave them my business plan, helped them to destroy everything I wanted to do."

"Technically, yes, I did use what I knew about your business to feed Centinela some information about how to break into the Bay Area market."

"And right after our breakup...that's when they came out in full force, calling all my clients, going after my locations. Was that just you twisting the knife after the pictures of you and what's-her-name came out?"

"Giselle."

"I don't give a shit what her name is! Jesus, Tom!" I was mad at myself for letting him rile me, but he was so frustrating.

He stood there in his pinstriped sport coat and expensive jeans and Ferragamo loafers, which I'd always hated. He crossed his arms and stared at me like I wasn't worth a response. Finally, ever so slightly, he nodded. "I was trying to get your attention."

"You can't be serious." I dated him for over a year and didn't know the man at all. "How are you that spiteful?"

"I'm completely serious. It's not spite, it's affection. I want you back. I can call off the dogs anytime. That's why I kept leaving you messages. I just wanted you to see me again."

I'd had enough. "Could you leave now?" I asked, pointing to the door.

"You're going to let Centinela shut you down? You don't want my help?"

"No. I'm good."

He shook his head, scowling at me. Not a hair was out of place, not a wrinkle in his starched white shirt. He ate people for sport all day long.

Nodding, he looked at me knowingly, as though he had one more bullet in his gun. "Heard you're seeing Owen Miller," he said, apropos of nothing.

I had no idea where he got his information, but Tom was nothing if not thorough. He did his due diligence, so if he wanted to know how I was spending my time, he'd find out.

"Not anymore. Not that it's any of your business." I hated having to put my time with Owen in the past, but I might as well own it.

He nodded, a satisfied smirk on his face. "Hmph."

"What's that supposed to mean?" I hated how Tom dangled information like bait. Everything was a manipulation. "You know what? Forget it. I don't care."

Nothing bothered Tom more than people who were indifferent to his wiles, but that wasn't why I was shutting him down. I really didn't care what he had to say.

Unfortunately, that only fueled his desire to tell me. "Just thinking that he must still be pretty pissed at me."

I knew he was baiting me. "I know you tried to do business with him and he turned you down. That's not news to me."

Now he smiled like a shark, savoring the sight of a minnow who was cornered. Tom waited a few moments for effect, nodding with that smug victorious expression. "He didn't tell you, did he?"

Rolling my eyes, I shook my head. "Just say what you're going to say. Obviously, you're enjoying this. Just get on with it. What don't I know?"

Tom could not have looked more satisfied. "I broke up his relationship back then. His girlfriend left him for me."

I couldn't help the shock that must have shown on my face. Tom looked satisfied, but I didn't care about him. Was this true?

"You're lying." He had to be. It was just another manipulation.

"Not at all. Why would I?"

True, he had no reason to lie.

Messing with someone's heart was a whole other level of cruel than playing business hardball. My heart broke for Owen, knowing that Tom had stooped to ruining his relationship.

No wonder he'd been so freaked about the text that said I was making plans to meet Tom. And I'd only confirmed his concerns by saying that Tom could offer me something, that it would be easier. Oh my God. How did I not see it?

He was a guy who didn't stay friends with his exes. Once they were done, he was done.

"Yeah. See? Don't ever underestimate me, Isla. I'll have Centinela be sure to sign the contracts for their new locations in the morning." If he'd been a wolf, this would have been the moment he bared his teeth to show me he'd always be the alpha dog.

Instead, he put his hands out. A concession. "It could have gone differently, you know. I told you I wanted you back."

He had. At the time, I hadn't known what I was up against. But now that I did, I just felt exhausted.

As long as I could hang onto my one original location and continue doing what I did well, I'd persevere. I'd find other places to expand. Tom would find some other pet project where he could unleash his wrath, and eventually, he'd leave me alone.

Tom took a step closer to me, his face still a maze of undecided feelings. "I'm . . . I regret that I took advantage of our relationship. I'd assumed we'd be together, and I could make it up to you. Anyway, it's . . . regrettable."

"You can't even say the words, can you?" It amused me that he was having such a difficult time trying to be a better man than he was. "It's good, actually. I'd hate to hear you apologize if you didn't really mean it. Better to say nothing."

"I am sorry. I've never doubted you, Isla. As I said, I regret that things didn't work out for us, but I know you'll land on your feet. You always do."

He was right. I did always land on my feet, despite guys like him.

So I didn't yell at him and I didn't smack his face, though in hindsight, I found it...regrettable. I opened the back door for him and silently stood there while he looked me up and down. After the standoff, he shook his head and walked out.

Then I went over to the pastry area where Camille kept a bottle of absinthe and grabbed one of the glass tumblers from the café.

I poured myself a healthy dose of what tasted like death and forced it down. Liquid courage. I'd need it because I was about to hand over my heart.

I hoped I wasn't too late.

CHAPTER 35

sla

I WAS RUNNING a risk when I knocked on Owen's door. He could fling the door open wearing only boxers, and I could catch a glimpse of the woman with the cool glasses and the mini skirt I'd seen him with outside the pizza place.

Or worse, I could hear them having sex from the other side of the door.

There were other possibilities, like Owen answering and standing there expressionless with his arms crossed, waiting for me to say what I'd come to say. I couldn't decide what was worse —seeing him with someone else or seeing him angry and indifferent to me.

It didn't matter.

I'd say what I needed to tell him and leave before I started sobbing. There was no question I was going to cry if he was as hard and unfriendly as he'd been the last time I'd seen him. I'd cried for a week after that.

I heard noise on the other side of the door and saw a brush of light cross the peephole. He saw it was me. Would he actually open the door?

Taking a step back for a hasty retreat, I was sort of surprised when the door whipped open. Owen stood there in a San Francisco Giants sweatshirt and gym shorts.

He didn't look angry or indifferent. He looked...like a guy I needed in my life and not just as a friend.

"I love you," I blurted. It wasn't how I planned to open, but that was beside the point.

It was the most important piece of information I had, and he needed to know.

He looked momentarily surprised, either at the admission or at my timing. "You do." He wasn't asking me, and I loved hearing that familiar voice telling me what we both already knew to be true.

I nodded. "I do. So no matter what happens from this moment forward, I just want to make sure you know. There's no doubt in my mind that I want to be with you—not as a friend or a friend with benefits or any of my other ridiculous titles. I want to be *with* you because you're the person I love."

He tilted his head, and his eyes roamed over me from head to toe, ending by locking on mine. That comforting blue. I'd missed it so much.

"Nice shirt," he said. I looked down at the T-shirt he'd bought me in Healdsburg with the lettering that spelled out, 'you had me at merlot.'

"Someone I like a lot gave it to me."

It got me the barest inkling of a smile.

He looked like shit, like he hadn't shaved in a week, and I could see from his wrinkled sweatshirt and messy hair that he'd probably given up on looking in the mirror. And I wanted him more than ever. I still didn't know if I'd get him back, but I had to try.

I couldn't look away from his eyes, which pinned me with an intensity I hadn't seen before. I had no idea what it meant.

"Owen . . ."

He didn't answer. Just watched me warily. I knew I was the one who needed to explain. So to start, I proffered my loaf of bread. "In case you still like this stuff."

He took it. "Thanks. I do still like it. I also like the woman who bakes it. Even more than the bread, actually."

I took a deep breath, then let it out and said what I came to say. "Owen, I'm sorry I didn't tell you how I felt that night at my house. I did love you then, but you caught me off-guard, and I was confused about Tom and—"

"I really don't want to talk about Tom." Saying his name seemed to visibly distress him. I put up a hand.

"This has nothing to do with him or anyone else. I wasn't fair to you and I apologize for not giving us real chance."

He folded his arms across his chest. "Did you want to? When we were spending time together? Did you want it to be something real?"

I nodded. I almost couldn't bear to look at him out of fear I'd need to blink and he'd be gone.

I'd missed seeing him so much it hurt.

"It never occurred to me that I could fall in love with someone on the same day as a breakup. But that was me and my titles again, which was unfair to you. I hate that I kept pushing you away. Loving you was never really up for negotiation—it just took over. And I get that it's been a month, and you've probably moved on, but at least now you know. Not that it changes anything."

I wasn't sure if there was any hope for a future, but I felt better letting him know how I felt—that he was wanted and valued.

"What do you mean? It changes everything," he said quietly, his expression softening.

I didn't see how. But then, I'd proven in the past that I could be a little dense about these things.

"Do you want to come in?" he asked, moving out of the doorway to make room for me to walk past him. I still felt like I ought to look out for girlfriends lurking in the corners but there was no one visible.

Just us.

Owen closed the door and walked over to where I stood in the middle of his living room.

I couldn't speak. My brain had gone AWOL. I couldn't articulate a single word to express my feelings when I saw what was hanging on the rolling white boards—three of them now—in his living room.

They were architectural renderings, in color, of bakery cafés with my logo painted on a shingle over the main doors.

There were bread kitchens and outdoor terraces. I looked closer and saw sustainable gardens detailed with a key identifying the different plants.

In all, there were six drawings attached to the whiteboards that took up most of the empty space in the room.

When I turned around to look at Owen, my eyes still round with disbelief, his gaze burned into me with the loving heat I'd missed every day for the past month. "Are these . . .?" I couldn't even ask the question, so dumbstruck by the idea that he'd done this for me.

Hands in his pockets, Owen took a step closer to me, tentatively, as though I was an untamed animal he might spook. He nodded. "Designs for six locations."

I shook my head, still in disbelief. Then I looked closer at the words at the top of each drawing and noticed something about the locations—Healdsburg, Calistoga, Bodega Bay, Sausalito . . .

"These are all places where you have hotels," I said, finally starting to understand. "You want me to expand Victorine in those locations?"

269

He rubbed the back of his neck as though he was reconsidering his plan for all of this. "It's not my decision. It was just a thought. Victorine could be adjacent to the hotels, supplying the restaurants, which are all gunning for their Michelin stars, and catering to the locals as well. The hotel properties are large. There's space for both."

I had a momentary bout of self-doubt and worried he was only doing this because he felt sorry for me. But before I could articulate that, he was shaking his head. "No, this is not a pity offer. I come out the winner here, trust me, and so do the hotel guests."

"I can't . . . believe this. I . . . don't know what to say."

"Say yes."

I'd spent so long making things complicated between the two of us, and the truth was that everything I wanted could be boiled down to that one word—yes.

Also giddy, excited, and overwhelmed.

"Yes." And because I couldn't stand to go one second more without touching him, I flew at him.

Luckily, he caught me. I wrapped my legs around his waist and my arms around his neck. "I'm so sorry for letting you walk away. I've regretted it every day since then and I shouldn't have been so stubborn. But when you didn't respond to my texts, I gave up hope a little bit."

He shook his head and cringed a little bit. "You texted me?"

"Um, yeah. I said I loved you, but you didn't respond. Obviously." Why was I telling him what he already knew?

"The night I left your house, I gave Raf my phone. For a month." He pulled a company phone out of his pocket and looked at the date. "I've got three days left with this one."

That made no sense. Who gives away their phone?

"Why?"

"I dunno. Raf had this theory that life is long, or some shit he told me when I was broken up over you and blitzed on tequila. I think he just believed we'd work things out, and he didn't want me deleting all evidence of you, which was my plan at the time. There are some really nice pictures from that wine cave in Sonoma." He smiled, and I recalled every one of those picture-perfect spots.

"Smart man. We oughtta get him a hooker as a gift."

His eyes nearly bugged out of his head. "What?!"

"Kidding. Sorry." I pushed my hands up into his hair and tipped my forehead to his.

"Listen, I know people have let you down. I know people have loved you and left, but that's not me. That will never be me. I love you and I will always love you, but it can't be from a distance. And it can't be as just a friend."

"You'll never be just a friend to me."

"Good, because this is the forever kind of love."

"Are you saying you'll be my forever girl? I can already picture that on a T-shirt."

I smirked. "That sounds suspiciously like a title. And . . . yes I will. Hard yes." I kissed him, sinking into his lips like I was home.

When we broke the kiss, I looked over his shoulder at the drawings. They were really beautiful, and I could envision exactly how each new space would look. "Are you sure these will work with your hotels?"

"Isla, I've never been so sure about anything. But it's not just because you're a talented baker. I know you'll raise the standard at each of these properties just by being there. I'm sure because it's you. Because I love you and I want you there, everywhere. Anyplace I go, I want you to be with me. I just do."

"I want that too."

His smile grew and it reminded me of the Grinch's heart swelling until it burst from his chest. Owen's smile almost outgrew his face.

He'd been holding me up all this time, so I released my legs from around his waist and slid to the floor in front of him. Owen reached for my hand and pulled me closer until there was no separation between us.

If I had my way, there never would be again.

EPILOGUE

Owen
Five Months Later

IT WAS A PERFECT SATURDAY MORNING. The early haze had burned off and given way to a pastel blue sky and a subtle breeze coming off the bay.

I was looking forward to spending the rest of the day with Isla.

Okay, truth—I wasn't crazy about what she had planned. In my defense, I was under duress when I'd agreed... after sharing a bottle of wine with Isla at dinner, worshipping her body for a solid three hours afterward, and sleeping for two.

No man should be expected to be of right mind to make a decision after that.

"Of course, sounds great," I'd muttered in a semi-conscious state. At least, I think that's what I said.

My brain was still drugged with sleep because it was three in the goddamn morning, which was still the middle of the night as far as I was concerned. Always would be. But she was awake, showered, and inexplicably perky, ready to head to the bakery and get the first run of bread into the oven while I dove back into a dream about us naked in the shower.

"We're going to Stinson," she'd whispered, and I remember muttering something about wanting to stay inside with her all day instead, or at least heading to a much closer beach to the south.

She kissed me. "Nope, Stinson. Meet you at my place at two. I'll bring the food. You're in charge of towels and beach toys."

These were nonsensical words.

Beach toys?

I didn't own beach toys, if what she meant was small plastic molds for making sand castles. In my dreamy state, I fantasized that what she really meant were sex toys we could somehow use among the ocean waves, and that kept me content enough to acquiesce. "Mmhmm... on it."

When she slipped quietly out the door, I drifted back to sleep, dreaming of all the things I would do to her body when I saw her again.

Now, sitting at a coffee place in the Haight, I let my grouch flag fly. Stirring an extra packet of sugar into my coffee, I glared at the steam coming off the top which made it too hot to drink. Then I glared at my phone, which had zero texts from Isla telling me we could forget about her beach plan and go with my plan.

Fine, I didn't have a plan.

Yet.

But I planned to have a plan. Jesus, I needed one. I was a wreck, and I had been for weeks. That's what meaning to propose and not actually doing it will do to a person. I didn't want to spend six hours at the beach if it meant delaying my marriage proposal for yet another day.

I had to grow a pair and do it, finally.

Shoving my hand deep into the pocket of my khaki shorts, I

felt for the familiar velvet-covered cube that had taken up residence in one pocket or another every day for the past month.

I'd been carrying around the two-carat, emerald cut engagement ring, trying to suss out the ideal time and place for a picture-perfect proposal that would give us an epic romantic story to tell our grandchildren.

I was being ridiculous, waiting for a moment that had yet to arrive, and talking myself out of the moments that already had because they didn't feel proposal-worthy.

After chickening out in Calistoga, where a sunset over the vineyards was only the first of several missed opportunities, we'd taken bikes down pastoral lanes flanked by grape arbors, tomato vines, and hedgerows of lavender.

We'd snuck onto the vineyard property next to the hotel and taken a midnight swim in a lake with swans. We'd had perfect moments, and I hadn't taken advantage of a single one.

Are you afraid she'll say no?

Pushing that thought aside because it certainly wasn't going to help matters, I decided to stop fucking around.

I'd get the words out somehow, some way, and it had to be this weekend. My overthinking brain had to get out of the way, and I'd just...propose.

The problem wasn't just *where* we were going, though that was certainly part of it. Beaches sounded great in theory, but in reality, sand was annoying and I knew I'd get a little carsick on the drive up Pacific Coast Highway. But Isla had invited her sister, Sarah, to join us.

It made no sense.

I knew Isla felt grateful to Sarah for handling the finances of Victorine's expansion into my wine country properties, but I couldn't imagine why she'd invite her along on our date.

I'd never mess with Isla's family bonds, especially after she'd done so much to help me reconnect with my own sister. Jen had become a regular fixture in our lives, and we had weekly Skypes where I talked to my new niece—not that she likely understood my explanations of what happened that week in the stock market or whatever else I decided to tell her.

Thanks to Isla, Jen and I had settled back into a sibling relationship that defied the years we'd spent apart. I owed her, and it seemed the repayment came in the form of Sarah coming on our date.

I fired off a text.

Me: G'morning, woman whom I adore.

Isla responded right away. She'd asked Becca to sew a tiny phone pocket into the aprons she wore while she was baking so we never missed a chance to connect.

It didn't make up for the pre-dawn departures, but it was something.

Isla: Good morning, man who uses perfect grammar. How'd you sleep?

Me: Horribly once you left. You have to stop doing that.

Isla: Doing what?

Me: Leaving.

Isla: Lol. I'll look into self-rising dough, but the bread will suffer.

Me: Blasphemy. Don't hurt the bread. Question: are we committed to this beach thing with your sister?

Isla: Oh yes. No way you're squirming out of our plans.

Me: But whyyyyy?

Isla: Because you love me and I want to go to the beach.

Me: I do love you. So... 3 of us at the beach.

After a few more exchanges of emojis and her promises to let me have my way with her as payback for an hour on winding roads and sand in our shoes for days, I gave in.

The only problem, however, was where to find the aforementioned beach toys, assuming I hadn't just dreamed up the conversation. Maybe I was supposed to bring beach *chairs*. Made much more sense.

I texted again.

Me: Were you serious about beach toys?

Isla: Yes. Buckets, shovels, sand sifters

I shook my head, a smile creeping over my face. My grumpy mood had no chance against her. If she wanted to build sandcastles all afternoon, I'd be her water boy, no questions asked.

Me: Don't forget the bread.

Isla: Forget? It's like you don't even know me.

Me: Oh, I know you. But I'm ever willing to get to know you in new ways.

Isla: Good to hear. I have a new recipe I want to try.

Me: I'll be here, waiting for anything you want to put in my mouth.

Isla: Why do I think we're no longer talking about bread?

Me: Were we ever?

A couple hours later, as my car idled on Steiner Street, Isla flung the door open and beamed down at me from the doorway. "You're here! I'm so excited for our date." She bounded down the stairs and flew into my arms.

I'd never get tired of hearing her refer to the time we spent together as *dating*—those days in the friend zone had left their mark. "And yet, you invited your sister to come on our date."

She laughed. "Well, only for the beach part. Our date will continue later without her. She's driving separately."

Her excitement was contagious and her promises of *later* were enough to make me agreeable. How was she supposed to know the ring was burning a hole in my pocket?

If I were a better man—or a more organized one—I'd have proposed weeks ago.

Sarah came out of the house and tilted her head to the side, studying us. Then she pulled down the neckline of her shirt to reveal the purple strap of a bikini top.

"Okay, comrades. I need to get some sun on this pale academic body. Let's get this show on the road."

Sarah carried beach chairs down the steps toward her own car, and I waited for Isla to lock her door. When she turned around, she dropped the oversized cotton tote filled with food at her feet and reached around my neck.

Her lips were soft and sweet as they grazed mine. I pulled her face closer at an angle that let me claim her mouth the way I wanted.

There was no end to my appetite for her, and even though I didn't say it, my eyes pleaded with her once more to abort mission and let me follow her back inside to her bedroom. I felt certain Sarah would understand.

She shook her head. "We should get going."

"If you say so," I said, wrapping my arms tighter around her and pressing a kiss to her forehead. She stood on a step above mine, making us the same height. I lifted her up and brought her down to my step, then leaned my forehead against hers. "Better."

"You always have to have an advantage, don't you?" Her tone was playful.

"I like the appearance of an advantage. I happen to know there's no one-upping you and I wouldn't even try."

She smiled and led me down the steps.

~

Isla

I HAD a good reason for inviting Sarah along on our beach date. Owen had been walking around with a ring in his pocket for weeks, and it was driving him crazy that he couldn't find the perfect place for us to get engaged.

Of course I knew.

It didn't help that more than a few nights when he pulled me against him I felt something hard that most definitely wasn't his throbbing manhood.

So I tried to come up with a way to make things easier for him. Easier, that is, once he got over the queasiness from the drive and gave into a beach day with my sister as the third wheel.

It only took two glasses of wine and the unimpeachable beauty of the California coastline, but eventually he loosened up.

"This was a good idea. How'd you find this place?" he asked, reclining on a towel under a rainbow umbrella we'd planted in the sand.

"I know people."

"She knows people," he said, rolling his eyes at Sarah, who shrugged.

The area was beautiful, a private beach in front of a cottage that belonged to a friend's parents. The property had been in the family for generations and sadly didn't get much use anymore. I'd proposed buying the place with Finn and we were working out the details.

"Never question Isla when she has her mind set on a plan," Sarah said.

He nodded, pulling me toward him so my head was resting on his chest. "I'm learning. In fact, I've given in."

For hours, we did a lot of nothing and I could tell Owen was happy. We watched a few dolphin pods migrating in the distant surf while the sun tilted lower until its golden rays stretched out over the water.

As the tide crept in, the waves ate at the mammoth sand castle the three of us had built earlier. Sarah encouraged us to go off on a walk alone and promised to start working on dinner.

"That's a lovely offer, and I'm going to take full advantage," Owen said, grabbing my hand and lacing our fingers together. We walked north on the beach past other homes in the next cove.

"Do you want your feet in the water or do you like the dry sand?" I asked him.

"Doesn't matter. I like *you*."

"I like you too. I love you." I stopped walking and reached around his waist, stepping close. He pulled me closer and took my face in his hands. The love in his eyes told me everything his lack of a proposal couldn't. The way he looked at me—the way he always looked at me, as if he was in awe—was something I'd never take for granted.

This was the kind of love I'd never dreamed existed in the years before I met him. I barely believed it now without having to pinch myself daily. Owen's lips covered mine in a deep kiss that was matched by everything I felt.

We walked and talked and kissed and walked some more until the sun had dipped below the horizon, and I knew we'd been gone for at least an hour.

When we were almost back at our tiny cove, I led Owen up a set of steps to the bluff so we could grab a couple blankets from the car. "You cold?" he asked, pulling me tighter against his chest and leaning down to kiss me softly.

"A little. And I want to eat dinner outside, so I'm preparing."

"I didn't even ask what you packed in that bag. What are we eating?"

I arched an eyebrow. "Not telling. But I think you'll like it."

Owen grabbed the blankets from me under one arm and held onto my hand as we walked back through the house and onto the bluff overlooking the beach. I stood back while he glanced down at the sand.

When he turned back toward me, I snapped a picture of him with my phone, wanting to remember the look on his face forever—a look of amazement, puzzlement, gratitude.

But more than that, he looked stunned...then besotted.

I joined him and leaned down to admire Sarah's work. It was perfect, exactly how I'd envisioned.

On the wet sand, Sarah had traced an enormous heart with our names inside. She'd outlined it with tiny votive candles and strung a series of twinkle lights from four tall posts she'd hammered into the sand. A wine bucket chilled champagne and a separate table held a bread, cheese, and charcuterie display worthy of a Pinterest board.

She'd set up the table for two with a silk table cloth, high-backed chairs, and more flickering candles. She'd left our plated dinners under silver covers.

And now she was already headed back to the city, leaving us to spend the night alone in the cottage.

Wrapping my hands around the back of Owen's neck, I let my fingers brush through his hair while I whispered in his ear, "Don't worry. I'll say yes."

He leaned away and his glistening ocean blue eyes met mine. "You knew...?" Then he shook his head. "It doesn't matter. I'm glad. I...needed to get my head out of my ass and stop waiting for the perfect moment, and here you created an even more perfect moment than I ever could have imagined."

I could feel the grin spread across my face. "I'm happy you like it."

When I'd dreamed up the idea of coming to the beach and having Sarah set up what I kept calling our "proposal landscape," I imagined Owen picking an opportune moment during or after dinner, among the tealights with the ocean lapping behind us. But he was caught up in the moment—finally.

With shaky hands, he reached for me, dropping to a knee and looking into my eyes.

He shook his head. "I wanted it to be perfect. I wanted to create a moment we could tell our grandchildren about...and now I realize that it's not about the venue or the romantic light-ing...it's not about *me* creating the perfect moment because all our moments are perfect. I want everything with you. You had my heart from the moment you said you loved that I was a bell-hop. My heart is yours. *I'm* yours. Will you marry me, Isla Finley?"

I blinked back the tears but it was no use. They spilled forth at his words and the love I saw in his face.

I nodded, feeling choked up but knowing I needed to give him a verbal response. "Yes, I will. I want you forever."

He kissed me, holding me like he'd never let me go.

And I knew he never would.

THE END

WANT a peek at Isla and Owen's happily ever after? Sign up for my mailing list at https://bit.ly/3cUT55Bnewsletter and get an exclusive Falling for You BONUS SCENE, plus monthly news about new releases, a free book from one of my fantastic author friends, and literary drink and snack recipes you will love.

THANK you so much for reading Isla and Owen's story! I loved writing this one and I really hope you enjoyed reading it. I'd love to see you in my Facebook reader group, Stacy's Saucy Sisters, so come join the fun: https://bit.ly/2B1psS4fbgroup

UP NEXT IS Sarah and Braden's story, which will be released in August. And ICYMI, Finn and Annie have their own book? In Trouble with Him is their story and it's available HERE.

AND...YOU can read on for a Sneak Peek at The Summer of Him, Book 1 in the Summer Heat Duet!

ACKNOWLEDGMENTS

Readers, thank you. I'm grateful for every word you read, every kind review, every thoughtful click and like and comment. Love you all.

Jay, Jesse and Oliver: You've put up with me working at all hours and leaving my shoes everywhere — thank you for forgiving it all and loving me anyway. Big love to you three giant men with the best hair ever.

To my beta readers, editors, proofers, givers of feedback, and supporters—Amy V., Amy D., Kristina Z., and Nancy S. - thank you for making the words sound better.

And enormous thanks to the SOS crew — a group that expands with every book — no matter when I send a desperate text or email, you respond and talk me off the ledge: Adriana L., Christine D.R., Dylan A., and Melanie H. I'd be a pile of unpublished mush without you.

Shannon, this cover is gorgeous - thank you, thank you. Thank you Jenn and the Social Butterfly team for expert advice, brilliant execution, and other superpowers. Hilary and Shan, I'm happy to have you in my corner - you make the PR part a breeze.

Bloggers and bookstagrammers—thank you for embracing my books and exposing my writing to readers, I couldn't. Glad to have you in my village.

And to my fellow authors: as always, I am honored to type among you.

ABOUT THE AUTHOR

Stacy Travis writes sexy, charming romance about grown-up nerd girls and the hot alphas who fall for them. Writing contemporary romance makes her infinitely happy, but that might be the coffee talking. She drinks a LOT of it.

When she's not on a deadline, she's in running shoes complaining that all roads seem to go uphill. Or on the couch with a margarita. Or fangirling at a soccer game. She's never met a dog she didn't want to hug. And if you have no plans for Thanksgiving, she'll probably invite you to dinner. Stacy lives in Los Angeles with her husband, two sons, and a poorly-trained rescue dog who hoards socks.

Facebook reader group: Stacy's Saucy Sisters

Super fun newsletter: Only the good stuff

Website: https://www.www.stacytravis.com

Goodreads: https://www.goodreads.com/stacytravis

Email: stacytraviswrites@gmail.com - tell me what you're reading!

ALSO BY STACY TRAVIS

The Summer Heat Duet

The Summer of Him: A Celebrity Romance

Forever with Him: An Opposites Attract Contemporary Romance

In Trouble with Him: A Forbidden Love Contemporary Romance (Finn and Annie's story)

The Berkeley Hills Series - all are standalone novels

Second Chance at Us: A Second Chance Romance (Book 1 - Becca and Blake's story)

Falling for You: A Friends to Lovers Standalone Romance (Book 2 - Isla and Owen's story)

Burning for You: A Brother's Best Friend Firefighter Romance (Book 3 - Sarah and Braden's story) - August 2021

Standalone Novels - Adult Contemporary Romance

French Kiss: A Friends to Lovers Romance

Bad News: An Enemies to Lovers Romance

BONUS CHAPTER - THE SUMMER OF HIM

A CELEBRITY MISTAKEN IDENTITY ROMANCE

Los Angeles International Airport
July

There was still time. The plane hadn't taken off yet. And that made me nervous.

He could still show up. Maybe he would.

I looked at my phone again. I'd already checked it too many times to remember, sneaking a look while dodging questions from my Lyft driver, going through security, and boarding the plane. Not to mention glancing behind me constantly like a fugitive who was being tailed.

I wasn't ready to give up on him yet. He could still get his act together. He could decide to apologize and admit that all the things he'd done and said were a blip in the larger, more important constellation of our love.

I hoped to God he wouldn't do that.

That's right. I hoped against hope that Johnny Royce, my now-ex-boyfriend, wouldn't call me or come to the airport or try to get on the plane. Yes, it was supposed to be our vacation together. And no, there wasn't a law against him traveling.

Except there was. It was the universal law of bad breakups: don't try to follow your ex-girlfriend to France, especially when the relationship ended badly. Especially when it was all your fault.

I'd been clear on that point, but logic didn't always mean anything to Johnny Royce. He was guided by different laws and principles than most people. He liked to do anything that seemed dangerous and fun. And while coming anywhere near me would definitely accomplish the dangerous part, I hoped—for once— that logic would pay him a visit and he'd see there was no fun to be had.

But I knew him.

He would think it was fine to travel together even after what had happened between us, which was a total shit show that I'd tried my best to block from memory.

Tried and failed.

So I didn't want him calling the airline and trying to reinstate the ticket I'd bought for him and later canceled. I didn't want to fight with Johnny in Paris or try to force the romance of an incredible city on the sad remains of what had sort of passed for barely-friends with mediocre benefits.

I looked down the aisle of the plane once more and exhaled an audible sigh of relief. He wasn't coming. Thinking about our yearlong relationship, I felt a mixture of 'we had our sweet moments' and 'wow, I should have seen that train wreck coming.'

If our breakup was as inevitable, so was our initial hookup. I'd walked into the bar where he worked and flirted with him. I'd planned it because I was a planner, and Johnny went along with it because, well… fun and sex. He wanted one thing from life—a party. He made a pretty decent effort to find a party on a daily basis, looking for a cliff to dive from or a door to sneak through if it seemed like something interesting lay on the other side. Johnny made everyone around him have a better time, no matter where he went.

What he didn't want was commitment. Or rules. Or sobriety, apparently. I told myself I was fine with that.

I was lying.

Johnny Royce worked as a bartender at Moby's, a tiny craft-beer and fancy burger place a dozen blocks from my apartment. He always looked like he'd just come in from playing beach volleyball—suntanned with streaks of blond in his sandy-brown hair and sunglasses on top of his head, even at night. He was always in motion, swinging out from behind the bar to wipe down three tables, scooping up empty pint glasses and dumping them in a grey kitchen bin, and wiping his hands on a long white apron without letting a single customer wait more than a couple of minutes at the bar.

He'd fill a glass, holding the tap open with the same hand so he could use the other to wipe off the bar or pop a napkin down for a newly arrived customer. Moby's had a steady flow of people, and Johnny kept up. It made me think he had to be smart if he was able to stay on top of everything without letting a task go unfulfilled.

The reality was he just didn't like people to go too long without a fresh beer.

His friends were bartenders or surfers or bartenders who surfed. After a few months of persuading, he even managed to get me on a surfboard. He guided me patiently and held onto the board until the waves came up and under me. "Okay, stand up now. Just hop into a squat, and when you're balanced, rise up and ride the wave." It took a half dozen attempts and more than a little water up my nose each time I fell, but I did get up on that board. I was having more fun than I'd had in ages, and it felt like the wave would keep on building.

That just showed how little I understood about relationships. Or surfing.

So I sat in my aisle seat on the plane—so far with no fellow travelers in my row—and thought back on the year that had led me to this moment: promising start, moments of irresponsible fun, differing life goals, and a crash and burn ending so bad it made me question my judgment for hooking up with him in the first place.

Final score: Judgment 0, Inevitable Realities of the Universe 1.

The plane was starting to fill up. Flight attendants were closing some of the overhead bins and I was telling my irrational self not to worry. He wasn't coming.

But I feared the grand gesture.

It was just the kind of thing that would appeal to Johnny's adventuring spirit, trying to ignite a dashed relationship—forever, this time—at the airport in the moments before the plane was due to take off. He'd buy a ticket he couldn't afford just so he could get past the gate. He'd push his way through the line of passengers, who would all turn to see his grand romantic gesture.

"Hold on. Don't close the door. I have to get on and tell this woman I love her... that I was meant to be with her... that I was wrong... that I was an idiot... that I want to spend the rest of my life with her... Nikki, it's you. It's always been you."

He'd bend his forehead to touch mine and look into my eyes, searching to make sure I felt the same way. I'd nod and he'd give me the best kiss of my life. People on the plane would applaud.

Then I'd have to deal with him again and look like the jerk who was turning away a guy with a cute smile making a grand gesture.

"Excuse me," said a voice to my left. My heart dropped to my feet because the voice was deep and sounded like Johnny trying to do a comedy bit: "Excuse me, Miss. Is this seat taken?"

I looked up at the tired, balding man staring at me and almost hugged him. His laptop case dangled awkwardly from his wrist while he waited for me to get up and let him into the window seat. He had a hipster beard and serious eyes, the kind that were focused on getting settled in and buckling his seatbelt.

"Sorry," I said, quickly unbuckling, standing, and moving into the aisle to let him get to his seat.

Then, because I was newly single, I checked him out. Above the beard, he wore nerdy glasses, maybe just for effect or maybe for reading, since he was leafing through a copy of *Sports Illustrated*. He'd already put his eye mask on his forehead in preparation for sleep. He'd already stuffed earbuds into his ears to block me—and anyone else—out of his life for the duration of the flight.

I turned back to the seat pocket in front of me and tucked in my iPad and the bottle of water I'd bought at the airport.

My thoughts drifted back to Johnny. Ten hours on a plane begs for topics to think about. I intentionally only remembered the best times—the sun-kissed afternoons sitting on the roof of his 1930s apartment building, where we'd have to climb out a window and hoist ourselves over a railing to crawl onto a flat patch that was perfect for watching the last half circle of sun slip into the Pacific Ocean.

At about six foot one with an athletic body he was lucky enough to have been born with, Johnny was good at pretty much any sport he tried without a lesson. I'd trained for months to get through a century bike ride, and Johnny hopped on a borrowed bike and joined me at the last minute without suffering a sore muscle. He could sink three-pointers easily and surf waves that would frighten most people.

But it was his smile that I found the most appealing. He had a blond-streaked shock of hair that fell over his green eyes and a guilty-looking teenage-boy ear-to-ear grin. His happiness felt contagious, and I was a born rule follower who was used to having things work out if I dug in and gave it my full effort. Maybe that was why it took me a year to figure out that Johnny and I should've only lasted a couple of dates or a couple of months at best. Instead, I convinced myself that if I tried, I could make a relationship work with a fun guy who brought out a playful side of me.

The rooftop always beckoned with another sunset. He'd stuff a couple of beers in his pockets and swing a leg deftly over the rail before helping me over. My legs were shorter, so I needed the boost. There was a perfectly placed half wall where he could rest while I leaned on him. Johnny would wrap his arms around me, and we'd sip our beers, silently watching the sky change colors, never disturbed by another soul venturing up there.

"It feels like we should be drinking rosé from tall wineglasses," I'd said more than once, thinking the chilled pink drink would look pretty set against the setting sun. And I liked the way it tasted.

He'd tip his pinky finger out like he was holding a teacup, mocking me. "Oh, *oui, oui*," he'd say, laughing at himself. "People who drink wine are kinda pretentious, don't you think?"

Like a million other things, I let the semi-insult go. Up on the roof, with the warm breeze wafting across my face and Johnny nuzzling my neck, I didn't think he meant to mock me or my interest in beverages made from grapes.

I didn't think he had a mean streak. I didn't think he'd ever cheat on me.

Until he did.

The Summer of Him is Book One in the Summer Heat Duet and is the perfect vacation read. Grab your copy at https://books2read.com/travisTSOH!

Made in the USA
Monee, IL
31 May 2021

69116290R00173